"She proves that love is timeless." —Nora Roberts

"Sh... ...s

"O'... ...s-
pen... ...e
that... ...e-
mer... ...y,
whi... ...es

"This should please those who appreciate a traditional romantic plot arc, as the author focuses primarily on romantic tension and the sacrifices of real love."

—*Publishers Weekly* on *Shifting Love*

"*Shifting Love* is unique, thrilling, and chock-full of emotion, proving O'Day-Flannery is still at the top of her
game!"

—*Romantic Times BookReviews* (4½ stars)

"*Shifting Love* reads like Deb Smith's *Alice at Heart*
crossed with *Touched by a (Sexy) Angel*. The dual heroes
in the book—Julian and Marcus—will leave you guess-
ing until the very end." —*Science Fiction Romance*

"*Shifting Love* is a tale that is magnificent with vivid
storytelling and charm. It is a powerful creation of fantasy, paranormal, and romance that offers so much for so
many readers. It is something that all readers should have
on their keeper shelves."

—*The Road to Romance*

Twice in a Lifetime

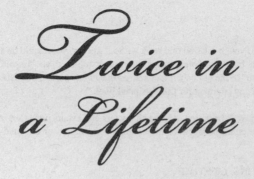

CONSTANCE O'DAY-FLANNERY

tor paranormal romance

A TOM DOHERTY ASSOCIATES BOOK
NEW YORK

This is a work of fiction. All the characters and events portrayed in this
book are either products of the author's imagination or are used ficti-
tiously.

TWICE IN A LIFETIME

A Tor Book
Published by Tom Doherty Associates, LLC
175 Fifth Avenue
New York, NY 10010

www.tor.com

Tor® is a registered trademark of Tom Doherty Associates, LLC.

ISBN-13: 978-0-765-35404-4
ISBN-10: 0-765-35404-7

First Edition: December 2006

Printed in the United States of America

0 9 8 7 6 5 4 3 2 1

For Patricia Trowbridge.
Dear friend, wise woman, courageous adventurer,
I hope you laugh.
It's not about you, just based on a woman
I admire greatly.

Twice in a Lifetime

Chapter

I

GIRLFRIENDS WERE WONDERFUL, ALMOST A NECESSITY for any woman struggling to survive in an ever-changing world, but when the girlfriends were closer than sisters, no punches were held. You were part of a spiritual family. You could take it.

Actually, you had little choice *but* to take it. It was what you had signed up for when you loved without question or judgment.

"Okay, so here's the way I see it, and I don't care if I am the first one to open my mouth." Claire paused briefly, as though to impart something important. "It's time for you to come out of the shadows, Isabel," she said in a matter-of-fact voice, her expression serious. "No one is suggesting you become a wild and crazy woman wearing purple hats. Just that you step up to the plate again, so to speak."

Isabel Calloway knew anytime one of them was the subject of discussion, especially if Claire was leading the discussion, it meant something unwanted was going to be exposed. It might be done gently, with compassion, yet it was still going to sting like hell in the end. No matter how the bandage is ripped off, little by little or all at once, it always smarts. "But I'm sort of used to the shadows now," Isabel answered, trying not to become defensive. This meeting was supposed to be about the direction of the foundation they had formed months ago, not about her.

"Really?" Kelly asked, leaning into the table all six of them were seated around. "How could you be used to the shadows?"

Isabel wasn't sure how to respond, or if they really wanted to hear her answer. Especially Kelly, red-haired single mom of a teenager, and still looking for her Mr. Right.

"So what's the big deal about speaking at this conference? You did it years ago, and now you have something important to say."

She heard Claire and smiled slightly before staring out of her gazebo to the tall oak and maple trees showing the last signs of autumn. Fall was nearly over, and everything in nature was preparing for winter. It was kind of like the way her life felt right now.

Bringing her attention to the women around her, she smiled again. How they believed in her, all of them, the Yellow Brick Road Gang, strangers who had come together eight years ago for a book club and who had morphed into a tight circle of friends who would support you in a crisis and call you on your crap when you were hiding from it.

Was she in hiding now? Is that how they saw it? She might as well ask. "Do you actually think I'm hiding from life?"

"Yes!" the chorus of female voices answered.

Isabel laughed self-consciously. "Well, I guess that's clear enough. But I don't think I am, not really. I see clients. I'm involved with the foundation, Cristine." She looked at her dear friend, who certainly wasn't hiding from her life after winning the lottery, giving birth to an adorable daughter, and forming a foundation that supported women in need. "I see you guys all the time."

"But there's more to life than work, Issy," Cristine said gently. "You still wear Chuck's clothes sometimes, and he's been gone for seven years. You refused the makeover in New York City and—"

"And you're too young to have that white hair," Tina interrupted in her "call it like it is" way of speaking her truth. "I mean, c'mon, Issy. . . . Why don't you at least have it tinted, try out a little color?"

Isabel grinned at Tina, noting the smooth milk-chocolate tone of her skin, which seemed to radiate now that she was in love with the doctor who had delivered Cristine's baby. "Tina, believe it or not, I happen to like my hair," she stated, running her fingers through the straight shoulder-length strands. And it was white, pure white, not gray and dull. "And what happens when I dye my hair and my roots begin to show? I'll look like Pepé Le Pew."

Everyone laughed.

"But your face is too young for white hair," Tina countered. "I'm just saying it wouldn't hurt to try something new."

"Why do you like it?" Paula asked.

Isabel thought about it a second too long.

"Is it like some badge of widowhood you insist on keeping?" Claire demanded, pouncing on her when she'd hesitated answering.

Even though she had a heart of gold in most situations, Claire always was the one to go for the jugular if you were hiding behind a mask. Isabel wasn't going to get angry with Claire, or with any of them. They simply didn't understand. Maybe it was time they did. "Listen, you're all younger than I am. Do you want to know what happens to women my age? We start to become invisible. We move through society, and no one pays us attention. It isn't that I want to disappear. Society doesn't shine a flattering spotlight on women approaching fifty or beyond."

"You're not old," Kelly insisted. "You're still a vital woman. That's what we're trying to tell you."

Paula crossed her arms over her chest. "Well, Isabel is right, in a way." All attention turned to Paula, the anthropologist with five kids who was finally finishing her thesis to get her master's degree. "It's not as apparent in Europe as it is in America. We're a youth-driven society here. The ads directed at women Isabel's age are for fighting wrinkles and age-related diseases. You see it everywhere, and it can be depressing. How are women who are approaching fifty supposed to feel vital in a society that treats them as has-beens? Just when was the last time that Meryl Streep had a leading romantic role portraying a woman who still grabbed life with both hands? Or Glenn Close? Or any other major actress that age? Think about it, ladies, because this is where we're all heading in a decade or more. Do you think women stop being sexual beings when they hit fifty? Where are the role models to tell society that women get better with age, not worse?"

"Men certainly have them," Claire muttered, her beautiful face transformed into a scowl. "Especially in the media. Michael Douglas. Harrison Ford. De Niro and Pacino are still leading men. They still have careers, because men become distinguished as they age and women just get old? Give me a break. Their faces are allowed to look like walnuts, but a woman has to go under the knife until she looks like the Joker? It's discrimination, that's what it is, and it's keeping the stereotypes in place." Her features lightened. "*You* could be a role model, Issy. For us. Become that woman who still grabs life with both hands."

"I don't want to be anyone's role model. I'm just trying to live out my life and—"

"And stay in the shadows," Tina interjected. "Your light is too brilliant to be overshadowed. That's why we're here, Isabel. To coax that light back out."

"I thought we were here to discuss the foundation," Isabel said.

No one answered her. They simply smiled and looked at her with love.

Isabel swallowed the lump in her throat. A part of her knew they were right. Somewhere in the last seven years she had capitulated, given up, given in . . . thought the best part of her life behind her.

"So will you consider going to the conference?" Cristine asked. "If it's a baby step, can you take it?"

"Please," Kelly asked, her blue eyes wide with hope. "You really do have something that needs to be heard."

"Do it," Claire said. "Or we'll put on our red high heels and be back here next week for another meeting."

"Do it," Paula added. "It's important work."

"Just do it, woman," Tina added. "You've got something to say, so say it."

She looked into their faces, and she felt tears forming. They were the closest thing to family that she had now. She didn't want to disappoint them, even if she also knew that going to the Regional Conference for Clinical Hypnotherapists at a local college was the very last place she wanted to be.

"All right, all right. I'll do it," she stated with exasperation, and sniffled a few times. "Then will you all get off my case?"

"Never!"

"Cha'right!"

"Like we ever would!"

"Get real, girl!"

"Honey, when your stuff begins to stink, who else will tell you except the people who love you?"

Isabel sighed deeply with surrender. She had signed up for this eight years ago, so she really couldn't complain about their interference. And she'd done the same to them. Now it was simply her turn under the microscope of friendship. But damn it, now she had to follow through with the conference, something she had successfully avoided for years.

It was a mistake. More than a mistake—it was turning into a disaster.

Her mouth went dry. Fear seized her diaphragm. Her heart slammed into the wall of her chest, and her breath seemed to stick against the back of her throat. Her hands were clutching the edges of the podium, as though it were the only thing keeping her upright. *Dear God, don't let me die now,* she prayed. *Not here.* Not in front of a bored audience of professionals who couldn't care what she was saying.

Seconds seemed timeless as she berated herself. Why was she doing this? She so disliked the spotlight, the undivided attention, the expectation, and then the signs of a wandering mind, as though she had lost the audience ten minutes before. *Wind it up, Isabel,* she told herself. *Get off the stage and get out of the room.*

"And so it is my belief some of these autistic children can be helped by clinical hypnotherapy, the gateway into the subconscious, thereby releasing them from, perhaps, years of isolation." She paused again, glancing down to her notes, amazed she had pushed those words out and wishing she had a dynamite closing or even a Dr. Phil saying like "It'll happen faster than flapjacks cookin' on your momma's cast-iron skillet," but she wasn't Dr. Phil. She was Isabel Calloway, widow, about to turn fifty the day after the seventh anniversary of her husband's death, and this whole experience of presenting her findings at the regional conference was turning into a classical anxiety attack.

"Thank you for your attention," she finally said, and listened to a polite smattering of applause as she gathered up her notes and walked off the stage.

Her face was burning with embarrassment as she placed

one foot in front of the other, walking past the moderator—who was smiling tightly, obviously disappointed—past the curtains, the backstage, and finally, blessedly, out an exit door.

When it slammed behind her, Isabel flinched and closed her eyes to the sun as she stuffed the index cards into her jacket pocket. *What a mistake to come here,* she thought, forcing a deep shuddering breath, as though to break through the wall of fear that had wrapped around her chest. Why had she ever let the group talk her into it? Thinking about the five women who had encouraged her to speak at the conference, Isabel smiled. Almost.

The Yellow Brick Road Gang, with their decorated red high heels that were mandatory footwear for meetings, had meant well—she knew that—and had truly thought her work with autistic children should be shared. Perhaps the best way was to write a book, alone in her own home without an audience, though that whole process scared the hell out of her too. She didn't know if she had the kind of discipline such a project would demand.

Opening her eyes, she sighed heavily and walked down the steps to a low cement wall that delineated the space between the main auditorium and a small park. She didn't have the energy to walk in the park, so she simply sat down on the wall and covered her face with her hands.

Why did she put this pressure on herself? she wondered, massaging her forehead with the pads of her fingers. Wasn't it enough that the dreaded week of hell was fast approaching? Why did she ever put herself though this torture of public speaking? No matter what the group had said, she did so much better in the shadows now, leading her quiet life, getting her excitement from the others. She'd had enough turmoil to last a lifetime. Anyone's lifetime.

She thought about the week from hell and wondered if she should just go away somewhere quiet to remember Chuck and, lest she forget, oh yeah . . . to turn fifty the very next day. She always wondered if Chuck had died the day before her birthday so she would never forget him . . . as though she could. So much of her loved him still, but a tiny sliver of her mind thought it was the dirtiest trick ever played on her.

She slowly shook her head, wishing she could click her heels, turn back time, and warn him not to go into work or walk that steel girder. He would only have laughed at her worry, because she'd always worried, always had a sick premonition one day that damn job would kill him and take him away from her.

Chuck. Charles Calloway. Tall, handsome, he had come into her life at thirteen and had swept her off her feet with his eyes, his smile. Older than her by eight years, he'd treated her as his equal, asking for her opinions and waiting for her to grow up, go to college, be engaged to the proper doctor of medicine her stuffy parents had thought was appropriate. Ten years after they'd first met, he returned to her life with the force of a hurricane, moving back to their hometown and right back into her heart. Her parents had been appalled when she'd broken off her engagement to the doctor and had told them of her plans to marry an ironworker. She'd never felt that kind of expansive love before, and had insisted she and Chuck would elope if her parents didn't give their blessing.

She'd loved him then with an innocent awe, and the love she held for him now was bittersweet, like a healed scar that sometimes itches, sending sharp threads of pain right below the surface of the skin.

How could he have left her so soon? He'd been too young. Too vibrant. Too essential to her life. She remembered how the first year after he was gone she could barely breathe, and constantly had to remind herself to inhale, to keep on going. Her hair had turned pure white by the first anniversary of his death. And then she'd begun wearing his clothes, his shirts, his jackets with the sleeves rolled up. The second year she could breathe normally again, but her body began to yearn for his so badly that she bought a new mattress, foolishly believing if she slept on something new she could dispel the memories and the terrible craving to be held in his arms. By the third year she had lost all carnal cravings, for Chuck or anyone else. Something inside of her had died along with her husband. She'd had the best, at least the best for her: best friend, best lover, best companion. Acceptance had come in the fourth year, and she now led a solitary life, staying alone in the big old Victorian house Chuck had loved. Since she and Chuck hadn't been able to have children, there was nowhere to see him reproduced in the curve of a smile or the tilt of a head, or to feel that dark silky hair she had loved to run her fingers through. No children, no grandchildren to come, and no one to wrap her in their arms and . . . damn it, she had thought she was done with pity parties.

Mentally shaking herself, Isabel stood up, stretched the muscles in her five-foot-nine body, and sighed. Time to get on with it. Put on a brave face, smile at the other conference attendees, and make her way home.

And think about writing a book . . . no more public speaking.

She climbed the steps back to the auditorium door and pushed the metal bar on the steel. Nothing.

It was an automatic lock.

She knocked, waiting to see if anyone would answer. No one did.

Sighing, she turned and walked down the steps, around the building, knowing she was going to have to use the main entrance to pick up her briefcase and her purse. Forget the closing cocktail party. The very last thing she needed was to mingle with anyone who had heard her poorly delivered speech. Which was odd in itself because once, a long time ago it seemed, she had considered herself at least a competent public speaker. There was a time she had been one of the *stars* of these conferences, winning Therapist of the Year twice, surrounded at the cocktail parties by others who seemed to value her opinion. That was when she had been full of herself and her confidence ran on a high level, and that had seemed to attract even more recognition. Then Chuck had died and she'd pulled back. It had been a trial to get up in the morning and get dressed, let alone muster the energy to attend a conference.

Had been. The past. What was the present showing her?

She was a has-been—a person whose star had lost its glimmer.

Now there were younger, more dynamic people who had marched in right behind her and had captured the attention. She hadn't realized how much of a has-been she'd become until she had looked out to an audience of perhaps fifty people, where once there would have been over two hundred. And she had failed to deliver her speech to those fifty with any real conviction. From the moment she'd entered the large auditorium and had seen the sparse audience, her self-confidence had plummeted.

No one had to tell her that basing one's self-confidence on the opinions of others was an unhealthy and unwise direction. She was very good at finding the answers for others. The problem, her problem, had always been taking her own advice.

Rounding the side of the building, she took a deep breath, then plastered a smile on her face as she walked through the smokers and headed toward the row of doors. If only she had thought to gather her things from backstage when she'd made her escape, she could be in her car now, heading back to Haverton.

"Isabel? Isabel Calloway?"

She heard her name called and turned her head, wishing she could ignore the female voice. Marcia McMillan.

Isabel stopped before opening the inside door to the auditorium. "Hello, Marcia. How are you?"

The younger woman excused herself from the crowd of

people around her and closed the distance between them. Marcia was dressed in her conference finery—smart business suit and high heels—had perfect wispy hair, and carried a leather designer attaché. "I'm fine. But how are *you*? I haven't seen you at one of these things in years, Isabel. I saw you were on the program, but my workshop was scheduled opposite yours and the place was jammed! Literally. It took me until now to get this far out of the room, and I think I just might have developed carpal tunnel from signing copies of my book."

Her book. A thin dissertation on family values that had been offered for sale at the registration table, along with all the other books written or self-published by attendees.

"Well, sorry about the aching hand, but congratulations on the book."

"Have you read it?"

Now see, Isabel would never have asked someone that question, afraid of the answer. Marcia was full of confidence following her successful presentation. "No, I'm afraid I haven't," Isabel answered truthfully as she opened the door that led into the room. "Good luck with it, though."

"Thanks," Marcia murmured with a satisfied smile as someone touched her arm for her attention. "I'll see you at the cocktail party?"

"I don't think I can attend," Isabel answered. "Have fun, though." And she entered the auditorium, now silent and less threatening. Marcia should have had this room for her presentation. At least it would have accommodated those waiting to hear her politically correct views on the reasons family values had degraded. Oh, she'd read the back cover copy when she'd registered for the conference and had put the book back. It wasn't jealousy. It was her disappointment that Marcia McMillan had once been a very promising student of hers, back in the years before Isabel's life had been turned upside down. Back when she'd easily conducted seminars with hypnotherapy induction of a crowd of two hundred professionals. It was, in fact, easier with two hundred than with one.

Politicians did it all the time.

Making her way to the backstage area, Isabel began looking for her briefcase and purse. They weren't where she had put them, on a chair by the curtains. She looked around her, searching.

"May I help you?"

Breathing a sigh of relief, she looked in the direction of the male voice. "I certainly hope so. I left my purse and my briefcase here earlier. I can't seem to find them now and . . ."

Her words trailed off as she saw a man approaching her, moving out of the dark shadows of the backstage. He appeared tall, lean, and he seemed to have a strange light surrounding him that looked like it faded as he came into the lights from the stage. He was also carrying her purse and briefcase, she noted with relief.

"Thank you so much for finding them," she called out as he came closer.

He looked like he was in his late thirties, with dark hair and a brilliant smile.

"And you saved me the task of finding you, Isabel."

He knew her name? Of course. He must have looked in her purse to find the identity of the owner. "Yes. That's me."

"I know it is you. I am most pleased to make your acquaintance."

Somewhere in the back of her brain she noted that his speech was almost formal, though his clothes were casual. Jeans and a blue shirt with the sleeves rolled up. Must be part of the clean-up crew at the college.

She forced her legs to close the distance between them. "And I'm very happy to meet you, especially since you have the keys to my car." She smiled. "You're a lifesaver."

And then his smile widened and she was struck by the

man's sheer magnetism. His whole being seemed to cast off rays of electrical attraction.

"Thank you for recognizing that so quickly."

Okay, what did that mean? And why was there this ridiculous tingling in her body, as if his nearness were pulling her closer? Wanting to correct whatever he was thinking, she said, "I meant that without my keys, my life would be difficult," she said, noting that his eyes were dark brown and kindly and he was handsome—like movie-star handsome with exotic chiseled features, like that man on television who had played a lawyer and then a detective. Jimmy something . . . Smits. That was it. Jimmy Smits. A part of her was shocked that she was even thinking about movie stars, like some awestruck kid.

"You are correct. Life can be difficult without the keys," he answered, smiling as he handed over her purse. "So many fail to even notice the doors when they are opened."

Was this some kind of riddle? She held out her hand for her briefcase and laughed self-consciously. "Well, thank you for keeping them for me. I do appreciate it." She had to recover her composure. What was she going to do next? Giggle?

He gave her the briefcase, and their fingers touched in the handover. Immediately, Isabel felt a frisson of electricity that was laced with pleasure. Surprised, she almost dropped the case, and when she looked up into his eyes he was still smiling.

"Would you join me for coffee?" he asked. "I would like to speak with you, get to know you better."

Isabel simply blinked, struck speechless by his unexpected invitation. Why did he want to know *her*?

"I heard your speech," he added, still staring into her eyes to the point of probing.

She inwardly cringed. "Sorry about that. I wasn't as prepared as I should have been. I'm afraid I'm not much of a public speaker anymore."

"I believe you may be onto something," he answered, as though he hadn't heard her apology.

"Are you a therapist?"

"Therapist?"

"Yes. The conference. Did you attend?" Maybe she was mistaken about the clean-up crew part, but he wasn't wearing a conference badge. Had he removed it, since the conference was technically over?

"I am here, am I not?"

"Well, yes . . . but . . ." She smiled and shook her head. "I really must be going. Thanks again for keeping my things."

"We will have our conversation another time, then," he said. "It was very good to meet you, Isabel."

"Yes," she answered, backing away. "Good to meet you too."

It wasn't until she was walking away that she realized he'd never introduced himself.

Bizarre.

Twenty minutes later she was looking for the ramp onto the turnpike when she saw him. Standing on the side of the road with one hand in the pocket of his leather bomber jacket and the thumb of his other hand out, looking for a ride. And damn it, he saw her too, she realized as she passed him and they made eye contact for a fraction of a moment. Within seconds her mind was in a tug-of-war. Pick him up? Give him a ride? Was she crazy? Who picked up hitchhikers in this day and age of serial killers and carjackers and rapists? But he had kept her purse and briefcase. He hadn't stolen anything—all her money and credit cards were intact. He'd been at the conference, so he must work for the college. Maybe his own car had broken down and he really needed help. . . .

Karma. It was her turn now.

She flipped on her turn signal and applied the brake as she made her way to the shoulder of the road. Watching him walk up to the car in her rearview mirror, Isabel prayed she was making the right decision to be a Good Samaritan, that she wouldn't wind up in some deserted gully with her throat slit.

Fear. It was a powerful force.

He opened the passenger car door and slid onto the seat.

"Thank you, Isabel," he said, grinning as he settled in next to her.

"I thought that was you," she answered with a smile. "Car trouble?"

Still smiling, he shook his head slightly. "No."

"Oh . . ." So he didn't have a car? He actually *was* thumbing a ride? "Where are you going?"

"Haverton."

Startled, she had to swallow to get moisture into her mouth. "Really? I live there."

"How fortunate," he answered, looking out the front window as though expecting them to get moving toward their shared destination.

"Yes," she said, staring into her side mirror and moving back onto the road. When she turned onto the turnpike entrance, she glanced at him from the corner of her eye and bit her bottom lip. He was smiling like a damn fool, as if very happy with the situation. And he spoke too properly, too carefully, as though he were a foreigner and English wasn't his first language, though there was no accent she could detect.

So who *was* this guy? He didn't seem like a serial killer or a rapist. She'd worked for six years in a psych ward, and he didn't show any signs of schizophrenia. At least not yet. And that's when she felt the heavy threads of fear winding up from her belly.

Oh God, what had she gotten herself into this time?

Chapter

2

OKAY, SO IT WAS TIME TO GET DOWN TO BUSINESS—THE business of her own sanity—because in the last five minutes her mind had become paranoid. If he wasn't a killer or a rapist, might he be a terrorist? And immediately she hated that the thought even crossed her mind. He could fit the profile. But what did she know?

Absolutely nothing . . . about him, at least.

Just because he spoke perfect English, had brown hair and eyes and an exotic olive complexion, she was programmed to be afraid of him? That wasn't her. She knew exactly what the government and the media were doing, hypnotizing the public with their repetition of key scare words—*terrorist warnings, security levels*—filtered into almost every speech. Repeat something often enough, and the subconscious takes it for truth. She'd done it herself with her students and later her clients to quit smoking or lose weight or to stop a stutter or nail biting. Just about anything could be programmed into the subconscious, but she didn't want to be a programmed citizen of fear. However, this guy next to her just wasn't . . . right.

Clearing her throat, she eased into the middle lane of the turnpike and set the cruise control to seventy miles an hour. Even at that speed, cars were whizzing by her, setting her nerves on edge even more. God, was she becoming an old fart? One of those annoying drivers who should be in the slow lane? No. Not yet. She was traveling five miles over the speed limit. Maybe this one time she wouldn't mind if a police car pulled her over.

"So . . . ," she began, trying hard to sound casual. "You haven't told me your name yet."

She waited for his answer with what she hoped was a casual expression.

He didn't say anything.

She darted a look at him, and he was still smiling as he continued to stare out the windshield.

"No, I haven't, have I?"

All right, not a good sign. Killer? Rapist? Terrorist? Amnesiac?

"You do have one, right?"

"I believe it is the custom that all are given names when they come into this world."

That answer didn't make her feel any more comfortable, especially the way he said it, like repeating a fact, so she decided to be more direct. "What is your name?" There. To hell with politeness.

"Joshua. You may call me Joshua."

Isabel expelled her breath. It was a beginning. "Joshua. So where do you live in Haverton?"

"I don't believe I said I lived there."

Again, she glanced at him from the corner of her eye. He was still smiling and seemed very interested in the passing scenery. "I'm sorry. I thought you did when you got in the car." She paused, wondering how she'd gotten that wrong. "So where do you live?"

"Is that important to our conversation?"

She blinked several times, staring at the rear of the car in front of her. "Ah, I guess not. I don't mean to be rude, Joshua, but I rarely pick up hitchhikers."

"You have nothing to fear from me, Isabel," he said, and she felt him turning his head to look at her. "I have come a very long way to meet you, and I would never harm you."

Isabel felt her heart rate increase as she clutched the steering wheel and tried to appear calm. "I'm sorry. I don't understand. You came to meet me?"

"Yes. That was my intention today."

"Why? I don't think we've ever met before and . . ." Her words trailed off while she tried to come up with possibilities. He had come to the conference to meet her? Meet *her*? It made no sense. "Why did you want to meet me, Joshua?" She eased into the right-hand lane, in case she slammed on the brakes and ran from the car. On the turnpike? Still, she'd get off at the next exit and ask him to leave her car. Politely, but firmly.

"Dear, Isabel . . . I have wanted to meet you like this for some time now. The conference gave me the perfect opportunity."

"I'm afraid I don't know what you mean." She swallowed deeply, beginning to feel like she was back at that podium and trying desperately to keep the lid on a panic attack.

He sighed. "You are afraid, and for no reason, Isabel. I mean you no harm."

"Well, you are frightening me and sounding like a stalker, or . . . or something."

"A stalker?" He seemed to think about it and then laughed. Laughed!

"I don't think that's funny," Isabel stated, not liking the whole encounter one bit. This was what she got for being the Good Samaritan. No good deed goes unpunished.

"Please stop allowing your fear to overwhelm you, Isabel," he said calmly, rationally, like *she* was the crazy one.

"I don't know what you mean," she answered in denial, desperately looking for an exit or a police car or something to help her.

"Of course you do. Your fear overwhelmed you when you were giving your speech at the conference today. And you're allowing it power again."

"Okay, I don't know who you are, but at the next exit you're going to have to get out of my car. I'm not comfortable with this." Why, on the Pennsylvania Turnpike, were the damn exits so far apart?

"On second thought, perhaps this wasn't such a good idea, especially while you are operating a vehicle."

"What does that mean?" she demanded, white-knuckling the steering wheel and looking at a passing car with desperation. Why was everyone in such a hurry that they couldn't even glance in her direction? See her frightened expression? Would anyone actually pay attention in today's world with its frantic pace and noninvolvement? Maybe she should put on her flashing lights and—

"It means, Isabel Calloway," he declared, interrupting her chaotic thoughts, "that we will continue our conversation at a later date." He placed his hand on her shoulder. "Now, please calm down. . . ."

And in that moment, Isabel felt a very pleasant tingle of energy enter her body and infuse it with waves of peace. She let her breath out. She released her death grip on the steering wheel. She blinked as her foot let up on the accelerator and the car coasted to the side of the road. And when she came to a stop, she turned her head to look at him.

Her jaw dropped.

He wasn't there. She was alone in the car.

Isabel blinked several times, trying to make sense out of the whole thing. Joshua. The tall, good-looking younger guy. She'd picked him up. He'd been in her car. She'd spoken to him. Looking around the roadside, she shook her head in disbelief. No sign of him. Had she blacked out, and he'd left her on the side of the road? What the hell was happening here?

She wasn't crazy! But nothing like this had ever happened to her before.

He *had been* sitting in her car moments ago!

Nobody could just up and disappear like that. Something had to have happened to her when he touched her arm. She remembered feeling peaceful and . . . and maybe she had coasted to the side of the road and . . . *and what?* Dozed off on the Pennsylvania Turnpike with cars speeding past at over sixty-five miles an hour? Not likely.

Don't think about it now, Isabel, she told herself firmly, willing her heartbeat to slow down and using her turn signal to get back into the traffic. She'd figure it all out later. Right now she needed to get back on the road, make it home, and then get a very big drink. *Bizarre* was a good word to use for the whole encounter. The entire day was completely weird!

She'd known she never should have gotten out of bed on a Saturday morning that was perfectly good for being lazy. But no . . . she had caved under pressure from her friends and had proceeded to make a complete fool of herself in front of her colleagues. Oh, and had picked up a hitchhiker for the first time in over twenty years, and he had turned out to be a stalker and then had disappeared right out of her car like David Copperfield!

Just get home, Isabel, she told herself.

So that was what she focused on, back on the turnpike, into the midst of speeding cars: *Get home, get undressed, have a drink, maybe a few, and go to sleep.*

Tomorrow would have to be a better day.

Forty-five minutes later, she pulled into her driveway as twilight seemed to cast her home in eerie shadows. For the first time since Chuck's death, the big white Victorian with its mulberry shutters and trim looked like the setting for a suspense movie. Sitting in the car, staring up at the house, Isabel sighed. It was far too big to live in alone. She'd known that for years. Too many rooms, too many floors, too much empty space for one person. Chuck had filled it with vitality, and had used every weekend to restore it and bring it back to life.

But there was no life in it now, save her own, and maybe she should finally think about selling it, letting a family fill its rooms with laughter and love.

Laughter and love . . . that time of her life was over.

Isabel leaned her head back against the seat cushion. She had realized several years before that part of herself had shut down. Certainly she laughed with others, especially the wild women in her circle of friends; but the laughter of intimacy, to just look at the beloved, read their thoughts, and burst into simultaneous giggles . . . that was the past. And love? She'd had the best. Well, her best anyway, and so what did that leave her with? A life struggling to find meaning and purpose? What made her get up every morning and get on with life?

Helping others, the children?

It wasn't a question she could answer, so she pulled the keys out of the ignition and opened the door. *Enough introspection,* she thought as she got out of the car and opened the rear door to pick up her briefcase. Pulling the strap of her bag onto her shoulder, Isabel closed the car doors and walked up to the front door of the house. She passed the scarlet and white mums she'd planted last month and reminded herself to water them if it didn't rain in the next few days.

She was still playing with the possibility of putting the place up for sale when she reached the wide porch that spanned the entire front of the house. It was when she was fumbling with her keys that she heard his voice.

"Hello, Isabel. I'm glad you returned safely."

She spun around as her heart seemed to jump into her throat, constricting it with fear. He was here! At her home! Rising from one of the wicker rocking chairs, as though he'd been an invited guest!

She could barely breathe, but she forced the words out. "What . . . are you doing here?"

"I am here to see you. I thought I had made that clear while you were driving."

"Look," she said, her mind racing to find something to defend herself with, "I think you'd better leave. I . . . I'll call the police." Why didn't she have a can of mace in her purse or pepper spray, or anything to use against him? She curled her fingers around her ignition key, clutching it between her first two fingers like a weapon. At least it was something.

"Isabel, please try to regain some composure. For a moment, stand outside yourself and see what your fear is doing to you. I would never, ever harm you. In fact, my intention is exactly the opposite." He came closer as he spoke, smiling at her.

He could be insane, she thought as panic again began to seize her vital organs, strangling her breath and making her freeze. "Go away," she muttered, thinking of the time she'd stood down a mental patient who'd grabbed a knife and how she'd talked him into surrendering to the orderlies. But there were no orderlies now, ready to take over and inject enough Thorazine to bring down an elephant. All she had was herself, her wits. . . .

"Enough of this," he whispered, as though to himself, as he reached out for her arm.

Suddenly, she wasn't frozen. It was pure survival instinct that made her raise her hand and use the key as a weapon as she sliced at his forearm. "Get away from me!" she cried, trying to break his hold. Yet as soon as his fingers clasped around her arm, she felt an immediate rush of energy infuse her body with peace and well-being. Her fingers unfurled, and the key dropped to the wooden floor of the porch as she stared into his eyes.

"What will it take for you to trust me, Isabel? How many times must I repeat I mean you no harm?"

She was breathing heavily as she stared at him, only vaguely aware that she had also dropped her briefcase when the sound of it hitting the floor registered. Her mind was calming, and for an instant, just a mere fraction of time, she felt a weird kinship with the man, as though it was perfectly natural for him to be on her porch, holding her arm, staring into her eyes.

"Are you better?" he asked with a slight smile, a friendly smile that made his eyes sparkle with something she couldn't name. Whatever it was, wasn't frightening.

Isabel could only nod.

"Good. Now I'm going to let go of you, and I would ask if we could sit down and have a discussion. I know you find it hard to believe, but I truly have come a very long way to speak with you."

"Okay," she answered stupidly, hearing her voice crack. She watched as he let go of her arm, and then he reached down to pick up her keys and her briefcase. In some distant part of her brain she realized she could have knocked him off balance and run for the car, but she was no longer afraid of him. Whatever he had to say must be important to him, and the sooner he said it, the sooner he would leave her alone.

He handed her the keys.

Isabel took them, almost afraid to look in his eyes again. Whatever that connection was they'd momentarily had, she wasn't ready to name it. "I . . . I'll make us some tea, and then you can tell me what is so important." She managed to unlock the door, then flipped on the light switch so her living room was illuminated. Only the outside of her home was Victorian. Inside was classic traditional in shades of brown and cream and moss greens. "If you want to wait here, I'll bring the tea. Do you like tea, or would you prefer coffee?" She didn't add that she, herself, would like a stiff drink.

"Whatever you're having would be fine, Isabel." He smiled again. "Thank you. For trusting me."

She simply nodded and walked away, through her dining room that seated twelve, and into her kitchen where, if she knew him better, she would have invited him to join her. Besides a large table and chairs, there was a sofa in front of the tall windows.

She turned on the light and remembered Chuck always keeping her company while she cooked, sitting on the sofa and reading a book or the evening paper, discussing the day's events. Shaking her head, Isabel proceeded to fill the teakettle. Another time and place. Those were the years of happiness, fulfillment, and knowing she was on the right path with the right person. The only thing that had been missing in their marriage was children, but she'd often wondered if having children would have altered them in ways that took away from the relationship.

Isabel shook her head, as though shaking out the past. Those memories were useless now. It was the present that needed her attention. Right now she had a very strange, good-looking younger man in her living room who had something important to say to her. *Concentrate,* she told herself, bringing down a silver tray and then reaching for the box of tea. All she had to do was treat him like a guest, listen to him, and then send him on his way. She looked at the kitchen phone. If he didn't leave she would call the police.

And then maybe she could have that large drink and get to bed.

Five minutes later, she walked back into the living room and saw him standing at the black baby grand piano by the windows. He was looking at the pictures on top of it, her gallery of loved ones, and for a moment, a split second, from the back he reminded her of Chuck. Tall. Dark. Lean. He must have heard her sharp intake of breath, for he turned around and smiled, breaking the spell.

"Here we are," she said, placing the tray on the coffee table and standing straight up to face him.

"You don't play, do you?" he asked.

She shook her head and smiled. "No. My husband did. Most of those pictures are of him. He . . . ," she paused and then just said it. "He died."

Joshua nodded. "You loved him very much."

"Yes," she murmured. "I did. I do," she quickly corrected. "He was the love of my life."

Joshua looked at the pictures once more and then moved away from the piano to sit on the sofa. Isabel felt him watching her as she poured the tea into the cups. "There's cream, light cream, and sugar."

"Thank you, Isabel," he said, watching as she sat opposite him on the edge of the seat cushion of one of the large club chairs flanking the coffee table.

She felt his gaze on her as she fixed her tea and brought the cup and saucer to rest on her lap. He appeared to like his tea just like hers, with only sugar. "Now, Joshua, what is it that you've come to tell me?" she asked as calmly as possible. *Treat him like a client. Be professional. In control.* And they might as well get on with this discussion. Enough of polite chitchat. She wanted to get out of her suit and climb into bed as soon as possible.

Joshua sat back, taking his tea with him, and smiled at her. "You're very direct."

"I've learned not to waste time and to get to the issue," she answered, then sipped her tea.

"What I have to tell you, Isabel, may be startling, but I would ask that you allow me to finish before interrupting with questions."

She simply nodded, giving him permission to begin.

"I have traveled a very long way to meet you because the time has come for you to acknowledge how extraordinary you are, why you came to this planet at this particular time, and how to use your skills in helping your brothers and sisters to evolve and recognize their purpose and their own extraordinary skills. It is now time, Isabel, that you put away the past and move forward." He finished his little speech and looked very pleased to have delivered it.

Isabel forced her fingers to relax around the fragile china saucer. She purposefully relaxed her shoulder muscles and took a deep breath. "Do you realize how arrogant you sounded, making that statement? As though you have some secret knowledge of the future when you know nothing about me?" Enough with politeness. Time to get rid of him, to end this ridiculous situation and—

"I know a great deal about you," he said in a calm voice, interrupting her thoughts. "I know that you are on a path of evolution, that you knew since you were a child there was more to this world than what you were being taught. I know that you fell in love when you were a young girl, that your future husband was older than you and worked in the movie theater you went to every Sunday, where you sat in the back row on the aisle. I know that he would come up and place his hand on your shoulder, never speaking to you with words, but you knew in your soul he was the man you would someday marry. I know that when you went to college you lost touch with him and pledged yourself to a man of medicine and that when your Chuck came back to Haverton, you stood up against your parents and married the man they thought was beneath your class. And I know, Isabel, that you were very happy married to him until he left you unexpectedly. And, most importantly, I know that you've had your life on hold since he's been gone. As I have said, Isabel, it is time to put the past behind you and move forward. You have a gift that needs to be shared."

She was barely breathing, staring at him in disbelief. How could he know all that? She had never told anyone about Chuck coming up to her every Sunday in that darkened movie theater and placing his hand on her shoulder. "How . . . ?" Her voice cracked. "How do you know all that?"

"I know that because I know you, Isabel. I have known

you since you were a young child. I have watched over you, guided you, protected you. And I have been so pleased with your progress until Chuck died. Then you stopped moving forward. You stayed static, remaining the grieving widow when you have so much life in you to share."

"I don't know what you're talking about," she said, her hand shaking so badly that she spilled tea onto her good Turkish rug as she put the cup and saucer back onto the coffee table. "I . . . I think you should leave."

"How can I leave, Isabel? I am always with you."

She felt like she was in a nightmare as she stood. "I don't want you with me!" she stated as firmly as she could. "You are an intruder."

"But you invited me in," he answered calmly, as though not fazed by her reaction.

"I invited you in when I thought you had something reasonably sane to discuss. Since that's obviously not the case, I'm now inviting you out."

He smiled with patience. "That isn't what I am talking about. You invited me in a very long time ago. Think back, Isabel, to when you were a small child, three years old in your perception of time. One splendid afternoon in the summer, you were hiding from your mother down by the stream, making mud pies, and we were laughing, you and I, playing together. Do you remember? You asked me not to leave, and I told you I wouldn't."

She felt like crying because her world, her once so orderly world, seemed like it was cracking and falling apart before her very eyes. "I had . . ." She swallowed. "It was an imaginary friend. . . ."

His head tilted slightly as he continued to smile. "Imagination is evidence of the divine."

"Who *are* you? Where did you come from?"

"Sit back down, Isabel, and I will tell you," he answered, standing up and coming around the coffee table.

She froze, afraid of him, of whatever knowledge he had about her.

"Relax. I'm not going to touch you," he said, passing her and walking toward the dining room. "I'm going to get you that drink you've been craving since you delivered your speech today."

And she watched in stunned amazement as he proceeded to the cabinet in the dining room and opened the door where she kept the bottles of alcohol. He removed a bottle and then went into the kitchen like he knew every inch of her house, like he knew every inch of her mind. He came back into the living room carrying a glass of ice and a bottle of Jameson's Irish whiskey. He opened the bottle and poured her a drink.

Handing the glass to her, he said, "Maybe this will calm you. Take it."

She noticed her hand was shaking as she accepted the glass and brought it to her mouth. She gulped, grateful for the warmth that slid down her throat, her chest, and settled in her belly. *"What are you?"* she muttered. "Like my guardian angel, or something?" The words, those very words, actually came out of her mouth!

He laughed gently. "If that is how you'd like to think of me, I can accept that label."

She sank to the matching club chair and stared up at him. "I want to know who *you* say you are."

"I am a being from a different dimension, one that is more evolved than this one. Your science has something it calls string theory, very unpredictable, but there is really an exquisite order to what appears to be chaos. You always knew, even as a child, that there was more to the physical world than what you were being taught, Isabel. And you were right. It is what made you question the accepted explanations you were being given by your teachers, your ministers, your politicians. And it has served you well by opening your mind."

"So you're like what? An alien from a different dimension?" Just saying the words out loud made her cringe. She was a professional! People came to her for sanity! This is what they shut people away for, delusional behavior. She didn't want to be crazy, to be shut away.

"Don't let your fear creep back in and take away your power, Isabel."

"How do you know what I'm thinking? And you didn't answer me. Are you an alien?"

"First, I don't always know exactly what you are thinking, but I can tell by your aura when you allow fear. It changes and becomes darker. And I'm not an alien from another planet. I am a being, like you, a sentient being, just from a different dimension."

"I don't believe you . . . ," she whispered, staring up at him and wishing she would just wake up from this insanity. *Wake up! Wake up, Issy!* she pleaded.

He only nodded, accepting her disbelief.

"How about this?" he asked.

Isabel could only blink as her jaw dropped in wonder. Joshua, the man who was standing in front of her, began to disintegrate into tiny white lights that swirled like magic fairy dust until he disappeared.

"Ohmygod . . ." she muttered, afraid to even breathe.

And in the next moment, he was back, staring down at her and smiling like nothing incredible had ever happened.

She just shook her head, unable to speak.

"I'm sorry. I thought you needed a more dramatic demonstration."

"What I need," she managed to croak out, "is another drink!"

"Yes, of course," he answered, and picked up the bottle of Jameson's. He poured her a drink, placed the bottle back onto the coffee table, and then moved away to the piano.

Still shocked, Isabel watched as he lifted the lid of the seat and took out a music book. He leafed through it and then placed it above the keyboards.

"Do you mind if I play?" he asked, sitting down. "It might soothe your mind."

She simply blinked, incapable of speech yet.

And then he began playing, slowly and beautifully, Chopin's "Nocturne in C Minor." She let her breath out and listened, waiting to hear a mistake, but there was none. He could have been playing at Carnegie Hall. He was . . . exquisite, his eyes closed, absorbing the music, playing with a skill that she had never seen in someone not classically trained and on a stage. His eyes opened and he smiled at her, locking in her vision, and Isabel instinctively felt that odd kinship again. She knew she had nothing to fear from him.

Whoever he was, *whatever* he was, he wouldn't hurt her.

Chapter

3

SHE SAT, MESMERIZED, WATCHING HIM PLAY THE PIANO. Somewhere in the back of her mind she acknowledged he was so much better than Chuck had ever been. And then she thought how bizarre it was that she was holding a glass of Jameson's in her hands, watching a . . . a dimension traveler who knew everything about her playing the piano in her living room. As if it were normal!

Like this happens in anyone's life!

She brought the drink to her lips and gulped again. She didn't care. This was a night for getting drunk, if ever there was one. Who was this man, this *being,* with magical powers? Why had he picked her life to invade, to turn upside down?

She finished the drink, then placed her glass on the coffee table and rose. She forced her legs to move and slowly walked up to the piano, wondering if she were sleepwalking, for it could only be a dream. Things like this just didn't happen in normal, sane lives, and she was supposed to be normal, at least sane. She'd made a living at it, for God's sake. She became fascinated, watching his long fingers glide over the keys until the song ended, captivated by the effortless movement to create such hauntingly lovely music.

"That was beautiful," she whispered, tears coming into her eyes. "Chuck would play for me sometimes."

"Yes, I know," Joshua answered in a gentle voice. "I had hoped you would like it."

"Where did you learn to play like that? It was . . . exquisite." That was the only word she could think of to describe his skill.

"Let me just say that I am able to absorb many things at once. I know you love the piano. You should have kept up the lessons after your husband died."

"I'm not even going to question how you knew that." She was too tired not to surrender to whatever was happening. She was carrying on a conversation with this handsome person from . . . somewhere, another world. And it was taking place in her once so orderly, predictable life. Besides, the Jameson's was working.

"Why didn't you continue?"

Isabel shrugged, glancing at a picture of her and Chuck together in France. "I don't know. The piano was Chuck's secret love. I always thanked his mother for insisting he had lessons as a child. An ironworker who loved to play classical piano. It was part of his charm, not mine."

"Would you like me to teach you?"

She shook her head and backed away to the sofa. "No. Now it's a lovely piece of furniture that holds pictures of a life long ago."

"It is a shame not to use it, Isabel."

"Then you can use it, if you come back for a visit." Had she just said that? Had those words actually come out of her mouth?

"I am still invited?" he asked, rising from his seat.

She grinned, trying to make the best out of her fumble. "Would it make any difference if you weren't?"

"It would make everything harder," he admitted, coming to sit next to her on the sofa. "I so did not want to frighten you, Isabel. But we needed to make contact."

"Contact. Is that what this is?"

He nodded, his eyes focused on hers, and she felt a frisson of electricity race through her veins, making the hair on her skin rise with a strange energy.

It suddenly came to her what was happening. She was attracted to him. Like in man/woman attracted! And she was shocked by something she hadn't felt in almost seven years: that insidious snaking of desire that rises so marvelously up from the core of a woman and awakens every nerve ending in her body. "What do you want with me, Joshua?" she whispered.

"I only want what you want, Isabel," he whispered back.

"What do I want, then? You seem to know me so well," she countered. Was she actually flirting with him? No, she couldn't . . . could she?

"You want what every being wants: to fulfill your potential, to feel loved and to give it in return. It's what makes you feel alive."

"So I haven't been alive?" she asked, feeling very . . . sexy . . . while staring into his eyes. Sexy. She hadn't felt that in years, many, many years. "I've given my love."

"Yes, you have, Isabel, to your husband and, since his death, to your friends, to those who come to you for help. Let me ask you something." He paused. "Do you believe you are worthy of receiving it again?"

Unexpectedly, looking at him so close, she felt something familiar take over her body, like an old friend who had gone away, but who'd now returned with even more presence. It was power. Sexual power. Something every female is aware of at some time of her life.

"Isabel?"

She blinked. Stared at him. And then blinked again.

Good God in heaven, she wanted the man with such desire that it was like an out-of-body experience to find herself leaning into him, grabbing him by the collar of his shirt, and slowly pulling him toward her, staring at his mouth, into his surprised eyes, then back at his mouth, only moments before allowing her own mouth to cover his in a kiss. Her hands rose to his hair, running her fingers through the silkiness, moaning as the kiss deepened and his hands pulled her in closer. When the kiss ended, she was gasping, staring into his eyes, mentally pleading with him to put out the intense fire within her before she spontaneously combusted!

"Isabel . . . I'm not so sure this is the way . . . to—"

"I don't care. This is *my* way," she murmured, sounding very unlike herself, like a bold woman who knew her mind and wasn't afraid to speak it. "It's what I want," she muttered, vaguely aware that she really didn't know her mind if *this* was actually a part of it. Blame it on the Jameson's. . . .

It was as though some stranger had taken over her mind and her body, an insane wanton with seven years of celibacy inside of her who was demanding release. It was exactly like riding a bike. It all came back to her: the scent of male, the firmness of muscles, the rightness of hard against soft, that her body was made to accept a man's.

Who cared if the man wasn't exactly from this world?

Nothing seemed to matter, except following the instincts of her body. She was like a drug addict, craving what she knew was right there in front of her, what every atom in her body was desiring. And it was too strong to fight.

Isabel was possessed to have sex, pure primal sex, pulling at his clothes and then hers. She simply could not stop herself from feeling his skin upon her own. She threw his shirt to the rug and tore her blouse off to follow it. She undid her bra and didn't even think that her breasts were no longer firm and perky. Nothing mattered. Not even that he was younger. He was male. That was all that mattered.

Surely, she had crossed some invisible line and was entering a place she hadn't known existed inside of her.

And once she had started this insanity, she had to have him, to finish it.

She ran her fingers over his chest with awe, studying it the way a collector must feel when touching a masterpiece. He pulled her to him, and she gasped with pleasure as her breasts were crushed against him. Clinging to him as he began kissing her neck and then her shoulder, she brushed away some rational part of her brain that was urging her to rethink her actions. She didn't want rational. Rational had been ripped away from her the moment Joshua came into her life. Now, all she wanted was to satisfy the burning desire inside her body that was calling out to him.

Still holding him, she fell back on the sofa, taking him with her. It wasn't choreographed; it was a fiery desire to feel his weight covering her body.

He was over her, breathing heavily, staring down at her.

"Don't speak," she commanded. "Please. Don't say anything. Just make love to me."

He seemed to understand her need and reached under her skirt for her panties. He pulled them down and off her legs, then unbuttoned his jeans. When he came back to her, he began kissing her breasts, but she was impatient. She didn't want foreplay.

"Please . . . I want you in me," she pleaded, pulling his face down to hers. There. She couldn't be any more clear about her intentions. No shame, no hesitancy was allowed. "Don't ask me to explain anything. Not now. I just . . . need you."

And then he filled her in one slow but magnificent motion, and she cried out her pleasure at the sweetly remembered sensation of fullness.

"Isabel . . ."

"Shh . . . ," she whispered, not wanting him to break the spell. Not now, not when she was so close. She began to move her hips in a sensuous dance, inviting him to follow the rhythm. He did.

Isabel closed her eyes, remembering it all now, the striving for something just out of reach, the slide of bodies working together as hearts pounded against each other, textures of skin and scent mingling, the absolutely magnificent sensation of a hard member teasing and coaxing a softer, hidden one.

Over and over, timelessness, sensations spreading and building, gasps of surprise, pleasure, near desperation . . . until she was clasping him tightly, throwing her head back into the sofa cushion, exploding in a shockingly mind-wiping orgasm of pleasure, waves and waves of pleasure that took her out of herself again . . . leaving behind the mundane of this world and transporting her into exquisite nothingness.

Her gratification only increased when she felt Joshua follow her, fusing his soul with hers as they traveled into the nameless abyss together, joined as one as they were thrust into joy and slowly, deliciously, returned to reality.

He was leaning on his elbows over her, his hands in her hair, breathing heavily. "I . . . I never . . ."

She opened her eyes and weakly smiled up to him, trying to catch her breath. "Never?" she gasped.

"No, not like that," he answered, and hung his head next to her own. "Not a physical communion."

"God, I've missed it!" she breathed and laughed out loud with relief. "I didn't know how much until now. . . ."

Joshua raised his head. He was sweating, his face flushed with pleasure. "It is good to hear you laugh," he murmured, and smiled down at her, his dark brown eyes confirming their connection.

And that's when it hit her.

She had just had sex with a complete stranger. Fast and furious sex she had initiated!

Her body stiffened with shock as her reality crashed in upon her. Oh, dear God, dear God, dear God . . . had she gone temporarily insane?!

"Please don't do this, Isabel," Joshua whispered, stroking back her hair. "I can't stay here any longer to reassure you.

I must leave now." He paused. "Please. Don't ruin the moment with fear or regret."

She closed her eyes to shut him out. How could she possibly deal with a person who knew every emotion she was feeling? Now all she wanted was for him to get off her and go away as pleasure was replaced with confusion and remorse. What the hell was wrong with her? What had she *done*?

He kissed her temple and whispered in her ear. "You are magnificent."

And then he must have moved off her, because she suddenly felt alone, as though something wonderful had been taken away. She reluctantly opened her eyes. He was gone, and she wondered if any of it had been real.

A grand delusion? A break with reality?

Stop thinking. . . .

Isabel lay on the sofa, not moving yet. It was as if her brain were sluggish, unable to direct the movement of her limbs. All she could do was feel.

And yet, despite her conflicting emotions, her body felt wonderful, alive, still tingling with vitality. She didn't care if it was real or the product of a very vivid imagination. It had been fabulous. She knew that science would say she was flooded with endorphins, but she'd never realized before how sex could energize the body. Of course, not having had it for seven long, lonely years might have something to do with it.

Embarrassed, she nervously giggled like a younger woman, and slowly raised her arms above her head, running her fingers through her tousled hair. Good God, but she wanted it again! How shameful was that? She lowered her hands and ran them over her breasts, her belly, remembering the exquisite feeling of Joshua inside of her. And then she moaned, groaned, grateful and yet ashamed as she rolled to her side and hugged herself.

She should get up, fix her clothes, clean the tea stain on the rug, but she didn't want to break the spell. And it was a spell—of that she had no doubt. It had to be. Nothing less could have made her act like a wanton, disregarding what she had known was right behavior.

But was it wrong?

Hadn't he come to her? Hadn't he messed up her head with his words, his knowledge, his incredible story about being her . . . her what? Guardian angel? But he wasn't an angel, was he? She couldn't have just had mind-blowing sex with an angel!

Suddenly she remembered Cristine telling her and Claire about Daniel, how he was different, and she did remember thinking she saw some strange light coming from him once. Could Joshua be the same? Could she ask Cristine about it, without Cristine thinking she had lost all reason?

No. She definitely didn't want anyone to find out about Joshua, and especially how she had behaved with him. That is, if Joshua was even real.

Whatever he was, angel or imaginary kook, he had to remain her secret.

She was turning fifty in a matter of days, and she didn't want anyone thinking she was having a midlife crisis. Everyone turned to her during a crisis. And right now, if this was a crisis . . . well, she'd gladly take one on a daily basis, thank you very much.

At least the sex part.

Eventually, she did rise and clean her rug. She did take the silver tray with two cups and saucers on it into the kitchen. That was proof she hadn't been alone, right? She did gather her discarded clothes and make her way upstairs to her bedroom. And for the first time in over seven years, she slept naked, relishing the sensuous feel of her good sheets over her skin.

As she fell asleep, Isabel knew this night had changed her.

Whatever actually happened didn't matter. It was like a faucet that had been rusted shut had magically been opened. Did any of it make sense? No, but she didn't care.

She felt alive again.

She felt like a woman again.

And she was grateful—very, very grateful.

§

Isabel awoke the next morning still feeling like she was wearing a cloak of enchantment. The sun was shining brightly. Birds that were not making plans to leave for the winter were singing. While washing her face and brushing her teeth, she had looked at herself in the mirror over the sink and thought her eyes looked brighter and her skin softer, silkier. She checked the weather outside, and it was one of those unseasonably warm days where the temperature hovers around sixty degrees when it should be in the thirties. Not yet ready to return to her normal world and still dressed in her bathrobe, she decided to take advantage of the warmth and took her cup of coffee out to the gazebo.

She didn't even want to read the Sunday paper, which was her routine. For once she didn't care what was happening to the rest of the world. There was this odd feeling swirling around inside of her that she couldn't quite name. It felt vaguely familiar, like an exotic spice she had once tasted. What was it? she wondered, sitting down at the table and staring out to the stream that bordered her back property line.

Suddenly, as she simply gave into it and didn't question it, it came to her.

She was happy.

How very odd to have forgotten what real happiness felt like. For years she had thought a part of her was missing, gone, and it was something she would just have to live with and get over. And now she found that it had always been there, waiting for her to reclaim it.

A tiny slice of her mind wasn't exactly pleased that it had taken a man, or the figment of her imagination or whatever he was, to show her. She'd never been a raging feminist, but shouldn't she have been able to find happiness without a man, without sex? She had thought she was content, but last night had shown her how mistaken she'd been. There is a difference between contentment with the way things are and happiness.

She was happy again.

And the insane part was that she was actually believing Joshua, that he came from another dimension and knew everything about her. What else could explain him disappearing before her eyes and then magically reappearing? There had been no smoke and mirrors. He'd disappeared from her car too and had reappeared on her front porch. Now, either what he was saying was true, or she'd had a huge mental blackout and lost an entire evening from the moment she'd gotten into her car at the college. And she knew, deep down, that hadn't happened.

This man—this *being*—had come into her life and had turned it completely upside down. Here she was, a woman about to turn fifty, and her body was still singing the "Alleluia" chorus after having sex with someone she'd just met, yet whom she felt like she'd known all her life. What was happening to her? Was it a blessing, or a curse? Because now all she could think about was whether or not Joshua would return.

And how would she ever look him in the eye again . . . knowing . . . ?

"Well, look at you. Communing with nature on this unexpectedly fine Sunday morning."

Startled, she turned and then waved, watching Claire make her way across the back lawn. Dressed in jeans and a white cotton sweater, Claire held a takeout cup of coffee and a bag from Starbucks.

"Good morning, Claire," Isabel called out, a little disappointed her time of contemplation was being interrupted, yet smiling at Claire's blond ponytail. She looked like a teenager, which wasn't hard with her petite figure.

"Morning. When there was no answer at the door, I figured I'd try out here. God, it's gorgeous today. Who would think winter is right around the corner?" Stepping into the gazebo, Claire slid her coffee onto the table and dropped the bag. "Goodies I couldn't resist. The slice of carrot cake is mine, but I'll share if you plead with me." She sat down and reached for the bag.

"The carrot cake is all yours. I'm not hungry yet," Isabel answered with a grin, wishing she had a pair of sunglasses on like Claire's, so she could hide behind them.

"Good, because I'm starved." Claire opened the bag and pulled out the cake. She broke off a piece with her fingers and asked, "So how did the conference go?" before putting the cake into her mouth and licking her fingers.

"It went," Isabel said. "And I'm glad it's over."

Claire swallowed and looked at her. "What does that mean? You gave your speech, right?"

"Right. Barely managed to get through it."

"And . . . ?"

"And it was received with politeness. Cool politeness."

"Really? I'm surprised. What happened?"

Isabel shrugged. "I'm out of practice, I guess. I just about had an anxiety attack at the podium."

"Oh no." Claire sat back and sighed. "Well, at least you tried. Next time will be easier."

"Next time? Whoever said there was going to be a next time?" Isabel demanded with a laugh. "I think my days of public speaking are over, thank you."

"Oh, for God's sake, Issy, you're a professional," Claire countered with impatience, reaching for more of her cake. "You know it's all in your head. You're good with people's heads, so deal with your own for a change."

"Can we drop the subject?" Isabel asked, sipping her cooling coffee. "You're ruining my perfectly lazy Sunday morning with your nagging."

Claire sighed loudly this time. "Fine. I'll just sit here and stuff my face while you commune with nature." She paused. "But you could have called me back yesterday."

"You called?"

"Left a message wishing you luck and told you to call me when you got back. So here I am, thinking maybe you got kidnapped or something and coming over to check on you, and you say I'm nagging." Claire chewed another bite of her cake. "See if I bring you goodies next time."

Kidnapped? Not exactly. Isabel turned to her and smiled. "I'm sorry I didn't get your message. I . . . I didn't even check the machine last night. And I'm sorry you were worried. As you can see, I'm fine."

Claire slowly sat up straighter and pulled down her sunglasses to the tip of her nose as she stared at Isabel.

Isabel found herself blinking and forcing herself not to look away with guilt.

Claire's mouth opened, and her jaw dropped as she seemed to inhale all the air around her. *"You've had sex!"* she exclaimed in a shocked voice.

Isabel blinked again and then had to look away to the tree line. She laughed self-consciously and shook her head. "Claire . . ."

"Don't deny it," Claire said, leaning in closer, as though seeing something unexpectedly rare, yet shocking. "You're positively glowing!"

"You're being absurd. There must be some chemical in your carrot cake that makes you delusional."

"Isabel Calloway, don't even bother denying it. I can always tell on a woman's face. Not a man's, unfortunately, which led to a delay in dumping my ex, but with women it's written right there to see." Claire grinned mischievously. "Who is it? My God, this is like losing your virginity all over again! I could not be happier! Tell me! Tell me every single juicy detail, or I'll stand up and yell it out to your neighbors."

"Claire . . . I'd rather not get into a discussion about—"

"Stop evading, Issy. This is the best news I've had since Cristine gave birth. Granted, I'm a little shocked, but what the hell. You got laid, girl, after seven years. I didn't even know you were seeing someone. Now dish out the details! Where did you meet him, what's he look like? Tell me everything."

Isabel laughed. "Oh for heaven's sake, will you calm down? I don't know why you think you've got this ability to see things in a person's face, because the simple matter is—"

"Isabel Calloway got laid last night and—"

Isabel clamped her hand over Claire's mouth. "Have you lost your senses?" she demanded, looking beyond her bare trees. The neighbors were too far away to hear anything, but still. . . . "You would think you're sixteen years old!"

Claire pulled Isabel's hand away from her mouth. "Are you going to tell me?"

"There's nothing to tell."

"Liar. And I've never called you a liar before, Issy. So tell me or I'll take out my cell phone and call an emergency meeting of the Yellow Brick Road Gang." Her eyes gleamed with mischief. "Right now. And you know I'll do it in a heartbeat."

"You can be such a bitch, Claire."

Her friend shrugged. "It's simply part of my charm. C'mon, Issy. You know I love you like an older sister. *Tell* me what happened."

Isabel sat back in her chair and looked out of the gazebo, not really seeing the beauty of nature any longer. Why did

Claire have to come and ruin everything? She didn't want to expose her memories of yesterday to the glare of reality. Not yet.

"Okay, I can see I'm going to have to do a root canal to get this out of you. Where did you meet him?"

Isabel sighed, still staring out to her trees. What was the use? Claire wouldn't give up, and she probably would call a meeting of the Gang. The very last thing she wanted was to deal with four more female inquisitors. But she would not look at Claire, who could read her too well. There was only so much she was willing to reveal. "At the conference."

Claire was swallowing her coffee, and she sputtered, sat up quickly, and coughed. "At the conference?" she demanded in a hoarse voice. "Yesterday? You met him *yesterday*?"

Isabel simply nodded.

"And you had sex last night? God, Issy, I didn't know you had it in you."

Isabel turned her head and looked at her friend, trying to see if there was any judgment in her expression. There wasn't, thank heavens. "Frankly, Claire, neither did I. It . . . just happened. In my living room."

Claire swallowed visibly at the admission.

"You're shocked," Isabel stated.

"Surprised."

"Do you actually think I'm too old to get carried away? That someone my age can't get as horny as a teenager? It happens."

"Hey, I'm thrilled it happened. Gives me great hope for my own future. So, who is he? What's his name?"

"Joshua."

"Joshua," Claire repeated and nodded. "Joshua what?"

Isabel blinked. "I don't know."

Claire burst out laughing. "Oh, you *are* precious, Issy! You finally have sex with someone, and you didn't even find out his whole name!"

Isabel cringed slightly and whispered, "If you think that's insane, I don't even know how old he is."

"Old? You mean . . ." Claire's eyes narrowed. "He's younger?"

"Oh yeah, definitely younger," Isabel said, and crossed her arms over her chest.

"Like Demi and Ashton young?"

"I don't know . . . ," Isabel murmured. "He looks like he's maybe thirty-eight, or thirty-nine, but that could just be wishful thinking." She shuddered. "Don't ask how it happened or why, because I can't explain it. It just happened. Fast and furious."

"And good?" Claire asked with a hopeful smile.

Finally, Isabel couldn't control her facial expression, and shaking her head, she laughed. "Dear God, Claire . . . it was fabulous!"

Claire hooted and slammed her hand down on the table. "All right! Thank God." She paused and sat back in her chair. "Now I'm the only one in the Yellow Brick Road Gang that's not getting any. Even Kelly's got a new boyfriend."

"He's not my boyfriend," Isabel insisted. "I don't know if I'm ever going to see him again."

"No exchange of numbers?"

Isabel hid another laugh and shook her head. Joshua didn't need a phone number.

"Well, he knows where you live."

"Claire, it was a one-time thing. I mean, I'm grateful, but this isn't something I intend to continue."

"Why not?"

"I . . . I'm too mature for this sort of thing."

"Jesus, Issy, you sound like some matron from the last century. You're still young and vital, and last night proves it. See, you really are becoming our role model, grabbing life with both hands. Don't stop because of outdated social convention.

Unless it's something else. You don't feel guilty, do you? Because of Chuck."

Isabel swallowed. "I do feel guilty." She paused. "Because I didn't think once about Chuck."

Claire reached out and stroked Isabel's arm. "I think that's healthy. It's been seven years. And you know that he would want you to live your life fully. Sex is a part of that, right? What's there to feel guilty about?"

Isabel shrugged, knowing what Claire said was true.

"Except that it was a one-night stand with a stranger," Claire blurted out, and giggled. "I'm teasing! I'm just teasing you, silly."

Isabel couldn't even be offended. "If you dare tell anyone else about this, I swear I will never speak to you again. Promise me you will shut your mouth."

"But this is *so damn juicy!*"

"Promise me!"

"Do you know how hard that's going to be? Isabel Calloway having a one-night stand with a young hottie. C'mon, Issy. . . ."

"Promise!"

Claire sighed. "Damn." She held up her hand in resignation. "Okay, okay, I promise not to tell anyone you slept with a younger man you don't know anything about, except he's fabulous in bed."

"Thank you," Isabel said gratefully.

"All right, so tell me what he looks like. Is he gorgeous? Intelligent? Funny? If I have to live vicariously, I want details. How tall is he? Tell me everything. . . ." Claire again slapped the table. "And does he have a brother or cousin or coworker for me?"

Chapter

4

IT WASN'T SUPPOSED TO BE LIKE THIS.

Isabel had thought she would mark the seventh anniversary of Chuck's death quietly, alone, remembering her husband with bittersweet memories. She would not be seated in a bar with the Gang celebrating her birthday one day early, after being kidnapped from her house by five insane women and taken into Philadelphia. Cristine and Claire had arranged rooms at the Four Seasons, and now they were all at some karaoke bar in Center City, listening to Kelly singing "I Will Survive"—and, Isabel thought, using the term *singing* was charitable.

"Oh, c'mon, Issy. Cheer up, will you?" Tina urged, nudging her arm as she sipped on a strawberry-and-banana daiquiri. She looked across the sea of people separating them from the stage. "Geez, just listen to Kelly murder that song!"

"This isn't exactly what I had planned, Tina," Isabel countered, still not believing she had allowed five women to pack an overnight bag, escort her to a limo, ply her with alcohol, register her at the hotel, and drag her to a bar.

"Did you really think we were going to let you wallow in another year's anniversary and then have you deal with the Big Five O the next day? Alone?" Tina arched an eyebrow, waiting for her answer.

"Still . . ."

"Oh, 'still' nothing, Issy," Cristine interjected, taking her attention away from Kelly at the mic. "Try something new, spontaneous. You're turning fifty! This is like a mini break for all of us. Do you know this is the first time I've left the baby overnight? And so far it feels wonderful!" She leaned back in her seat and raised her leg above the table, showing the mandatory sparkly red high heels. "Surrender, Dorothy."

"You do know that was the witch's line?" Isabel countered.

"Tonight I don't care who said it. Just surrender and have fun, okay?"

Realizing she was putting a damper on the festivities, Isabel shrugged her shoulders and stated, "Just so no one thinks I'm getting up there and singing."

"Honey, you're next," Paula said matter-of-factly. "So pick your song."

Everyone looked at her horrified expression and laughed.

"There's only so far I am willing to go with this adventure, and singing is out of the question."

"Well, we can't force her," Cristine said.

"Nope. Must be an old fart gene kicking in, or something," Tina said with a teasing smile as she looked at her watch. "And it's not even midnight. Only twenty minutes to go before you turn fifty."

"Oh, Issy's not an old fart," Claire piped up with a sly grin. "Maybe she should sing 'It's Raining Men.' "

Isabel glared at Claire. "I think we should be paying attention to Kelly."

Tina giggled. "She's right. Kelly's going to need our support when she completes this gruesome massacre. Poor Gloria Gaynor. Never knew a skinny, red-haired white woman with absolutely no singing voice was going make ears bleed. Bless Kelly's heart, though. Just look at her."

Everyone turned their attention to their friend, who was,

seriously, murdering the song with great relish, putting her hand over her heart to emphasize the lyrics. When she ended her performance, they all clapped, hooted, and whistled as Kelly bowed dramatically and accepted the good-natured laughter of the crowded bar.

Returning to the table, her face was flushed. "Thank you, thank you, thank you. It's my anthem," she declared breathlessly, sliding back onto her seat. "In case any of you have been in a coma for the last eight years."

"But I thought you were dating someonc ncw," Isabel said, placing Kelly's drink back in front of her.

Kelly's pretty face transformed into a scowl. "I am still the biggest loser magnet on the planet. Do you know what this guy said to me? On the second date?"

Everyone just stared at her, waiting for her next words.

Kelly inhaled dramatically. "He said the new second base is oral sex. I should ask around."

"Get outta here!" Paula exclaimed.

"And so I hope you told him he'd just struck out?" Claire asked, shaking her head.

"I told him not only did he strike out, he was out of the game and being sent back to the minor league."

"Good for you. Should have added he was being traded for a new player with some maturity and class," Tina stated.

"That's just it. I'm so tired of meeting players," Kelly moaned, picking up her drink. "Aren't there any decent, regular men out there? Unmarried?"

"Sure there are," Cristine said, touching Kelly's shoulder with sympathy. "Look at Tina. She's dating a great guy."

"Right," Kelly moaned. "But she hit the jackpot. A great guy *and* a gynecologist." She looked at Tina and smiled. "I love you, lady, but you have to admit I have a right to be envious."

"Hey, if it happened to me, it can happen to you. . . ." Tina's words trailed off when she turned her attention to the stage and listened. "There ya go, Kelly. Say hello to the sex-iest man in the joint." She paused in appreciation and then added, "And he can sing."

They all looked at the stage. A tall, good-looking man was standing at the microphone, singing with his hands in the pockets of his bomber jacket, very comfortable, very sexy.

"Don't be so hard on yourself; those tears are for some-one else. . . ."

"Melt my heart," Cristine breathed.

"My, my . . . ," Claire whispered.

"He's probably gay," Kelly muttered. "All the great-looking ones that age are."

Isabel wanted to answer he wasn't gay. And she should know. . . .

Her heart was pounding with a strange mixture of excite-ment and panic. What was Joshua doing here? *Here!* Singing in front of strangers. And her friends!

"I think he's looking at this table!" Paula whispered.

"He is!" Tina confirmed.

"Don't cry; you're not alone. . . ."

"What song is he singing?" Paula asked, not taking her gaze off the man.

"It's Seal, right?" Claire asked Tina.

"Right. 'Don't Cry.' I have the CD," Tina answered. "Man, this guy can sing."

Isabel noticed that the more Joshua sang, the quieter the bar became. It was as though everyone knew they were hear-ing someone with a gift, and they paid attention. Her own boisterous table shut up and listened in silent appreciation. All Isabel could do was freeze, as if her veins had been shot through with ice water.

It was as though once Joshua knew he had her attention, he lowered his face and sang directly into the microphone, while with every word he attempted to break through the wall around her heart.

"Those memories, they seem so long ago . . ."

Isabel kept blinking, unable to look away, hearing the words clearly.

Did he know it was the anniversary of Chuck's death? Of course, he must. He knew everything about her. She had waited for him to reappear in the last few days, a part of her wishing he wouldn't, that he was simply made up, a figment of her imagination. Now, seeing him again, she couldn't deny the attraction, even on this day, and she felt that traitorous hot snaking of desire melting the fearful ice water in her veins.

He was singing to her, communicating in song what he wanted her to know, and Isabel felt tears of confusion burn her eyes.

"Don't cry tonight; you'll still be loved. . . ."

The song ended, and after a moment of stunned silence, the bar erupted in thunderous applause.

Joshua simply raised a hand to acknowledge the applause and walked off the stage and through the tables. Just as he headed for the door, he stopped, looked directly at Isabel, and placed his hand over his heart. Then he walked out into the night.

"Did you just see that?" Paula whispered in astonishment. "Who was that meant for?"

"I don't know," Cristine breathed. "Someone at this table."

Claire looked at Isabel. "Any ideas, Issy?"

Isabel shook her head. "Nice voice, though."

"Nice voice, nice face, nice body," Kelly said, picking up the remainder of her drink. "Mysterious. And exotic. God, he was gorgeous, wasn't he?"

"I'll say," Tina agreed. "Probably sings in a band here in the city." She giggled. "I could become a groupie, following him from bar to bar."

"Hey. You've already got a man," Kelly countered. "I'll be the groupie."

"But *who* was he directing that heart gesture at?" Claire persisted. "Anybody ever even see him before?"

Everyone shook their head, save Isabel. She continued to stare down into her daiquiri. "Maybe he was just being dramatic. It was quite an exit."

Cristine nodded. "Maybe. But I would swear he was looking at one of us. Too bad it was so far away we couldn't see his eyes."

"What do you think, Issy?" Claire asked, as though her weird instincts were kicking in again.

Isabel was not going to look directly at Claire. This was not the time or the place. "I already said what I think. It was quite an exit."

"Hmm," Claire murmured. "I thought he was looking right at you."

"And I think you're all making too much out of this," she countered. "Nice-looking man. Nice voice. And now he's disappeared. Who's going to sing next?" She looked around the table.

"You know, Issy, I think Claire's right," Tina said, ignoring the last question. "And the song. Was that not perfect for tonight? About not crying, not being so hard on yourself?"

"Yeah," Paula added. "He could have been singing those words right to you."

"Maybe he was your angel tonight, Issy. Giving you a message," Cristine said. "There really is no such thing as a coincidence, you know."

"Great-looking angel," Kelly added with a sigh. "He could give me a message any day of the week."

Isabel inhaled deeply. "You know, I appreciate everything you're doing for me tonight. It's been a blast, but I'm really tired. Would you mind if I made my way back to the hotel now?"

"You can't leave your own party!" Tina exclaimed.

"The night's still young," Kelly added. "And your birthday is in a couple of minutes."

"I really want to go," Isabel answered. "I just want some time alone, okay?"

"She's right," Claire said. "This is her night. Let her do what she wants."

Isabel gave Claire a grateful smile as she pushed her chair back and picked up her purse and the heavier sweater coat that matched her dress. "I want you guys to stay and have fun. Believe me, I really had a great night, but it's time for this old lady to hit the mattress. We'll have breakfast in the morning before heading home? My room?"

"We'll come with you," Cristine said, reaching for her purse.

"No. Please," Isabel said firmly. "The hotel is right up the street. Stay and have fun. I'll see you all in the morning."

"I'll walk you to the door," Claire said, standing and waiting for Isabel to join her.

Isabel kissed each woman and thanked them, then joined Claire as they made their way to the exit. At the door, Isabel turned to Claire. "Really. I'm fine."

"Are you sure?" Claire asked. "Maybe this wasn't such a great idea after all."

"No, it was wonderful. I needed to be kidnapped, or I would have been sitting at home looking at old pictures and feeling alone. Like every other year." She kissed Claire's cheek. "I'll be a wild and crazy fifty-year-old tomorrow, okay? I just want a little time alone."

"See you in the morning," Claire answered with a returning kiss on the cheek. She held Isabel's arm. "It was you he was looking at, wasn't it?"

"Can we talk in the morning, Claire?" she asked with sincerity. "I'm really beat."

Claire slowly smiled. "He's gorgeous, Issy. I understand

completely why you lost your head, but how did he know we'd be here tonight?"

Isabel was really too tired to deny anything more. "I have no idea," she answered.

Claire opened the door for her with a wide, admiring grin. "Old lady? Damn, Issy. You give me hope!"

"Good night," Isabel murmured with a tired smile, squeezing Claire's arm as she left the bar.

All the way back to the hotel, Isabel focused on only one thing. . . .

Saying good-bye to the love of her life.

Tonight she had seen Joshua was real. Everyone had seen him. He existed. And for some bizarre reason, he had come into her life. Seven years of mourning were weighing too heavily on her heart now. She would always love Chuck, the memory of him, but he was gone. Incredibly, her body was teaching her mind that she was still a vital woman. She had thought when she turned fifty she would simply slide into whatever women that age are. Did she have her own prejudices about turning fifty? Did she think it would be a slippery slide into old age? What a surprise. No one could have told her that she would still feel like a younger woman, still have the desires and urges of someone thirty years her junior. In her head she was in her late twenties, despite the reflection in the mirror. That never changed. Now her body was reminding her that age made no difference. She was a woman, and before it was too late, it was time to come out of the darkness of mourning.

Pulling the long sweater coat around her, she gulped at the burning in her throat, the heaviness in her heart that was demanding release.

I'm sorry, Chuck. I'm sorry you left too soon. But I'm here . . . left here to deal with it all alone. I've been so angry with you for dying and leaving me with all my emotions, all my desires, intact. What was I supposed to do? I didn't know—I really didn't—so I shut down. I've even worn your clothes to feel close to you, but your scent is gone now. Like you . . . You're really gone, and nothing is going to bring you back into my arms, arms that have ached for so long for human contact.

She ignored the strangers passing her, her eyes filmy with tears.

I've spent seven years loving you still, wishing you alive again, paying tribute to you and making you into a saint. But you weren't a saint, were you? A saint wouldn't have died in a stupid accident.

She sniffled, walking in a daze toward the direction of the hotel. *I've missed your presence, your infectious laughter, the way I felt so at home in your arms, and I still miss it. But I need to connect with someone again, before it's too late. Wherever you are I hope you can see I need to move on now. I can't live like this anymore. Something's happening to me, and I'm scared. I don't know what the future is going to bring, but I do know if I pass up this opportunity I might regret it for as long as I live. I know he's younger. I know he may not even be normal. Okay, I know he's not normal, but if I'm crazy or having a breakdown, I'm willing to find out. It's better than being half alive.*

She reached the hotel entrance and wiped at the tears streaming down her face.

I'll always love you, but I have to let you go. I have to. I . . . I'm so sorry if I held on to you too long.

And then she saw him, waiting for her by the elevator.

She walked past the reception desk, the Swan Lounge, the late-night guests having a drink or making their way to their rooms.

He simply held out his hand to her.

And she took it.

Neither of them said a word as they rode the elevator up to her room. Joshua held her hand in silence as others got off on their floors. Not even when they were alone did either one of them speak. Isabel didn't question anything. When the doors opened on her floor, Isabel withdrew her hand and opened her purse. She took out the key card, and they walked to her room.

She slid the card into the door and opened it. He followed.

Isabel dropped her purse onto a chair and removed her coat. In the darkened room, she stared out the large windows to the colorful gold dome of Saint Peter and Paul's across the street, illuminated by lights.

"You've changed," he murmured from behind her. "Your aura is different."

She blinked, almost mesmerized by the beautiful mosaic of colors on the dome. "I said good-bye to my husband," she whispered as tears once more began to blur her vision. "I let him go. Finally."

"You released him, Isabel. He has moved on . . . and now you can."

She sighed, and her shoulders sagged. "So all my grieving and holding precious memories were really a disservice to him?" Shaking her head, she added, "Great, I even screwed up widowhood."

He didn't move to come near her, simply stood somewhere behind her in the darkened room. "Holding precious memories was not a disservice," he answered in a gentle voice, "but you didn't allow the essence of him to leave this dimension because you thought you needed him to validate your past."

She thought about that. Maybe he was right.

"Is he . . . gone now?" she asked, trying to push the words past the tightness in her throat.

"Isabel, sweet gentle soul . . ." His voice sounded closer. "He has been gone for some time now. The grieving you have been doing has been for yourself. When you could not let loose the ties that bound you together, he did. He left you."

She spun around. "He left me . . . *again?*" she demanded in shock.

And not just by Joshua's words. Joshua, the man, the being, *whoever* he was, appeared to be outlined in the most beautiful haze of light. Her heart began pounding against her chest wall, and her ears began ringing. Reminding herself to breathe, she held onto the back of the chair for balance. *"What are you?"*

He smiled. "I have been trying to tell you, Isabel. I am a being of information and energy. I use this—this body suit you recognize as a man—to commune with you, to not frighten you. I will do whatever it takes to help you evolve and realize your potential."

"What are those lights around you?" she breathed in awe.

"Electrical energy. You see them now because this room is darkened, and since you have already seen them in your living room, your brain accepts them. Should you turn on a light, they may disappear."

"But why are you here? Why me?"

"Why not you, Isabel? I have achieved unity with your soul, and it is exquisite, open, willing to expand and evolve."

"Is that why Chuck left me? To evolve?"

Joshua smiled. "See how intelligent and perceptive you are. He remained with you in spirit as long as he could, until the urge to expand was overwhelming and drew him to another level of his soul experience. This plane of earth is simply one dimension of many. In this dimension you need this body suit to keep you grounded against the force of gravity. It is a magnificent mechanism, but it is not who you truly are. That you already know."

Isabel was trying to find some order in her frazzled brain to comprehend what he was saying.

"Your brain is part of that mechanism, but it is also not who you truly are."

"How did you know what I was thinking?" she asked,

wanting to turn on a light, but still in awe of the colors surrounding him.

"It's in what you call your aura. You too have beautiful lights surrounding you. You are an electromagnetic masterpiece that you cannot yet comprehend. Everything about you—your health, your emotions, your state of being—is available to anyone with the perception to see."

"Then why can I see them around you, but no one else?"

"You see them now, Isabel, because you know they are possible. I allowed you to see them at your house. Your brain imprints what it has the ability to see with no judgments. It's wired up so you only see what you believe is possible. With the speed of light you match patterns that exist within yourself through your conditioning, your previous experiences, like at your house. You accept it now, and so does your brain." He paused and smiled. "But it is available to everyone, Isabel, not just you. Sit down and I will tell you a little story your scientists tell themselves. It will help to explain."

She walked over to the edge of the mattress and sat down, holding her hands together in her lap. She felt like she was in school, but no schooling ever involved being alone in a darkened hotel room, illuminated only by the lights across the street and the awesome lights surrounding the sexiest teacher she'd ever encountered.

Joshua pulled a chair from the desk and sat down across from her, straddling the seat and folding his arms over the back. He was still wearing his bomber jacket, and if it weren't for the lights she would swear he was normal. Normal? Nothing in her life right now was even close to normal. . . .

"Columbus' ships arrived at the Caribbean islands and were anchored some distance from the shoreline. The native Indians couldn't see them; not ever having seen ships there was no experience in the brain for such a thing. The shaman kept wondering what was creating ripples in the surf, what was the cause and effect, and he opened himself up to the possibilities. Eventually, he then saw the ships in the distance. The native Indians trusted this wise man when he told them, and then they too were able to see the ships. That wasn't magic, Isabel. It was what you call quantum physics. That shaman was playing in the realm of possibilities. He opened himself up to anything and became the observer . . . who he truly was. Who you truly are. You are using this marvelous body suit and the extraordinary mechanism of your brain to process what you, the real unchanging eternal you, observe. You see the lights surrounding me because you, the observer, opened yourself up to the possibility of who I really am. Everyone can who has not closed off their mind."

"So everyone can see you, like in the bar tonight? I didn't see the lights then."

"You and everyone else saw what was expected. A man. An ordinary man."

Isabel slowly smiled. "No one, Joshua, thought you were ordinary. You should have heard my friends. They thought you were wonderful. I didn't know you could sing like that."

"I can and will do whatever it takes to get through to you, Isabel. You have a purpose. You made a conscious choice to come into this dimension to fulfill it."

"So my purpose is to see lights surrounding people?"

Joshua shrugged. "I don't know your purpose, but it would prove to be a useful tool."

Isabel thought about it. "Imagine knowing, reading a person, who's talking to you."

"Imagine a world of people reading one another before they ever shook hands. You would know who would lie to you before they ever spoke. It would make duplicity obsolete."

Isabel got excited by the possibility of it. "Imagine knowing if world leaders or heads of industry are corrupt or simply feeding you what they think you want to hear."

Joshua didn't immediately answer her. He removed his jacket and tossed it onto the bed. "Isabel, please listen carefully to me. You are living at a precarious time in the earth's history." He paused. "*History* . . . that is a strange word, is it not? *His story?* Humans spend a great deal of time reading the past of men, locking in their expectations by studying what has already taken place. Very few think about infinite possibilities in creating a different future. What about *her* story? The contributions of women? A new paradigm is being born in the human consciousness, and it's going to come in mainly through the female."

"The female?" she asked, trying to understand what he was saying because he sounded so serious.

"Yes. Females are genetically wired for this. Their chromosomes are thriving, while men's are dying off. Your science has already verified this. Ever since you were a little girl, you knew there was something more to what you were being taught. I played with you, and you sensed me being there. You have always been open to the unexplainable. It is why you chose to marry Chuck, who was more open than you and encouraged you to explore. It is why you and your friends banded together and began a search through the mysteries, some of them forbidden by your religious leaders, who would prefer to keep control to themselves. And it is why all of your friends have come to the conclusion that the answer is within themselves, not out there in what is perceived by most as reality. What if everyone is searching in the wrong direction, looking outward toward something big or huge and the answer is inward toward something so tiny yet infinite that it cannot be found by any scientist with any microscope? What if . . . the intangible you that has been with you since you attained consciousness, the observer who never changes or ages . . . what if *that* is the answer humanity has spent millenniums searching to find? You can't hold it or see it, but you and every other human know it exists. It *is* your true identity. What you don't know—what the majority of humans don't know—is the power of that observer. It will create whatever you desire."

"The power of the mind?" she asked, truly attempting to get what he was saying. "I do understand that. That's why I chose to use hypnotherapy, to bypass the conscious mind and go straight to the subconscious and deal with the fears there."

"And you have done so well, Isabel. You deserve great credit for leaving the clinical world of accepted medical procedures and daring to use something that has been ridiculed for ages."

"It's becoming more accepted now," she answered, pleased by his compliment. She wanted to show him that she knew what she was doing was a bit off the middle of the road, but it was credible. "Let me tell you a little story now," she said with a smile. "There was this big experiment in Washington, D.C., in the summer of 1993. Washington was the crime capital of the country then, and over four thousand volunteers came from a hundred countries to collectively meditate for long periods of time. It was predicted that with such a large group there would be a twenty-five percent reduction that summer in violent crime as defined by the FBI. The chief of police said a two-foot snowstorm in the summer would be the only thing that would drop crime by twenty-five percent—by keeping the criminals inside. In the end the police department became collaborators as authors of this study because results did show a twenty-five percent drop in violent crime. And it's been done with patients in hospitals in controlled groups. The group that is prayed for or meditated over, seen as healthy and whole, gets better much more quickly."

"So people are now learning they can affect the world of reality that they see," Joshua answered. "Every single one of you affects the reality that you see, even if you try to hide from that and play a victim of your circumstances. And you're doing it all the time. The thought, or intent, is the driving force and affects the molecules of matter. You are creators, Isabel. All of you. You are creating this dimension in this world all the time. The question is, what are you creating?"

She knew what he meant. All one had to do was turn on the news to see the answer. But it was now her birthday. Her fiftieth birthday. And the last thing she wanted was to continue discussing issues that made her feel heavy with concern.

One night. Couldn't she have just one night for herself?

"Am I creating you, Joshua?"

He grinned. "You have altered your aura."

"And what do you read in it now?"

"That you are tired of this serious discussion?"

"Very good," she whispered. "I'd like to create something a little different right now. It's my birthday; did you know that?"

"Yes."

She slipped out of her red high heels and scooted up the bed to the pillows. Patting the mattress beside her, she murmured, "I want to be held tonight," she said, feeling shy, yet desperately wanting him next to her. "Don't worry; I won't attack you again. Just hold me, okay? Please . . . ?"

She watched him take off his shoes and come to her. He moved over the mattress until he was spooning her, surrounding her with his arms and the beautiful lights that seemed like a magical reverse shadow. She felt an awesome sense of peace, of belonging, and she thought she had created exactly what she'd wanted. Feeling almost dizzy with joy, she sighed in gratitude.

Joshua whispered into her ear. "Happy birthday, Isabel."

Each word sent tiny shivers of exquisite desire through her body, and she had to concentrate really, really hard to keep her word.

I cannot ravish him again. I can't . . . I can't . . . I can't.

"Do stop fighting it, Isabel. I admit I've thought of little else myself. . . ."

She giggled. "I didn't know you'd . . . well, you'd be thinking of such things."

"I didn't either," he admitted with amazement in his voice. "Not until I had experienced it."

Turning around to face him, she stopped fighting what her true self demanded.

"Joshua?" she whispered.

"Yes?"

"You don't mind that I'm older than you? That my body isn't as firm as it used to be?"

"Older? Isabel, you are a magnificent creation. Your soul is ageless, as is mine. We are equals, only you are just beginning to remember it now. Would you like me to appear to you as older? I can, you know."

She slowly shook her head. "I don't want you to change anything about yourself. She reached out and ran her finger lightly across his cheek. "You, Joshua, are the magnificent creation."

He turned his head and kissed the palm of her hand. "I have done research since our . . . time together. There are many ways to achieve physical unity."

"Research?"

"Yes. Many of your writings explain it. This physical uniting of bodies is possible in many ways, is it not?"

She nodded. "It is and . . ." Her words trailed off when his mouth kissed hers.

"I would like to try all of them," he whispered against her lips.

She opened her eyes and blinked in disbelief. "*All* of them?"

He nodded.

She prayed for courage and strength.

This time she was the one who was going to be ravished. Turning fifty wasn't so bad after all, she thought as his lips took possession of her again, and she moaned with gratitude and a desire for more.

She wished someone, some wise older woman, had told her she would still feel like this, that turning fifty could be simply glorious!

Chapter

5

ISABEL HAD ARRANGED FOR A WIDE ROUND TABLE TO be set up in her room to seat them all for a private breakfast. The hotel had done a superb job, and she was grinning as everyone sang her happy birthday. She then opened her presents, which ranged from a crazy purple beret decorated with a sprig of flowers to sex toys she had never even heard of before.

"Don't ask me," Paula said, staring down at the box being passed around the table. "I'll take mine without a string of pearls being inserted in any orifice, thank you."

"Where's your adventure?" Claire demanded. "There *are* more positions than the missionary one, you know."

How well Isabel knew the validity of that statement. It was not the first time that morning she was grateful for the thick and comfy cushion of the chair.

"It's a joke gift," Kelly said to Paula. "Just like that crotchless teddy you gave Issy. It's just more . . . adventurous, like Claire said."

"I'm with you, Paula," Tina added, passing the box to Cristine after peeking inside. "I'll wear my pearls around my neck, like nature intended."

"Well, thank you, Claire," Isabel said with a laugh. She took the box from Cristine and placed it on the floor next to her chair with the other presents. "I think I'll read the instructions before making up my mind. The teddy . . . ," she said with a grin, "now that I might try."

"Good for you!" Tina cheered.

"Seriously?" Paula asked. "I really did buy it as a joke."

"So you all bought me sex gifts for my fiftieth birthday as a joke? Thinking I'm over the hill and would never use them?" Little did they know. Maybe she would. Especially after last night. *No, no, don't think about last night. Not now.* The blush would give her away to all of them.

"Well, the rabbit vibrator . . ." Kelly laughed. "You could use that. They said at the store it was a big seller."

"Oh, Issy, you should have seen us in that place," Cristine said with a grin. "We were like ten-year-olds, giggling and laughing and embarrassing everyone else."

Tina burst into laughter. "And Paula . . . honey, I love you, but you were a trip!" She looked at Isabel and added, "She kept apologizing to the men she passed in the aisles, who seemed embarrassed by five women descending on their turf and acting like adolescents."

"Well they *were* embarrassed!" Paula insisted. "They turned their backs to us!"

Claire laughed. "Embarrassed? Or guilty?"

"Who really cares?" Kelly asked. "We had a great time. You should have been with us, Issy."

"But then she never would have allowed us to buy all these goodies," Cristine said, leaning her elbows on the edge of the table. "Don't worry, we got the beret at the Irish Store. You can actually wear that."

"Right," Tina said. "Cristine added the flowers. . . . You know, like the book *When I Am an Old Woman I Shall Wear Purple?* There's your purple. Now you can be wild and crazy and eccentric."

Isabel looked down to the remains on her plate. "Like wearing Chuck's clothes for the last seven years wasn't eccentric?" she whispered with a smile, and looked up at her dear friends.

Kelly shrugged. "You pulled it off because of your height."

"You looked kinda artsy-fartsy, bohemian," Paula added.

"Hold it. Wait a minute here," Claire said. "Who said wearing a crotchless teddy was eccentric? Are we not Women of the New Millennium?"

"That's right," Tina joined. "We're the Yellow Brick Road Gang, and we don't have rules to live by anymore. If we want to wear crotchless panties or teddies or . . . mess with pearl sex toys, we can and will, without guilt!"

"Hear! hear!" Cristine called out, raising her mimosa flute. "To the Yellow Brick Road Gang."

"To the Yellow Brick Road Gang!" they all toasted.

"And to Issy, our role model for how to age gracefully and still be her own woman," Claire added with a sly wink to Isabel.

"To Issy . . ."

"Thank you," Isabel answered, grateful for each one of them surrounding her. If only they knew that even raising her arm and holding the flute out into the air was creating a pain in her shoulder. She thought every muscle in her body ached, but it was a good ache. Even sitting comfortably was a challenge, and she tried not to show her discomfort . . . let alone think about last night and the fact that she had only gotten three hours of sleep.

Good God, it had been fantastic.

Joshua had been fantastic, making love to her, holding her, talking to her, and then making love all night long. It had been quite some time since she'd felt like this: truly pleasured and paying the sweet price for it afterward. And, a part of her admitted, she just might be infatuated by some- one who was not even of this world, because she was already wondering if he was going to show up at her house tonight. Like some lovesick teenager. Now that was pathetic.

"That's a sly smile, if I ever saw one," Claire remarked. "What are you thinking?"

Not wanting to look at Claire and have her friend guess, Isabel leaned down and picked up the hat. She put it on her head and said, "I was just thinking about walking through the lobby of the Four Seasons wearing a crotchless teddy and my fantastic purple beret."

And two hours later, she did just that when they all checked out.

She wore clothes over the teddy, of course.

There was only so far she was willing to go to be wild and crazy.

§

"I don't know why I keep biting my nails. I've tried to stop. And the weight gain since I stopped smoking . . . It's like I'm turning into someone else. A stranger who can't seem to control herself."

Isabel smiled at the woman across from her. "Don't you think you're being a little hard on yourself, Lori? You've gone through such a dark time, and you're on the other side of it now. Give yourself credit for the courage it took to get here."

The middle-aged woman shook her head, causing her thick, brunette, shoulder-length curls to bounce. "But I didn't think if I got *here,* I'd be twenty pounds overweight and have nails that look like this."

Isabel inhaled softly and crossed her legs as she leaned toward her client. "I'm simply asking you to look at yourself differently, be a little gentle with yourself. You left an abusive relationship and are beginning a new life. That took courage."

"I know, I know . . . ," Lori murmured, staring at her fingers and then curling them into fists to hide them. "I just wish I could see myself the way you do."

"Okay, maybe I can help there," Isabel said. "Why don't you lie back and get comfortable."

Having been in the chair before, Lori pulled the small lever on the side, and the chair slid back into a lounging position. It was wide, and the leather was soft as butter, designed for comfort.

"Would you like a light blanket?"

Lori nodded. "It's always so nice here, and I love the way you have it decorated. So exotic."

Isabel got up and lifted the cashmere blanket from the back of her wing chair. She placed it over Lori's legs and smiled. "Thanks."

She sat back down across from Lori and looked around the office in her home, decorated with mementos she and Chuck had accumulated through their travels to Africa, Malaysia, and Europe. Blinking, she brought herself back into the present. "Okay, get comfortable," she said to Lori. "Uncross your legs, and let your hands rest at your sides, or on your stomach."

She waited as Lori fidgeted for a few seconds and then became still.

"Now let's take a nice *deep* breath. . . ." And she inhaled with her client.

"And another one. A deep cleansing breath . . . inhaling fresh air to nourish your body and . . . exhaling all toxins, all stress."

"And another . . . deep, cleansing breath. . . ." She watched Lori, breathing with her. In a controlled, low voice, she continued. "With each breath, you're going to feel yourself relaxing, sinking back into the chair. There is no stress, no tension, just a deep, peaceful feeling of relaxation. If you feel sleepy, it's okay to close your eyes. Just listen to my voice. Any other sounds you hear will only allow you to sink deeper and deeper into a soothing, relaxing state. . . ."

Lori's eyelids fluttered closed.

"Now I'm going to ask you to feel your toes, to place your attention at your toes. Feel them. Wiggle them if you want."

Isabel saw by the movement of the blanket Lori was wiggling her toes inside her shoes.

"Good. Very good. . . . Now, imagine a warm feeling of relaxation beginning at your toes, wrapping around each one. Slowly this deep feeling of relaxation works up your feet— warm, soothing relaxation over your arches, around your ankles—and sweeps slowly up your calves, relaxing the muscles. It feels like warm, soothing honey as it rises up to your knees, swirls around them, and up your thighs to your hips. . . . Warm, soothing relaxation loosening all muscles, taking away all stress, all tension. . . ."

She watched Lori's breathing deepen and slow.

"Good. Very good. . . . Feel how relaxed and comfortable you are. Now imagine that deep, warm relaxation coming up your torso, relaxing your abdominal muscles, your chest muscles. Deep, deep, warm comfort as you breathe easily, deeply. The muscles in your back now relax, like unwinding rubber bands, each muscle falling naturally into place . . . one by one, so easily . . . so comfortably, releasing all stress and tension. Very good. . . ." Isabel paused for a few moments, watching Lori's breathing.

"Now I would like you to imagine the big muscles in your shoulders loosening. Feel the relaxing warmth spreading over your shoulders, taking away all the cares and worries as the comfort spreads slowly down your arms, over your elbows, and down your forearms to your hands. Feel your fingers relax, each one letting go all stress or tension. Good."

She watched Lori's fingers jerk for a moment and then relax.

"Very good. . . . And now I would like you to imagine that

warm honey at the crown of your head, slowly, ever so slowly, spreading down your head, bringing with it a deep, comfortable relaxation . . . over your forehead, your eyes, around your ears, relaxing your jaw so your mouth is slightly open. So comfortable, so soothing. . . ."

Isabel waited a few moments until Lori's lower jaw dropped slightly. "Very good. Feel how good it is to be you. No stress. No worries. So comfortable inside your own body."

She paused for a few moments, letting Lori really feel her body in a relaxed state. "And now I would like you to imagine before you a flight of stairs, ten steps in all, and at the top of the stairs is a beautiful doorway. With each step you take, you will feel even more relaxed, more comfortable, more healthy and whole and at peace within yourself. Are you ready? Let's take the first step. *So* relaxed. Now the second. A deeper relaxation. Climb the third and now the fourth. Deeper . . ." With each step she brought Lori into an expanded state of guided imagery. "Take the last one, Lori, and when you feel ready open the door."

Now into Lori's subconscious, Isabel inhaled and said in a soft voice, "Before you is a beautiful pristine beach. A soft breeze plays with your curls, lifting them back from your face. The sand is shimmering in the warm sun as you walk toward the welcoming blue ocean. There's a beach chair waiting for you at the shoreline, low, so when you sit down the warm surf bubbles and washes over your feet and your legs. You're now seated before the tiny waves. Feel the surf as it lightly tickles your skin, bringing wholeness as it washes over you and, as it recedes, taking away any remaining thoughts that don't serve you. In, bringing wholeness . . . and out, taking away any thoughts. Let it continue to wash over you as you listen to my voice."

Isabel paused. "I want you to remember when you were little, when you were in love with yourself and the world around you. Remember your innocence? See that precious little girl.

Can you remember your happiness to walk out of your house and play in the sunshine? Can you remember the joy you felt when you inhaled the scents of the earth and you knew you were a part of everything you saw? That you were safe, protected, and loved?"

She paused again. "Remember feeling whole and complete. That is who you are. Remember looking at your body and knowing it is just fine the way it is, how it has taken care of you. Feel your gratitude for your body. Remember looking at your fingernails, little fingernails that were shaped perfectly. You knew wholeness. You knew you never had to worry about what your body looked like because it was perfectly you."

Isabel paused briefly, waiting for Lori to fully remember herself as an innocent child. "Now, when you're ready, I would like you to see yourself as the woman you want to be. You already know how strong you are by the recent decisions you've made for yourself. As the waves continue to wash over your legs, see yourself eating healthy foods that nourish your body, and imagine the pounds washing away as easily as the surf recedes off you now. See your fingernails whole, shaped and buffed into the style that most fits this wonderful new image of you. Every time you think of yourself from now on, you will see this whole woman who loves herself enough to become who she wants to be. Spend some time with this image of you; take it within you and feel it meld into every cell of your body. This is now you, Lori. Whole again. Healthy again. Loving again . . . especially to yourself."

Isabel sat back and closed her eyes briefly, seeing her client as she'd imagined. "And in the future," she whispered, "should you be tempted by something unhealthy, that wouldn't serve you, you will simply place your thumb and forefinger together and the desire will immediately be gone . . . because you value yourself now more than you ever have, more than anything that might tempt you into old habits. And it is right and appropriate for you to now show that love to yourself. You are an extraordinary woman deserving of an extraordinary life."

She opened her eyes to observe her client. Before her gaze became focused, Isabel thought she could see hazy lights around Lori, getting brighter and brighter around her heart. She swallowed in awe. Was that what Joshua saw when he looked at her? Did her aura around her own heart get brighter when he was around her? Blinking, Isabel sat up straighter and focused. She had a client. She couldn't daydream about Joshua.

The lights disappeared.

"And when you accept you are an extraordinary woman, deserving the very best life has to offer, I want you to raise one finger. Take your time, until you feel it in every cell of your body." She waited, and almost a full minute later, Lori's finger moved.

"Very good. This is who you are, and you will now always remember it."

She allowed Lori to spend some time with her new image. "Now I'm going to count to three," she said in a brighter, slightly louder voice. "And with each number you will feel yourself waking up, coming back to consciousness, remembering everything, feeling wonderful, whole, free, happy, without worries. One, coming up, feeling harmonious within yourself. Two, waking, filled with balance and purpose. And three, fully awake now, feeling peaceful and stress-free, alive and vital and ready to go forward with your life."

She watched Lori blink, then close her eyes, as though not wanting to wake up and rejoin the world. It was a common reaction. "How do you feel?" Isabel whispered with a smile.

"Fabulous . . . ," Lori murmured sleepily. "I want to go back to that beach. It was like a mini vacation."

Laughing softly, Isabel rose from her chair and stood by her client. "One you deserve." She patted Lori's knee over the blanket. "When you're ready, I'll be at my desk. Take your time."

Isabel walked across the large room to the floor-to-ceiling mahogany bookshelves and her desk in front of them. She sat down and looked out the large window to the trees. The leaves had already turned color, and the cooler wind was quickly stripping the few that clung stubbornly to the branches. She could hear a car driving down the rain-soaked road in front of her house, the tires making a whooshing sound on the asphalt. This was not her favorite time of year—this reminder of life's cycle. Soon the tree limbs would be completely bare; the grass would become dormant and lose its color. All of nature would soon lose its color, as the days grew gray and the temperature drastically dropped, plunging them into deep winter. In the past she would have hung on through Christmas, impatiently waiting for signs of spring. On days such as this, she would've loved staying in bed with Chuck, drinking coffee and reading the Sunday paper, discussing articles and the state of the world.

That had been a very hard thing to surrender over the last seven years.

No one to intimately share her life.

Today, however, she was actually lighthearted as her mind foolishly thought how nice it would be to snuggle up with Joshua on such a dreary day and watch a movie in bed. Silly thought, she chided herself as Lori drew the blanket off her legs and began to sit up and stretch her arms. Joshua was not her boyfriend. She was too old for a boyfriend.

"God, Isabel, I feel so . . . wonderful," Lori murmured, sitting sideways in the chair as she folded the blanket.

"Good," Isabel said with a smile. "I have a CD I want you to use. It's basically the same induction."

Lori slowly walked over to the desk and sat in one of the two chairs in front of it. "Did you make it? Will it be your voice?"

Isabel nodded. "Yes. And I would like you to add the image of yourself as whole and healthy. Do you remember what to do if you might be tempted by something that doesn't serve you, either a person or food?"

Lori raised her hand, touching her index finger to her thumb.

"Good. So you're set." She slid the CD across the desk. "How do you feel? Alert? Ready to drive home?"

Lori nodded as she took out her checkbook. "I just don't want to drive home. I wish the sun was shining and I could drive to the shore."

Isabel laughed. "Not too much fun there today, I'm afraid." She added, "It will be twenty dollars more for the CD, Lori. Use it when you go to bed at night. No sticking it in the CD player in your car, okay?"

"I'd probably drive off the road," she answered with a laugh while writing out her check.

Isabel wrote out a receipt as she waited for Lori to finish.

"That's why I want you to use it when you're in bed. Don't worry if you fall asleep in the middle of it. Your subconscious will take it in."

Lori handed over her check. "I think it's amazing what you can do. When Marti told me about you, I was more than hesitant, but her daughter isn't so nervous anymore and is off all medication, so I thought I'd give this hypnosis a chance."

"And look at the progress you've made. How is it living with your mother again? I know it must have been a hard decision."

"My mom's great. You know, it's funny. She knew about the abuse and tried to get it out of me, but it wasn't until I came here that I had the courage to leave Jim and tell my mother the truth, and she opened her arms to me." Lori took the receipt and put it in her checkbook. "Sometimes I look around my old bedroom and feel like that insecure teenager all over again."

"Hey!" Isabel corrected. "Did that thought just serve you?"

Lori grinned and held up her hand, touching her index finger to her thumb. "Sorry. Hard habit to break, just like the others."

"I know." Isabel grinned back at her. "Don't tell me you're sorry. Tell yourself. Listen, Lori, you're in transition. You went to college, got married, and you thought that was the beginning of a great new life. Unfortunately, you married a man so insecure he had to take out his frustrations on you. But you got out; you made a healthy decision for yourself. You knew you deserved better, right?"

"Right."

"Okay, so every time you think something that doesn't serve the new, whole you, you stop yourself. You rewire your brain." It was what Joshua was trying to teach her to do. "I know it's not easy, but what does the whining and complaining and worrying do, save reinforce those very damaging feelings inside of you? Transition isn't easy, but it does mean something wonderful is on the other side of it: a new Lori, the person you are meant to be."

"I know you're right. It's a bad habit."

"Habits can be broken."

Lori took the CD off the desk and rose. "I'm going to play this every night. Thanks, Isabel."

Isabel stood up and shook Lori's hand. "Take care of yourself." How weird—she felt slightly dizzy, and so she held onto the desk.

"I will. I promise." Lori put her jacket on and picked up her purse. "Can I call you if I need you?"

"I don't think you're going to need me, but you can call anytime."

"Thanks, Isabel. I'll see myself out."

Isabel sat back down and sighed, rubbing her hand over her stomach. Now if she could only do what she asked of others. See herself as whole and healthy and not too old for a magnificent being who had popped into her life and turned it completely inside out and upside down. She shouldn't be surprised at the dizziness or that her stomach ached. Still, there was a part of her that worried something might not be right. She was, after all, fifty and acting like she was in her twenties. Maybe her body hadn't yet adjusted to sex after seven years of abstinence. What did she know for certain any longer?

Absolutely nothing.

She wanted to talk to Cristine about Daniel, who had appeared out of nowhere and had won the whole gang over with his devotion to their friend, but what if she wasn't right? What if Daniel was simply a man with some extraordinary talents? Would Cristine think she was crazy if she told her friend about Joshua, about how he could pop in and out of her life? About how he was turning it around and exposing all her misconceptions?

Her hand reached for the phone, and then she stopped herself.

She wasn't ready to share Joshua with Cristine, or with anyone. Not yet.

And how could she possibly explain it? Or him?

She was supposed to be the more grounded one in the group. She knew she was looked upon as the sane one. *Sane? What about any of this could be termed sane? And grounded?* What a laugh that was now! They would think she had lost her mind if she told them about Joshua and his abilities. And what would happen to the fragile thread that held them all together? Would it strain and snap? No, the group was more important than her need to find answers. Besides, she really didn't want anyone else's opinion right now about her secret life with Joshua. It was too precious, and it might not survive a reality check.

Reality? Now there was another concept that had been turned inside out.

Chapter

6

SHE THREW HER HEAD BACK AGAINST A PILLOW, AND her breath left her in rush of gratitude as she stared up to the ceiling of her bedroom. Her body still tingled with delicious waves of endorphins washing over her. "Thank you," she breathed as her hand reached out to rest on his bare chest.

He was lying opposite her with his head at her hip, his shoulder neatly fitting the curve of her waist, like two smooth pieces of a puzzle. "What a magnificent mechanism the body is," he whispered in wonder. "It is surely a gift."

She smiled, feeling the beat of his heart begin to slow under her hand. "Yes. It is a gift," she agreed, and giggled like a younger woman. "And I have *so* missed this!"

She heard him chuckle. "I can see how you would," he answered, placing his hand on top of hers. He paused, then added in a more serious voice, "I am sorry you remained alone all those years. Alone, and not experiencing this."

Isabel sighed and closed her eyes, blocking out the midday sun. "I suppose I never thought it would come again into my life. That I'd had my time, a good time, and it was over. That I should be grateful for what was and not look beyond that."

"Oh, Isabel . . ." His fingers caressed her hand and ran up her arm. "How sad you denied yourself, for it could not be healthy to keep this . . . this magnificent energy trapped within."

She shook her head and grinned. "After a time, the craving for it goes away," she said, opening her eyes again. "Becomes dormant, I suppose. You don't think about it anymore. Or at least not as much as you used to."

"But it didn't go away, Isabel."

Her grin froze, and she blinked several times. "No, it didn't. Maybe I was in denial. Maybe it was the only way I could deal with losing everything when Chuck died. To shut down those feelings and urges . . ."

"Well, I am glad you have released them again. It is a most marvelous form of unity, is it not?"

She laughed, changing her mood once more. How odd to have a male so honest. "Yes, Joshua. It is *most* marvelous." And she felt the muscles of his chest contract as he laughed with her.

"You think of me as amusing?"

"I think of you as marvelous," she corrected, running her fingers ever so lightly up his arm.

"And I think you are very clever, Isabel Calloway, in keeping me distracted from my mission."

"Oh, so I'm a mission now?" she asked with a grin, loving this feeling of intimacy after sex, where everything seemed to function on a higher level. No body aches. No worries. No thoughts of a world in chaos. In the magical glow of aftersex, peace reigned. If only she could postpone reality from creeping in and zapping it away.

"You know I came to this dimension to help you, Isabel. We began our discussion, and every time I attempt to get back to it, you seem to have the ability to once again divert me from my course."

She stroked his arm gently, feeling the muscles relax under her touch. "Is this such a bad diversion?" she whispered.

He pushed himself up on his elbows and looked at her. "It certainly isn't bad. It simply isn't helping us move forward."

"Move forward? And where are we going?"

"You are to expand your consciousness. You already know that."

"Joshua . . . every time we are together . . . like this . . . my consciousness expands."

He shook his head and sat up fully. "That isn't what I mean, and you know that. You came here—you *chose* to come here, to this dimension—for a purpose."

Isabel thought about his answer as she watched the dust motes swirling in a beam of sunlight. "If I chose to come here, then that means I existed before that choice."

"Of course you did. You already know that. The you, the real you, Isabel, has always existed and always will in different forms of energy. You chose to use this body in this particular time frame to express yourself and fulfill your purpose. None of this is random."

"So what is my purpose, then?" she asked. "I try to help others whenever I can."

"It's more than that, and you know it."

"It is?"

"Only you can discover what it is. I will tell you that you are headed in the right direction. Actually, there's no wrong direction. Every choice will lead either to a discovery or a lesson that will illuminate a course correction. You already know there is no judging what is right or wrong. In the end it all serves."

She raised her head slightly and stared at him, his dark tousled hair, his kind expression, his lips. . . . Dear God but she wanted to kiss him again. What in the world was she becoming? Even with Chuck, she hadn't been this . . . this *hungry* for a man. Fifty. Turning fifty had brought her a very unexpected gift: the return of sexual desire. And not just the return. It was even more intense now than when she was younger. She cleared her throat. "So you have always been with me, Joshua?" she asked, needing to bring her mind to a higher level. "Since I was a child?" There, that should change the mood. Think of childhood.

He nodded. "You called out in your soul, and I heard you. You were a delightful child." His smile was endearing.

She grinned. "And then I became a rebellious teenager."

"You were trying to discover yourself. You didn't call out as much then."

"Ego," Isabel whispered.

"Ego," Joshua confirmed. "Which isn't such a bad thing if it isn't out of control."

"I can think of a few times I was out of control," she answered with a grin.

"Like when you stole some of your father's Scotch whisky."

"Ewwww . . ." Isabel covered her face as the memory rushed up and seemed to slap her. "It was the beginning of my teenage rebellion. I had never drank alcohol before. I think I was sixteen, and we were going to a school dance. I didn't like the smell of it, or know what to mix it with, so I thought lemonade would mask it and make it bearable. Oh, God, lemonade and scotch . . ." She curled into a ball and held her stomach as even the thought of it made her retch. She had been so sick that night, never knowing how she had wound up in her own bed in the morning. To this day, the very smell of scotch would turn her stomach. It had also taught her a lesson and had made her a wise consumer of all alcohol for the rest of her life.

The nausea grew stronger, like a wave of internal distress washing over her, so she immediately pushed herself upright and rushed into the bathroom. Kneeling at the toilet as she lost her lunch, Isabel shuddered, thinking how powerful the mind was that a memory could actually make her physically sick.

"Are you all right?" Joshua called out from behind the closed door.

"I'm fine," she murmured, waiting for her stomach to settle. "I'm sorry. . . . I'll be out in a minute."

She reached up to the vanity and grabbed a tissue. Blowing her nose, she thought how perfectly she had managed to kill off desire. The very last thing she was thinking about was sex. She even wished Joshua would disappear so she could crawl back in bed and wrap herself in the covers.

"Are you sure you are all right, Isabel?" he called out again.

"Yes. Just give me a minute."

"Isabel, if you need me . . . you will call out?"

She sighed, hearing the concern in his voice. "Yes, Joshua," she answered dutifully, maybe a little impatiently.

"Then I hope you feel better."

And she knew he was gone. She could feel his absence, like something light and joyful had been sucked out of the house. It was as if he knew she had wanted him to leave her alone in her misery. Throwing the tissue into the toilet, she grabbed another and wiped her mouth before flushing it all away. *God, that was weird,* she thought, pushing herself upright. Was it simply a reaction to a memory, or was she getting sick? She didn't do sick well. On the rare occasions when she'd had the flu, she had hibernated in bed, wanting to be left alone. She was a much better nurse than patient.

After brushing her teeth and throwing water on her face, she left the bathroom and went back into bed, pulling the cover up over her shoulder. Within moments her stomach settled; the shivers ended. She no longer felt sick and was thankful. So just a strong reaction to her teenaged rebellion. . . . *No, no, don't think about it again!* She was struggling to find something else to occupy her mind when the phone rang. Grateful for the interruption, she leaned across the bed and picked up the receiver.

"Hello?"

"Isabel?"

She didn't recognize the voice. "Speaking."

"Isabel, this is Marcia McMillan. How are you?"

Isabel blinked. She hadn't seen Marcia, save for that brief encounter at the conference, or had a call from her in years. "I'm doing well. How are you?"

"Well, since you asked, I'm about to tear my hair out at this point."

Wasn't Marcia supposed to say *Fine, just fine?* Wasn't that the accepted social lie we told one another, instead of the truth, when speaking to those who weren't close friends? Marcia seemed to have skipped over that programming. "I'm sorry to hear that," Isabel answered. "How can I help?"

As soon as the words came out of her mouth, Isabel screwed up her face with regret. It was obvious Marcia wanted *something* from her.

Marcia let out her breath. Isabel could actually hear the relief through the phone. She knew it was a setup, and she'd fallen for it.

"I have a problem, Isabel," Marcia began. "I don't think you know about my sister, Jennifer. She's slow. Beyond slow. And sometimes she shows signs of regressing into an autistic state. I know that's your field now, and I was wondering if you could take a look at her."

Isabel was surprised, and she sat up in bed, leaning back against the pillows. "Of course I'll see her, Marcia," she said, regretting her earlier feelings of being set up. "I can't promise anything," she added. "Most of my clients now are young. How old is your sister?"

"She's about to turn eighteen. Midlife baby for my mother. Not a great experience since my mother never really recovered and died when Jen was five. And I'm not asking for promises or miracles, but something has to be done. She was in quite a respectable facility, and now I find out she's pregnant."

"Oh . . ." Isabel could only stare at her mussed bed linens. "I'm sorry."

"So now she's here with me again and . . . well, Isabel, I have a book tour lined up. It's national and will last for ten days. My publisher is flying me all over the country doing interviews. Print. TV. You name it. This could not have happened at a worse time. I'm afraid if you can't make any headway with her, I'm going to have to institutionalize my sister and then get her an abortion when I get back. You can see now why I'm about to pull out my hair."

"Good heavens, Marcia, I'm so sorry. How dreadful for your sister. Was it . . . ?" She left her question hanging, not wanting to offend.

"Rape? Of course it was rape. My sister isn't in any state of mind to give her consent. Probably one of the damn orderlies in the place. When I get back I'm going to raise bloody hell about this and demand an investigation and sue them. She was supposed to be safe there."

"I can't blame you," Isabel whispered, truly in shock. "Look, how's this afternoon? Can you get your sister to my home today? When are you leaving for your book tour?"

"Two days from now. And yes, thank you so much. How does four-thirty sound?"

"Sounds fine, Marcia. I'll see you both then."

"Great. Thanks, Isabel."

She hung up the phone and blew her breath out in a rush of compassion. That poor girl. She must be so confused. What in the world could she say to her? Glancing at the clock, Isabel realized she had better get her act together.

For the second time that day she headed for the shower.

This time her heart was heavy, and she called out to Joshua and any other source in the universe that could help her communicate with the young woman who had been abused by those she had trusted.

§

Her hair was still damp, and she'd pulled it back with a thin headband to keep it from falling onto her face. She had dressed casually in a pair of jeans and a soft cashmere hoodie the color of the sea. In the shower she had decided that it was best not to appear like a professional. Jennifer had probably had enough professionals in her life who had frightened her. The most she could hope was for the young woman to trust her . . . though it would take a miracle to accomplish anything significant in two days. Her heart ached when she thought of Marcia institutionalizing her sister.

Years ago Isabel had worked in such a facility, and the experience had changed her life. Sometimes she'd thought the only difference between her and the patients was that she had the keys and could get out. Back then anyone with money could put away a family member who refused to conform with society's dictates. When she was younger, anyone with dyslexia or depression or any number of now-accepted challenges could find themselves living with truly mentally ill patients. It had been a scary experience for her and . . . she'd had the keys. Perhaps that was why she had begun her journey into the subconscious, why the mind fascinated her. The keys. She was always looking for them.

The doorbell rang, and Isabel blew out her breath with anxiousness. Walking toward the door, she prayed for guidance, for some inspiration to show her the right path to follow. She smiled as she opened the door and saw Marcia standing next to a thin young woman who was looking down.

"Hi," she said in a friendly voice as she held the door open wider. "Come in, come in. Far too cold today to be standing on the porch."

Marcia took her sister's wrist and led her inside the house.

Isabel closed the door behind them and smiled. "You must be Jennifer."

Marcia didn't even give her sister a chance to nod. Instead, she began unbuttoning Jennifer's coat. "Can you say hello to Mrs. Calloway?"

"Isabel, please," Isabel quickly responded. "We're all friends here."

"Can you say hello to Isabel?" Marcia asked, removing Jennifer's coat.

"That's all right," Isabel murmured, observing the pretty girl, her long dark blond hair pulled back and off her delicate face into a ponytail. Jennifer was thin and dressed in tailored brown slacks and a white sweater. And there were pearls. Isabel wondered if Marcia had dressed her sister for the occasion. She took their coats and led them into her office. "Why don't we all sit down and get to know each other?"

Isabel put the coats on a hook by the office door and smiled. "Would anyone like a cup of tea, or hot chocolate? It is getting bitter out there, isn't it?"

Marcia, dressed in a dark brown business pantsuit that matched the color of her hair, sat down on the sofa with her sister at her side. "We're fine," she answered for both. "And I hope to God it doesn't snow before I can get out of here on a plane in two days."

"Are they calling for snow?" Isabel asked, sitting opposite them in her usual wing chair. It seemed that since Joshua had entered her life, she wasn't even watching the news as much.

"The possibility," Marcia said. "It would be just my luck."

Isabel simply nodded as she watched Jennifer. The girl seemed withdrawn, allowing her older sister authority over her. "And what about you, Jennifer? Do you like snow?"

The girl didn't look up from her lap, where her hands were clasped together. She didn't even appear to have heard the question. She was somewhere in her head, Isabel figured, somewhere safe.

"Jen, Isabel asked you a question," Marcia said, patting her sister's leg as though to awaken her. Marcia looked up at Isabel and shook her head, indicating it was useless. "I've tried everything with her. You would think with my abilities I could reach her, but nothing. . . ."

Isabel didn't say anything for a few moments as she attempted to get her patience under control; then she took a deep breath. "Marcia, could you leave your sister with me for about an hour? Is there someplace you could go? Get a cup of coffee and relax? Run to the mall for last-minute shopping?" She paused and added, "And congratulations on your book and your tour. I forgot to tell you that on the phone earlier."

Marcia appeared to like the last part, as she sat up straighter. "Well, I could run and get a manicure. I didn't think I would have the time, but . . ."

"Why don't you do that?" Isabel interrupted, and stood up. "There's a place right in the Willow Grove Center that takes walk-ins."

Marcia looked at her sister.

"She'll be fine with me, even if we just sit together in silence the whole time."

"But you'll try?" Marcia asked, running her fingers through her short brown hair, which was styled into fashionable wispy points to frame her pretty face. "I've never done this before. A book tour. There's so much to do before I leave."

"Well, get your nails done. That'll be one thing to check off your list." She crossed the space between them and sat down on the floor by Jennifer's shiny penny loafers. Yes, the poor girl must have been dressed by her stuffy and professional older sister. "Is it all right if you spend some time with me, Jen?" she asked softly.

The girl only blinked.

"She'll be okay," Marcia answered, already reaching for her coat. "She's isn't violent, or anything."

Isabel only nodded, not wanting to hurt Jennifer by answering such a statement.

"I'll be back as soon as I can. If it's a little over an hour, you won't be upset?"

"Not at all, Marcia. It must be important to an author to have nice hands if they're signing books."

"I know," Marcia answered, buttoning her coat. "But who has time, especially with this . . . *emergency* thrown at me last minute?"

Isabel forced a smile as she heard the resentment in Marcia's voice. "Take your time, then, and enjoy this bit of pampering."

"Right. Then I'm off." She headed out of the room. "Should I lock the door, or anything?"

"We'll be fine," Isabel called out.

When she heard the front door close, Isabel leaned her arm on the sofa cushion next to Jennifer and moaned, "God, I thought she'd never leave."

Then, realizing what she'd said aloud, she quickly glanced up to the girl to see if she'd heard.

Jennifer simply blinked, but Isabel could swear she saw a slight turn up at the corner of her mouth.

Hmm. So Jennifer wasn't completely withdrawn, and maybe Marcia had just given her a clue how to proceed.

"I never had an older sister," Isabel said quietly. "Or a younger one. I was an only child. It was pretty lonely sometimes." She paused, watching for a reaction. None came. "I even made up an imaginary friend."

Ah, again the slight upturn of the lip.

"I think sometimes an imaginary friend can be most helpful when a child is lonely or confused or frightened. Did you ever have one?"

Jennifer simply blinked.

"Mine's name is Joshua," she murmured, more to herself than to her client. Realizing she had used the present tense, she cleared her throat and continued. "I mean I didn't know his name at the beginning. It happened one day when I was out in the yard, making mud pies. I think I was three years old. My mother would have had a fit if she'd known I was playing in mud. My mother was a little like Marcia, I think. She wanted everything to fit into its proper place, and little girls wearing pretty dresses weren't supposed to be squatting in the mud, slapping it all together to make pies I really thought I could sell to a bake shop." Isabel chuckled. "Well, I thought they were very pretty. I'd even sprinkled them with a fine coating of dry dirt like powdered sugar. Anyway, that's when I remember giggling with my imaginary friend for the first time." She looked directly at Jennifer. "Do you remember your first time?"

Astonishingly, the girl nodded. Barely nodded, but it was an answer.

And that's when Isabel knew the doorway had opened a crack, and if she was very careful, she might be able to open it enough to get in. "I didn't think there was anybody else like me, so of course I didn't say anything to my mother. It became my secret. Was it like that with you?"

Jennifer blinked several times and then again nodded.

Isabel waited a few moments before continuing. "It seems when we're little there's so much we don't understand: what the adults and even the big kids around us are doing or saying. I found for me it was best if I didn't say too much of anything, didn't get anyone around me upset. It can get pretty lonely living like that."

No answer, no movement of eyes or mouth. Isabel tried another tack. "Do you think our imaginary friends are real?"

Jennifer nodded.

"I think you might be right." Who was she to argue when she'd made exquisite love to hers only a few hours before? No therapist worth her salt would encourage such thinking, but experience, as outrageous as it was, now far outweighed educational training, and Isabel was in uncharted territory now. "You know, Jen, you're the first person I can talk to about this, the imaginary friends. Anyone else would think me foolish, maybe even a little . . . unbalanced. But sometimes what you know is true in your soul doesn't have to be true for anyone else. I think, many times, people don't want to hear about the unusual because it frightens them. I just want you to know I'm not frightened, and if you choose, you can talk to me about anything. You do talk, right? I know you understand me now."

Jennifer nodded.

"Good. That's a beginning for friendship. In fact, it's how most friendships begin—by communicating with another person."

Jennifer simply blinked.

"I would like to be your friend. Would you like to be mine?"

Several more blinks and then another nod.

"I'm glad of that." She paused, wondering how to proceed. Usually there was an intake form and discussion with the client or parent. All she had to work with was that short phone call with Marcia. "I know some things about you— things Marcia has told me. I'm sorry about your mother. You were very young when she died. Is your father alive?"

A short shake of the head was the answer.

"So it's just you and Marcia now?"

A nod.

Isabel paused. "You know I knew Marcia many years ago. She was a student of mine. She was strong willed and impatient to learn then. Is she still like that?"

Already knowing the answer, Isabel didn't need Jennifer's reaction, but wanted to keep the girl engaged. Jen nodded, and her clasped hands became tighter.

"I think she only wants what's best for you, Jen, but perhaps doesn't go about it in the most patient way."

No reaction.

Isabel took a deep breath. "She also told me what happened to you. That you are pregnant. Do you understand what that means?"

After a short pause, Jennifer nodded.

"And what do you think should be done now?"

The young girl shook her head so fast that her ponytail began swinging.

"It's okay, it's okay," Isabel soothed. "Do you mean you don't want to be pregnant? It's completely understandable after being violated."

Jennifer was now rapidly blinking, her mouth a thin line of agitation.

"Do you know what that means . . . violated?" Isabel asked, knowing at any other time she wouldn't have proceeded so quickly. But with only two days . . .

A nod . . . and then the furious shaking of the head.

"I'm confused, Jen. Do you mean you know what the word means, or that you weren't violated?"

Jennifer nodded.

"You understand the word?" Isabel asked as a tingling sensation raced up her back.

Another nod.

"You were not violated?" Isabel whispered, feeling her heart begin to race with excitement.

Jennifer shook her head.

Isabel bit her bottom lip, struggling to find a way to proceed. Marcia was not going to like this at all. She had plans for her younger sister to terminate the pregnancy.

"Listen, Jen, you need to tell me who the father is." She swallowed deeply to bring moisture back into her dry mouth. "I won't tell Marcia. I promise. She thinks you were raped."

Jennifer began breathing heavily, blinking rapidly, and Isabel knew if she touched the girl's wrist her pulse would be elevated.

"Whatever it is, whoever it is, you can trust me, Jen. Your secret will be safe with me."

And then Jennifer exhaled, stopped blinking, and looked up for the very first time.

Isabel was stunned by the intelligence she could read in the pretty girl's now-focused gaze. She had to remind herself to breathe.

Jennifer smiled shyly. She opened her mouth once, as if to speak, and then shut it.

"You can trust me," Isabel whispered, waiting to hear the girl's voice for the first time.

"It was . . . ," Jen murmured, and then stopped.

"It's okay," Isabel whispered back, swallowing deeply again. "Was it someone you know?"

A nod.

"Was it someone who works at the home you were staying at?"

Jen shook her head.

Isabel's mind was racing with questions now that Jennifer had actually said two words. It was communication. "Was it another person who lives there?"

The young woman closed her eyes and shook her head. "Friend," she whispered, opening her eyes and then bringing her hand up to cover her lips, as though she had revealed a great secret.

"A friend . . . ," Isabel repeated. This was not the scenario Marcia had described. "Have you known this friend a long time?"

Jen was back to nodding.

"Since you went to live in that home?"

She shook her head in the negative.

"Before that?"

A nod. And then Jen sat up straighter, breathing in deeply through her nose.

"My . . . my imaginary friend," Jen whispered, releasing her breath with a secretive smile, as if those three words were the key to her universe.

For a split second, Isabel thought she was going to faint as her ears began ringing and her vision tunneled with darkness and then, thankfully, expanded. Now she was the one blinking rapidly, clutching the sofa cushion, feeling her heartbeat thudding against her chest wall. Had she planted that idea by talking about her own imaginary friend? Was it a handy answer, or was Jennifer truly delusional? Any other professional would immediately make that diagnosis, and a month ago she would have immediately agreed.

But Isabel now knew something those others didn't, and the knowledge terrified her.

Imaginary friends can become real.

Chapter

7

HER HEAD WAS A CHAOTIC MESS, AS IF THE RECEPTORS couldn't make any logical connections, like a hard drive on a computer that keeps whirring on overload. She had to stop, get control, and she tried to clear her mind. Within seconds Isabel's brain made a connection and registered something she had read a long time ago, during her years of studying. According to Emil Crué, the expectation of something tends to bring about the realization, because the imagination is stronger than willpower. When the will and the imagination are at war, the imagination always wins. The force of the imagination is in direct ratio to the square of the will. Or, the harder one tries to do something, the less one is able to do it.

The answer seems to be in *allowing* the answer to surface.

But *this* answer? Jennifer's *imaginary friend* had gotten her pregnant?!

How could she possibly tell this to Marcia, who was already prepared to put her sister away? How could she protect this young girl until Jen, herself, allowed the real answer to surface? It would take more than two days.

Isabel cleared her throat and tried to slow her heart rate. She simply had to stay calm. "Jen, I'm going to keep your secret, so don't worry about Marcia right now, okay?"

Jennifer nodded.

"I would ask a favor of you, though. Do you think you could sit in that chair over there and let me talk to you? I'm not as young as I used to be, and my knees are starting to hurt from sitting on the floor."

Jennifer looked at the chair where Isabel's clients usually sat and nodded. Slowly, she rose and walked over to it.

"Would you like to take off your shoes? I have this great little blanket I can put over you to keep you warm."

Jennifer looked down to her shoes.

"They're very shiny," Isabel said with a grin. "Like brand-new. Are they stiff? Do they hurt your feet?"

The young woman nodded.

"Then kick them off and let's both get comfortable," Isabel directed. "I'll take mine off too." And she did, just as Jennifer took off her shoes and lined them up perfectly on the side of the chair.

When Jen sat down in the chair, Isabel pulled the warm cashmere blanket over her and tucked it in around her thin stocking-clad feet. "There, that's better, isn't it?"

Jennifer nodded, and Isabel pulled a sweater from the door hook and sat down. Wrapping the sweater around her own feet, she took a deep breath and mentally prayed for guidance on how to proceed. "Has Marcia ever hypnotized you, Jen?"

A nod.

"Did you enjoy it? Was it relaxing?"

A shrug.

"Okay . . . would you allow me to give it a try? Do you trust me?"

Jennifer nodded several times.

"Good. So you probably know how this goes, but just listen to my voice. If you feel drowsy close your eyes and relax. Any other sounds you might hear from outside this room will only drift away and increase your relaxation. Are you ready? Shall we give it a try?"

Jen nodded and closed her eyes.

Isabel thought she could probably use a quicker induction, since Marcia had most likely put her sister under any number of times, but something told her to begin at the beginning, to do it her way. "Let's take a deep cleansing breath together. Breathing in fresh clean air to nourish all parts of your body, and exhaling to release any tension or toxins we're holding in our cells. In . . . clean, cool air. Out . . . warm releasing air . . ." After a few more deep breaths, she said in a low, soothing voice, "Now I would like you to focus your attention on your toes; imagine the tiny muscles in your toes relax with a wonderful warmth. Feel it wrap around each toe and move up to the arches of your feet . . . soothing, relaxing warmth. . . ."

Isabel worked all the way up Jennifer's body, watching the young woman relax each muscle. She was a very good subject, and when Isabel directed Jennifer's imagination to the beach, Isabel told her to see a large comfortable hammock between two sturdy palm trees. She asked Jennifer to climb into it, to lie down and relax, hearing the soft ebb of the waves on the shoreline, feeling the gentle warm breeze slowly rocking her back and forth as she went deeper and deeper into relaxation with each slow sway of the hammock.

"How do you feel, Jen?" she whispered, then held her breath with anticipation. Would Jennifer actually speak? In complete sentences?

"Good," she murmured with a slight smile. "Pretty here."

Isabel let out her breath in relief at the young woman's words. "It's your special place, so it must be. Do you like the slow rocking feeling?"

Jen nodded. "Mommy . . ."

Isabel felt a lump in her throat, and her eyes began to burn. Poor girl had lost her mother at five years of age. Had no one ever rocked her since? "Yes, that's how it feels, doesn't it, like being held in the soft, warm arms of your mother?"

Jen nodded.

"You're protected here, Jen. This is your space. Nothing can hurt you here, and you can return to this place anytime you want. May we talk about your mother?"

Jen didn't answer immediately, and then she barely whispered, "Sick."

"Yes, your mother was sick. But she must have loved you very much, right?"

A definite nod.

"Do you know what happened to your mother?"

The young woman's breathing became less relaxed. "Went away."

"A hospital?"

A nod.

Good grief, the last place Marcia should send her sister was into an institution. Marcia could lose Jennifer forever.

"So you were about five years old when your mother went away. Did you speak before that? Did you talk to your mother?"

"Yes."

Good. They had moved into verbal answers instead of head movements.

"And after your mother left you, did you speak then?"

"Just . . . my friend."

"Your imaginary friend?"

"Not imaginary."

"A real friend?"

"Yes."

"Could anyone else see him? Like Marcia?"

Jennifer shook her head. "Marcia's bossy. Knows everything." A pause. "But she doesn't."

"I don't think any of us knows everything. We are always learning, don't you think?"

"Yes."

"I would like to learn something today. Do you think you could help me?"

Jennifer shrugged. "Don't know."

It never failed to amaze her how once a person's conscious mind was relaxed, the subconscious readily responded, as if waiting to be recognized. "I believe you could help me, Jennifer. All I want to know is who your imaginary friend is. Does he have a name?"

"Not imaginary. Not anymore."

"Right," Isabel murmured, trying to stay objective. "Does he have a name?"

"Yes."

"Could you tell me?"

"It's a secret."

"And I have promised you that all your secrets will be safe with me. You can trust me. All I want to do is help you, Jen."

"Don't tell Marcia." Jennifer's voice lowered, as if imparting something very confidential. "She's still sleeping."

Isabel blinked. "Sleeping? Marcia is sleeping?" Jen didn't remember her sister bringing her here?

"She thinks the answers are big, and . . . and they are really very small."

Hadn't Joshua once tried to tell her something like that? Isabel's own mind was starting to shift in a different direction, and she had to force herself to stay on topic. "Well, I won't tell Marcia anything you don't want her to know. But you were going to tell me the name of your . . . friend."

Jennifer inhaled deeply, and Isabel could see the young woman's muscles tensing.

"Come back to the hammock, Jen. Feel it gently swaying you in the soft breeze, like in your mother's arms. You can relax again. You're safe now. You can tell me."

Within moments, Jen's breathing became more shallow and her muscles relaxed. "His name is . . ."

Isabel held her breath and leaned forward. ". . . Is?" she prompted.

"Manny."

"*Manny?*" Isabel asked in disbelief. She had expected something a little more profound.

Jen nodded.

"Manny," Isabel repeated, this time calmly. Maybe Manny was the name of someone who had been nice to Jen as a child. A friend of the family, an uncle. *Manny?* Mentally shaking her head, Isabel asked, "And Manny is the father of your baby?"

"Yes."

Isabel was now beyond uncharted territory. She was into the deep unknown. "So you and Manny made love to each other?"

Isabel nodded, a slight smile of remembrance upon her relaxed face.

"Was that the first time you were . . . with someone? Like that? Intimate. Sexual," Isabel added. "Sexual intercourse."

Jennifer shook her head. "Not the first time."

Isabel took a deep steadying breath. "There was someone else?"

"No. Just Manny. I love him."

Isabel bit the inside of her lip and stared at the face of a young woman in love—the secret smile of believing you are the very first person on the planet to have felt such wondrous emotions. "So you've made love with Manny before?"

"Yes."

"And it's just now you've found out you're pregnant?"

"Manny told me I was going to have a baby. Our baby."

Isabel blinked. "Is Manny a doctor?" That would explain a lot.

Her eyes still closed, Jen shook her head and grinned at the silly suggestion.

Isabel felt like she was playing twenty questions. Is Manny bigger than a bread box? Is he animal, vegetable, or mineral? *Does he even exist?* "So Manny doesn't have any medical training?"

"No. He doesn't need it."

Again, Isabel bit the inside of her bottom lip. Hmm. "Does anyone else see Manny? Besides you?"

"Cathy said she saw him. She said he was beautiful."

"Cathy?"

"She lives with me. Lived with me," she corrected, "before Marcia came and took me away."

"So Cathy saw Manny," Isabel repeated. "Did she speak with him?"

Jennifer shook her head. "But Manny talked to her and touched her face." There was a pause. "She doesn't cut herself anymore."

Isabel stared at her client in stunned silence. She honestly didn't know how to proceed. For the first time she was not questioning the state of the person in the chair. She was questioning her own sanity. A part of her—the trained part of her, the professional part of her—wanted to help Jennifer see that she had made up Manny to cover up and deny being impregnated by a real male. Another part of her, something deep and instinctual, was wondering if it all might be true. That was the insane part.

Isabel knew she hadn't made up Joshua as some kind of fulfillment fantasy. The Gang had seen him singing in that bar in Philly. Joshua was real. If Joshua was real, might there really *be* a Manny?

Everything she had ever been taught, everything she had ever learned in her many years of studying the psyche, told her the opposite. But how could she deny what she knew to be true? She had met an extraordinary being who claimed to have been with her since childhood—a dimension traveler who had manifested himself to her by using what he called a body suit. And he'd come to her to help her expand her consciousness. Joshua knew everything about her—things she hadn't revealed to anyone else, not even Chuck. Joshua *was* real.

She brought her attention back to Jennifer. "Do you want to have this baby?" she asked softly.

"Oh yes," Jen immediately answered, her hands moving to her abdomen as though to protect the cells multiplying inside of her.

"Do you think you could take care of a baby, Jen?"

"I will take care of my baby." A pause followed that statement. "And I won't ever, ever leave it and go away."

Oh God . . . if Marcia had her way Jennifer would be so traumatized that she might become catatonic and never recover. "Babies can be difficult sometimes to handle, especially if you're doing it alone."

"Manny will help me," Jen answered with confidence. "He said I shouldn't be afraid or worry."

"He did? What else did he say?"

"He said our baby will be different, special. He said the world is waiting for our baby."

Isabel's jaw dropped. She forced herself to swallow. "Different? How different?"

"He said I was born different, but when my mother left me I forgot. And now our baby will remind me."

Isabel realized she was slowly shaking her head as she stared at the lovely young woman across from her. She honestly didn't know what to say next, and was saved by the sound of a car engine pulling into her driveway.

Marcia!

Suddenly Isabel stood up, kicked the sweater covering her feet aside, and walked over to the chair. "I'm so glad we talked today, Jennifer. I'd like to do it again. Would you?"

Jen nodded.

"Good. Now I'm going to count to five. With each number you will feel yourself waking up. One . . . leaving the hammock and waking up. Two . . . becoming more awake, feeling all parts of yourself coming together in harmony. Three . . .

more awake, remembering everything we talked about. Four . . . opening your eyes. And five . . . awake, alert, feeling calm and good about yourself." She smiled down to Jennifer. "How do you feel?"

Jennifer blinked sleepily and smiled. "Nice," she whispered, just as the doorbell rang. Suddenly, she tensed and stared up at Isabel. "You promised."

Isabel nodded and stroked Jen's silky hair. "I promised. Don't worry about Marcia right now. I'm going to talk to her, but I won't tell her any of our secrets. Now, let me get the door."

Isabel felt like she was pulling in all the air her lungs could handle as she opened the front door and saw Marcia standing there, holding her red-lacquered fingers out in front of her.

"Good color, don't you think?" Marcia asked. "Couldn't decide on a French manicure or the red. Decided to go for the dramatic."

Isabel smiled as Marcia passed her into the foyer. "It is dramatic," she stated, thinking she'd have gone for the more subtle French manicure herself. "A touring author gets to be dramatic, if she chooses."

"Would you mind helping me out of this coat?" Marcia asked, presenting Isabel with her back. "They're still not a hundred percent dry, and I don't want to smudge them."

"Sure," Isabel answered, carefully removing each sleeve of Marcia's coat and then carrying it over her arm.

"And the paraffin wax dip on my hands. God, it was heavenly. You were right about the pampering."

"Listen, would you join me in the kitchen? I could use a cup of tea, and I'd like to talk to you in private."

Marcia glanced toward the office door. "Did you make any progress?"

"Some. Let me just tell Jennifer where we'll be for a few

minutes." Without waiting for an answer, Isabel walked into the office and grinned at Jen as she hung up Marcia's coat.

"Marcia's here, and I'm going to make all of us a cup of warm tea. Do you think you could wait here for a few minutes?" She went to the bookshelves that lined two walls and picked up a large book. "I think you might enjoy this," she said, handing it over. "I went to Easter Island in the South Pacific a long time ago. There's some beautiful pictures of beaches."

Jennifer took the book and then looked up beseechingly.

"I promised you, Jen. I won't break my promise," Isabel whispered with a smile.

Jen simply nodded and opened the book.

Satisfied that Jennifer would be occupied, she walked into the foyer and jerked her head to the side, indicating that Marcia should follow her to the back of the house.

When they reached the kitchen, Marcia said, "This house is huge."

Isabel took the teakettle from the stove and opened the fridge to dispense filtered water into it. "I know. I've been thinking it might be time to downsize." She paused. "Marcia, how did you find out Jennifer is pregnant? She isn't showing."

"The facility she was at does routine testing, to see if anyone has brought in drugs. Sometimes visitors will try to do that, especially with the teenage patients and teenage visitors. Because it's coed, pregnancy testing is part of the urine analysis on the females. I was stunned, believe me."

"I can only imagine."

Marcia sat at the table and sighed. "So what happened with Jen? Did she tell you anything? Sometimes I swear she knows everything I'm saying and just refuses to communicate. It's so damn frustrating."

With her back to Marcia, Isabel turned on the gas burner under the kettle. "I think I might be able to help her. I did get through and—"

"Damn it! Now why won't she let me in?" Marcia interrupted. "It's not like I don't have the experience."

"This isn't about you, Marcia," Isabel stated, the words blurting right out of her mouth before she could censor them. "This is about your sister." She then turned around to look at her former student, who appeared apologetic for speaking her mind.

"I know you're right, but it's so . . . so damn embarrassing, Isabel. I mean, here I am, about to go out all over the country during prime Christmas season promotion, print and TV interviews, book signings, lunching with book distributors, touting my book—a book about the degradation of family values—in the hopes they keep it on the shelves and reorder it. And my own sister, my learning-disabled sister, winds up pregnant. Do you know what a disaster this could be?" Marcia looked horrified, and then it was as though a light turned on in her head as her eyes widened with an idea. "Or . . . it could support my thesis, you know? My poor sister is violated by some person without any values at all, whose parents obviously never instilled in him the concept of right and wrong because they were too busy making money to raise their children properly."

Isabel only held on tightly to the back of a chair as she stared at the attractive woman sitting at her table.

"It's a thought," Marcia murmured.

"It's a shitty thought, Marcia, and you should be ashamed of yourself for even thinking about using your sister like that." *Screw her and her book tour and her red nails,* Isabel thought, losing all patience. "Why does everything always come back to you and your ambition? There's a young woman in my office who needs help. She's your sister, for God's sake. Doesn't that mean anything to you?"

Marcia straightened her shoulders, as though pulling her defenses together. "Don't talk to me about what my sister means to me. You get an hour with her and you think you know anything about the last eighteen years? I was there as a fifteen-year-old kid, watching my mother get sicker each month after Jen was born. And who do you think years later had to take on the major responsibility of raising that child when our mother died? My father?" Marcia laughed bitterly. "It's a miracle I made it through school, until he hired a nurse for Jen. But not a full-time one," Marcia added with more bitterness. "Oh no . . . at night I had to watch a five-year-old who'd regressed into silence and try to learn chemistry while my father sat in front of a television set to escape." She took a deep breath. "That person in there has been my responsibility since I was a child myself. And now it's my turn, Isabel. Finally, it's my turn. And, by damn, I'm taking it."

Isabel sat down opposite Marcia. "I'm sorry," she whispered, slowly shaking her head. "I know there's always two sides to a story. I should have remembered that."

Marcia sniffled and held up her hand. "Don't feel sorry for me now, Isabel. I know you think I'm one pushy broad. You always have, even when you were my teacher. Why do you think I even entered into the psychology field? To try and break through to Jen."

Isabel nodded. "It fits, but sometimes we're way too close to our subjects and we can't be objective."

Marcia sighed deeply. "I'm just going to have to have her admitted to a private hospital. I can't do it anymore, at least not now. This is my shot, and I don't care how selfish it sounds, I'm going for it."

"Of course you should go for it," Isabel murmured. "It's a great opportunity, and you'll be fine, Marcia."

"But what about Jen? Did you get anything out of her?"

Isabel nodded. "Actually, she's an excellent subject and went into induction easily. We spoke about . . . well, your mother. And it appears you've both been traumatized by your mother's death. I'd like to keep working with her."

"I've only got one more day before I leave, and then—"

Marcia's words were cut short by the whistle of the teakettle. Startled, Isabel jumped up and turned off the gas. She placed the kettle on a cool burner and brought out three teacups. Making the tea, she said, "I think I might have a solution. A temporary solution, but it's one I think could work for both you and Jen."

"And what's that?" Marcia asked. "A miracle? I don't believe in miracles, Isabel, not since I stood at my father's side, holding my little sister's hand while they threw flowers on my mother's casket. And fixing this situation at this late stage will take a miracle."

Isabel took a deep breath, turned around, and faced Marcia. "What if Jen stays here with me while you're on your book tour?"

Marcia's jaw dropped. "Here? With you?"

"Sure. Why not? You said the house is huge. I have four empty bedrooms. Jen's a sweet girl, and—"

"A pregnant girl," Marcia interrupted. "She needs special care now. At least until I get back from the tour and can fix that mess."

"Marcia, need I remind you I was a registered psychiatric nurse before going for my doctorate? I am perfectly capable of seeing to your sister's needs."

"If she gets agitated, she's been given Xanax."

"I remember how to give a patient a pill," Isabel answered, thinking Jennifer would have to go into a raving anxiety attack before she'd hand over that medication.

"You're serious?" Marcia asked in disbelief. "You'd do that for me?"

Isabel smiled. "I'd do it for both of you. I only have one client in the next ten days, so I can use that time to get to

know Jen better. It would be like intensive one-on-one therapy without the clinical setting. Who knows what could happen in that time?"

Marcia's eyes filled with tears of gratitude. "I can't believe it. I was so worried, racking my brain about her. And
now . . ."

"And now you've allowed the answer to come to you."

"How can I ever thank you?" Marcia asked, sniffling and
wiping her nose on her freshly paraffin-waxed hand.

"You can carry this tray into the office, and we can both
tell Jen, in a calm way, that she's going to be my guest for
ten days."

Marcia stood up as Isabel placed the teacups on a silver
tray, along with the sugar bowl. She took milk from the fridge
and poured it into the matching creamer.

Marcia sniffed again loudly, and Isabel grinned as she
opened the cabinet door under her sink and pulled out a paper towel. Handing it over, she said, "This will have to do.
No tissues in the kitchen."

Marcia blew her nose, then pointed her perfectly red
glossy nail toward the front of the house. "Just see if you can
get out of her who raped her. That's all I want. When I get
back I want to haul that bastard into a jail cell, and he'll be
lucky if he gets there with his sac still attached to his body!"

Isabel blinked. "Let's have our tea and calm down. First
things first. See if Jen is agreeable to staying here."

"Oh, she'll be agreeable," Marcia muttered, picking up
the heavy tray and following Isabel out of the kitchen. "It's
either here or a hospital. And she's terrified of hospitals."

"Let's not even mention the word then, okay? Why don't
you let me talk to her?"

"Good idea," Marcia whispered. "I'm too emotional right
now. No predicting what will come out of my mouth."

No kidding? Isabel thought, wondering how Marcia was
going to conduct interviews with anyone who challenged

her. *Not my problem,* she thought. One thing at a time. And the very next thing she was going to do once Marcia left with Jen was talk to Joshua.

And it wasn't going to be like anything they had talked about before.

Chapter

8

She closed the front door, leaned back against it for a moment to calm down, and then pushed herself into the foyer as she called out, "Joshua! I need you!"

"I'm right here, Isabel," he said from behind her. "There is no need to shout."

She jumped in fright, even though she'd been expecting him to appear—just not right behind her back like some ghost. Holding her hand over her heart, she said, "I need your help."

"What is it you want me to do?" he asked, studying her face with this strange smile, like she was some experiment he was very pleased with.

Isabel took a step back, to create some distance between them, because his *nearness,* just being so close to him, was magnetic, pulling her mind into memories of being held in his arms, touched by his hands, kissed by . . . *Stop it!* She commanded her mind back in the right direction. "Do you know what took place here this afternoon?"

"You had a visitor. I stayed away."

"Then you don't know about it?"

His eyes narrowed. "About what? All I can perceive about you right now is your mind is chaotic and you are very agitated."

She grabbed his wrist and led him into her office. "Sit down and I'll tell you."

He chose her client chair, and she sat down in her usual wing chair, glad not to chance sitting next to him on the sofa. It was better to keep some distance, at least for this conversation. "After you left me I had a call from an old friend, actually an old student of mine, and she asked if I'd see her sister. It was an emergency because she's going away on a book tour and . . . well, her sister had been classified years ago as being slow, learning disabled, and she was staying in a home, a homelike facility, and Marcia, my old student, just found out her soon-to-be eighteen-year-old sister is pregnant."

She told him all the details, everything she could remember pouring out of her in a rush, up until she put Jennifer under hypnosis.

"So she says she is pregnant by . . . get this, Joshua . . . *her imaginary friend!*"

Joshua leaned forward, resting his elbows on his knees. "She told you that? Are you sure, Isabel?"

Isabel's head sort of wiggled in disbelief. "Like I would get *that* wrong? She said she had made love with her imaginary friend. She calls him Manny." She held her hand up, like a traffic cop. "I know. Manny. What kind of name in this day and age is that for a kid to make up? That is, if he is made up. And now she says she's pregnant with their baby, who—oh, and you're gonna love this—is *special,* right? And this baby is going to help Jennifer remember how special she is."

Joshua simply stared at her.

"I know I shouldn't be telling anyone this. Client privilege, and all that, but I mean . . . *c'mon,* what am I supposed to think? If I hadn't just made love to you, to *my imaginary friend,* a few hours earlier, I would have immediately thought the girl was delusional and in need of intense psychiatric care. But . . ."

"But you know differently now," Joshua said, filling in when her words trailed off. "You know I'm real."

"Well, if you aren't, then all my friends are crazy too, because they saw you that night in the bar when you were singing. If you're real, Joshua"—She paused and gulped before continuing—"then, maybe, *just maybe,* Manny is real too? And Jennifer is troubled, but perfectly sane?"

He sat back in the chair and blew out his breath as he looked up to the ceiling. "There is so much I should have told you before this, but you are such a lovely distraction, Isabel."

"Thanks for the compliment," she said, now leaning away from him, her spine straight against the back of the wing chair, feeling like he was going to say something she didn't want to hear. "So, what are you thinking? What is it, Joshua, that we should have been discussing, instead of making love?"

He lowered his face and stared at her. "Is it so hard to believe Jennifer is telling you the truth? I'm not the only one coming to this third dimension to assist humanity in ascending into a higher one."

Isabel tensed as a weird sensation began racing up her spine, like a tiny electrical current that seemed to rush upward to bathe her brain. "A higher *what*?" she asked in a whisper, and had to remind herself not to be frightened.

"A higher dimension," Joshua answered sympathetically, as though aware she was fighting for clarity. "You're all stuck here, Isabel, like prisoners of your own fearful thinking. There was a time in your so-called history when mere survival depended on a highly developed stress response. Every single human alive in this moment is here because they come from a stock of people that had a well-developed stress response. Otherwise they would have been eaten by animals or killed by a fellow human, but in this present time that stress response is proving out of control, and it could destroy humanity, not to mention the delicate balance of the planet. Choices produce actions, and those actions have consequences. It appears humanity stopped at what you call the Age of Enlightenment, and hasn't gotten much farther along the path." He shook his head slightly. "And now the alternate path of fear-based thinking is heading toward becoming a threat to the rest of this universe. Cause and effect."

Isabel tried to bring moisture back into her mouth. "Are you . . . talking about something . . . like Armageddon, or the end-times?" She hardly believed those words came out of her.

Joshua shook his head. "This isn't about any religious belief system, which are all man-made. This is something much more provable, more real. The irrefutable law of cause and effect." He paused for a moment. "Fear. Fear of lack produces greed. Greed is the misuse of power and harms the planet and those you share it with. How else does the majority of the world's wealth find itself in the hands of the very few? Humans fear so much, and you look upward to the sky for your answers, to either praise or blame an entity you created in your own image. You give away your power so easily, especially the females. The time has come in this far corner of this particular universe for the women to take their rightful place and bring balance back to the earth."

"So Jennifer . . . and her baby . . . ?"

Joshua nodded.

"They *are* special? They're a part of . . . this transition to a higher dimension?" she asked, hardly believing she was actually accepting what he was saying. But after the unexplainable things she'd already experienced with him, she wasn't about to challenge anything. At least not yet.

He smiled slightly. "Jennifer and her baby are special, as you call it. But then so are you, Isabel. So are your friends. And that man who just drove by your house," he added, tilting his head slightly to the window.

Isabel looked beyond his shoulder and saw a red SUV passing out of view of the window.

"Every single one of you is special . . . or none of you are. It's that simple and, perhaps, that complicated. And if you are all the same, regardless of your status or wealth or education, or the country you live in, why then do you fear one another so much?"

Isabel stared at him and shook her head as she waited for his next words.

"Because you've been programmed to forget your true identity. You've been taught to see and recognize differences in race, religion, education, culture. No matter who you are or where you call home, you are prejudiced. You have been programmed by your society to prejudge, especially yourselves. You have forgotten what you knew as a new being coming into this dimension: that the spark of electrical energy beginning the first division of a single cell is your true identity. And that spark, in true reality, is exactly the same in each being. It is alive and creative. In the reality of this universe, in this dimension, you are all expressions of that spark of infinite energy and intelligence. Within every cell of that body suit you and everyone else wears is a majestical display of dancing electrical energy. What changes it and every molecule in your bodies is fear. Without fear, you are all one, the same, and you would no more violate another, for it would feel like self-violation. With fear, you separate from one another, and you tell yourself you no longer feel another's pain. It isn't your problem. You are just trying to survive."

"Not all people are like that," Isabel muttered, feeling she had to defend her species, at least a little.

"No, not all people. But many have forgotten, and it is that loss of identity which has caused most of humanity's fears. The separation has now become critical. You live in what your culture has called the most influential country, with the most wealth, the most opportunity. Imagine how others who are looking to this country for guidance are feeling as they watch what is happening here, the surrender of freedoms most would envy for the false promise of tomorrow's safety. Have you not noticed the stress level is increasing? The psyche, the collective soul of this noble country, is under great stress."

"Of course it is. One only has to open a newspaper or watch television to realize something profound is happening. We see corruption at the highest levels of government, and no one really seems to be doing anything about it. It's just accepted now. Everyone's stressed out and frightened about what tomorrow might bring."

"What if there is no tomorrow?" Joshua asked.

Now she was the one who was blinking like Jennifer, unsure how to answer.

"What if you didn't have to worry?" he asked, as though trying to get her to see something. "What would life be like without worry?"

Isabel shrugged. She couldn't remember a time of not worrying about something. Maybe when she was very, very young. "I don't know . . . heavenly? Normal? Whatever that might mean anymore."

Grinning, Joshua asked, "What if normal, real normal, is just that? What you have termed *heavenly*? No worries about tomorrow, because the present is a continual present to yourself and everyone you encounter?"

"Wouldn't life be . . . well, a little boring? Don't we need conflict and tension to move us along?" That's what she'd always heard.

He tilted his head. "Boring? What about a life that was exciting with creativity? Solutions? Discoveries? What if every new acquaintance brought you a gift, expanded your knowledge about yourself and your world?"

Isabel saw a mental picture of adults giggling like children, rushing around, wanting to meet others and discover their gifts. It would certainly not be considered normal. In fact, white coats and nets might be called out. "But there have always been those who prey upon the weak. Not everyone would accept such a world that evened out the scales and made us all equal."

"No, not everyone would. For some the ego is their sole reality."

"They would fight to retain power."

He smiled gently. "They are already fighting, Isabel. That's why they have created this environment of fear. This isn't something new that began in this period of time. It has been ongoing for generations, but has now reached a critical point, and everyone who has not closed down their minds can feel it. The energy surrounding this planet is heavy with fear, and the result is that feeling you named as *stressed out*. It is up to the females this time to achieve balance, to recognize and take back their innate power."

"The females . . . ," Isabel murmured, seeing women all over the world coming together and protecting their children from war, compromising and not allowing anyone's child to starve to death or die of preventable disease or—

"So back to your new friend Jennifer," Joshua said, interrupting her thoughts. "Will you help her?"

"I'm going to try," she answered, still rattled by the conversation. She attempted to get back on track. "Marcia, the sister, leaves for her trip the day after tomorrow, so she's bringing Jennifer to stay here with me for ten days. Maybe in that time we can find a solution and a way for Marcia to accept what's happening to her sister." She paused and pressed her lips together tightly. "She wants Jennifer to terminate the pregnancy because she thinks her sister was raped. Somehow, we have to figure this all out in ten days."

"What can I do?"

Isabel straightened her shoulders and sat up straighter. *Finally* they were getting to the point of why she had called out to him. "Okay, here's the thing. You need to find Manny."

"I do?"

"Absolutely. How else are we going to figure this out?"

"Isabel, no matter how it turns out, you don't have to worry. If it isn't Jennifer who brings this being into this dimension, it will be another female who does."

"But you didn't see her, Joshua! She wants this baby and . . . and I think if Marcia forces a termination on her, Jennifer will be lost forever. She'll never recover from the trauma of it." She looked pleadingly at him. "If I knew she was violated and raped I would take her for an abortion myself. Can't you see? We *have* to help her. You have to find out if what Jennifer said about her imaginary friend is true, if he's the father, and then go out there and find this Manny and get him back here."

"This universe is vast, and there are others beyond this one, Isabel, each with levels of dimensions. I cannot say how long such a request might take."

Her jaw dropped. "I don't care if you have to do a *Vulcan mind meld* with the girl to get to the truth!"

He turned his head sideways, exposing more of his ear. "A Vulcan mind meld?" he asked in a confused voice.

Shaking her head impatiently, Isabel said, "Get in her mind. See if this Manny is truly who she says he is, where he came from. And if that's the case, then go out there and get him back."

"You are giving me this mission?"

She exhaled, realizing how she must sound. "Well, it's more like a strong request. This girl needs us, Joshua," she said in a pleading voice. "I know this isn't what you expected. It certainly isn't what I expected! But it's here now. In our laps. We have to do *something*."

His smile was tender, loving, as he seemed to inhale the air between them. He stood up and reached for her hand. Holding it, he brought her to stand before him and murmured, "And now you see why I had to come to you in this way, why I have been so attracted to you and distracted by being in your presence. You are one of the most beautiful and compassionate beings I have ever encountered."

Completely taken aback, Isabel actually blushed. She could feel the heat rising to her face. "Joshua . . . I'm certainly not beautiful any longer and—"

"I wish you could see yourself the way I see you," he interrupted, as though taking great pleasure as he gazed at the space surrounding her. "Your colors are magnificent. You *are* beautiful, Isabel. . . . Never, ever again forget that."

She lowered her gaze self-consciously.

He reached out and gently raised her chin. "And every time I am near you I physically want you. Inside and out . . . you are most lovely to me."

Isabel swallowed down her emotion. "We're getting off track again," she whispered.

He grinned. "I shall miss your presence as I attempt to complete your assigned mission."

"Will you be gone a long time?"

"Time, your concept of time, is different than mine. I don't know how long it may take for my return."

She sighed as she rested her head on his chest while staring at the fireplace hearth and the sculpture of a woman balancing a basket on her head. She and Chuck had bought it on their trip to Africa so many years ago. Balance. Women and balance. That was the message Joshua was bringing her.

"I'm going to miss you," she whispered in amazement. "I didn't think I would ever say that to a male again." And in that moment, Isabel realized her feelings for Joshua went beyond the joys of physical intimacies he had reawakened.

Heaven help her. She was falling in love again.

And it was troubling—wonderfully, foolishly troubling.

§

Standing at the doorway, Isabel stared into the guest bedroom on the second floor, down the hallway from her own.

She had decorated it years ago in pale aqua and coppery browns, a combination she had been unsure of until she'd put it all together with the aqua in accent pillows and the dust ruffle on the bed. It was a balanced room, not too feminine or masculine, just a bit formal because of the furniture, which had reminded her of an East Indian English plantation. Would it be too much for Jennifer? Should she let the girl sleep on the third floor in one of the more informal bedrooms? Instinct told her to keep the girl on the same floor as herself, not to isolate her or let her think she was being banished upstairs.

No, she thought, this would have to do. And she'd already put fresh linens on the bed and emptied the dresser drawers of her personal things. Isabel was nervous about spending ten days with someone who was virtually a stranger. What had made the invitation pop out of her mouth like that to Marcia? At the time it had seemed the only solution to an immediate and bizarre situation. Hadn't she learned a long time ago that she couldn't save the world? And now here she was, being the caregiver again, thinking if she helped this one girl maybe the world could change a little for the better.

Damn, she'd thought she was done with the messiah syndrome that most women suffer from—that innate desire of saving another. She had let it go, believing it had died with Chuck. If she couldn't save the one person she had loved the most, who the hell was she to think she could help anyone else? Especially a young adult who had years and years of programming and emotional trauma. It was so hard to break down the barriers. Maybe that's why she had altered her career to assist younger children, who had no advocate save their parents against the system that wanted to classify them, typecast them, and drug them. Not that drugs couldn't be useful at times. It was just that she'd seen too many kids who were too easily diagnosed as trouble. But trouble for whom? The teachers? The parents? A society that demanded conformity at all costs in order to succeed in school, SAT testing? Sometimes the enormity of those with learning problems seemed overwhelming, as the statistics continually showed a higher and higher percentage. And now here she was again, not just trying to help a young woman who had been boxed in with that label, but who also believed she was pregnant by her imaginary friend.

You might have taken on more than you can handle this time, she told herself, and then felt the urge to laugh at her vast understatement. She was diving in way over her head, for what was at stake wasn't just Jennifer. It was her own balance, years of study and practice colliding with what could only be termed the supernatural. She might very well lose herself, she thought, just as the front doorbell rang.

Startled, even though she was expecting it, Isabel gulped down her anxiety and inhaled deeply as she raced down the stairs. She was in it now and prayed for some guidance, because she felt like she was flying by the seat of her pants on this one.

Plastering a friendly smile on her face, Isabel opened the door to Marcia and her sister, who was carrying an old-fashioned leather suitcase.

"Hi," Isabel said, opening the door wider to let them in. "It's good to see you both again."

Jennifer was staring down at Isabel's shoes, and Marcia sighed with exasperation. "Good to see you too, Isabel, and I can't tell you how grateful I am for taking in my sister like this. Last minute, and everything . . ."

"Well, why don't you both come inside?"

They walked into the foyer, and Isabel smiled at Jennifer. "I'm so glad you're going to stay with me while Marcia's on her business trip. Would you like to see your room? We can put your suitcase upstairs."

Jennifer was back to her nonresponsive state. Isabel didn't

know if it was Marcia's presence, or the young woman's confusion at the sudden change again in her living arrangements.

"Jennifer," Marcia said, holding her sister's upper arm. "You could at least nod when Isabel is speaking to you."

"Why don't we just go up anyway?" Isabel asked, to break Marcia's tension. She led them toward the staircase. "This house is so big, it will be good to have company again," she added.

"Well, I don't know how I can ever repay you for this," Marcia stated, following her sister up the steps. "I couldn't call my publisher and tell them to cancel all their arrangements. It isn't just bookstores. There's local television and radio spots in A.M. shows, and newspaper interviews. . . ."

Isabel was barely listening as Marcia droned on about herself again. When she reached the upper hallway, she turned and smiled at Jennifer. "Your bedroom is right here. And mine is down the hall, at the back of the house."

She led them into her guest bedroom.

"This is really nice," Marcia murmured, looking around the room as Jennifer simply stood like a good, silent child, still holding her suitcase.

"Why don't you let me take that and put it on the bed? We can unpack later," Isabel suggested as Jennifer released her grip on the double handles. Isabel put the suitcase on the queen-size bed and ran her hand over its old, soft leather. "This is really lovely," she murmured.

"It was my mother's," Marcia answered. "Jennifer took it over years ago, even though it's heavy as all hell."

"I think it's wonderful," Isabel replied, walking over to the dresser. "Reminds me of a more glamorous time in the forties and fifties when style seemed to mean something a little more elegant than today." She then opened a few drawers. "You can put your things in here, Jen, if you want. Take your time and make yourself at home, okay?"

Jennifer blinked, staring at the suitcase on the bed.

"Take your coat off and put your clothes away, Jen," Marcia commanded, giving Isabel a look of exasperation before checking her gold watch. "I'm going to have to run soon."

Isabel nodded, glad Marcia was going to be leaving. She'd thought she might have to put up with her longer. "Well, I'll leave you two alone to say good-bye," she said, moving toward the door. "I'll be back, Jennifer, after Marcia leaves."

The young woman didn't even acknowledge Isabel's words.

Marcia shook her head and blew out her breath as she approached her sister. "Now, listen. . . . I want you to behave yourself. Isabel is doing me a great favor by taking you in like this and . . ."

Isabel didn't want to hear any more as she headed for the stairs.

Marcia couldn't leave soon enough for her. And, probably, for Jennifer too.

After getting a detailed information page containing Jennifer's doctors' numbers, Marcia's cell phone number, and a copy of her tour itinerary, Isabel led Marcia back to the front door, assuring the woman Jennifer would be fine and that Marcia could call whenever she wanted to check.

"You know I'm leaving her with you, Isabel, because, even though you and I have had our differences in the past, I really do respect you. I want you to know that." She paused. "You shouldn't have backed off after your husband died." Marcia shrugged as she buttoned her coat. "You could have had a stellar career, maybe even your own talk show by now."

Isabel smiled. "But I didn't write a book. You did." She didn't want to add that Marcia's subject was slightly offensive to her, blaming parents who were simply caught up in the struggle to survive an economy that had been phasing out the middle class for almost a decade. And then entertaining them with mindless escape in the hope they didn't notice working longer hours, getting paid less, and paying more for health insurance and drugs to keep them getting up the next morning and doing it all over again. Instead of shining a spotlight on that, it was easier to place blame on the loss of family values. Make scared, guilty people more guilty and scared. Marcia was probably going to be very popular in certain states.

"Well, I just wanted you to know. And I will find a way of repaying you for this favor. Whatever your going rate is, I'll double it for taking in my sister."

It must have been quite a book deal for Marcia to make that offer, Isabel thought, holding open the door. "Why don't we talk about that when you return?"

"Okay, well the limo is picking me up in three hours, and there's still a lot to organize yet. Thanks so much, Isabel. I'll check in with you every day."

Isabel's hand on the doorknob tightened. "Good luck on the tour, and every other day should be fine. I know how busy you're going to be, and I do have your cell number if I should need you."

"Right, right . . ." Marcia walked outside to the porch and turned around.

"I don't want you to think I don't care about my sister. I do. It's just that all this unraveling right now is . . . well, more than I can handle."

"Why don't you concentrate on yourself for the next ten days?" *Shouldn't be too hard,* Isabel thought, and then immediately chastised herself. "Besides, as you said, this is your time, and you deserve it."

Marcia's eyes began to fill with emotion. "I really do," she murmured.

This time Isabel's smile was sincere. "Yes, you do. So go break a leg, or whatever one is supposed to say to a celebrity. You'll be fine."

Marcia simply nodded and turned to walk down the porch steps.

Isabel watched her get into her shiny new red Jag that sparkled in the winter sun.

It must have been one hell of a book deal.

Chapter

9

JENNIFER WAS SITTING ON THE BED, STARING OUT THE window to the now-bare branches of the trees that surrounded the property. Her winter coat was neatly folded on the bedspread. Again Jennifer was dressed too formally, as though she were interviewing for an office job. Isabel quietly walked into the room and sat down next to her. "It's so pretty here in the springtime when that soft color of green starts to come back to the trees and the birds return. I think they're so happy to have the weather turn warmer, their singing wakes me up every morning like an alarm clock."

Isabel glanced sideways and saw Jen's mouth turn up into a small smile.

"But I really enjoy their songs. Too bad we have to wait a few months for that, but I think you'll like it here for the next ten days—at least I hope you will."

No answer.

Isabel inhaled, searching for a way to break through again. "Marcia just left. I bet she gave you a whole list of instructions on how to behave."

Jennifer nodded slightly.

Good. A nod.

Isabel lightly poked Jennifer's arm with her elbow. "How about you just be yourself?"

Jennifer blinked, but didn't seem to mind the contact.

"Talk if you want; don't talk if don't want to . . . though I hope you choose to speak with me again. I really enjoyed it the other day. I felt like we were becoming friends."

Jennifer breathed deeply, then whispered, "You didn't tell Marcia."

Great. A complete sentence. Isabel shook her head. "I told you I could be trusted with your secrets."

"Marcia . . . she said she's going to do something so I . . ." Jennifer seemed to gulp down the word, as though it were too painful to repeat.

"So you . . . ?" Isabel prompted. ";You can tell me."

Jennifer touched the small swelling at her abdomen. "She doesn't want me to have my baby."

Isabel exhaled and gently touched Jennifer's back, barely stroking in sympathy. "It's because she thinks someone hurt you. Maybe in the next ten days we can come up with a plan Marcia can accept."

"I . . . I'll run away."

Closing her eyes briefly with compassion as she felt the girl's pain, Isabel said, "Let's not think about it now, okay?" She opened her eyes and smiled slightly. "The more you worry about it, the more scary it's going to become, Jen. Let's try to stay right here, right now in the present. Right now you're with a friend who's trying to understand you and your situation. Why don't you unpack and you can get into something more comfortable. Do you have a pair of jeans in that suitcase?"

Jennifer nodded.

"Good. Let's put your things away, and then we can go downstairs and I can show you the rest of the house." She rose from the bed. "I hope you're going to like it."

Jennifer obediently stood up and turned to her suitcase. She flipped the locks back and opened it out on the bed.

Inside, Isabel could see everything folded in precise order.

Now either Marcia had packed it with an anal meticulousness, or Jennifer had been trained to do it and not displease her older sister. Then again, maybe this was one place in her life Jen could have some control. Whatever, it was odd to see such precision, not one thing out of order. Even the shoes were enclosed in felt bags and strapped to one side. Isabel had to fight the urge to reach out and muss something, just so Jennifer could see the world wouldn't fall apart with a little chaos. Instead, she turned to the dresser and reopened a few drawers. "You can put your things away in here. Take as much space as you want."

She watched Jennifer methodically pick up each item and place it in a drawer. "I'll leave you to it, then, and come back in a little bit. Would you like to take a tour of the house?"

Jen simply nodded.

"Maybe we'll have a light lunch. Would you like something to drink? Some herbal tea or a soft drink?"

Putting a pretty pink sweater away, Jennifer shrugged.

"Okay, I'll be back in a little while. And, Jennifer . . . ?"

The young woman stopped what she was doing and looked up.

Isabel smiled. "I'm really glad you're here."

Jennifer nodded self-consciously and then continued her unpacking.

Twenty minutes later, after showing Jennifer the third floor, Isabel's own bedroom, and then leading her downstairs and through the living room, the office, the dining room, the walk-in pantry, and into the large kitchen, Isabel pointed to the small sofa by the window. "Why don't you sit down and I'll make us something to eat for lunch. Do you have any favorites, or things you don't like?"

Jen, who had remained silent throughout the tour, said in a low voice. "I like peanut butter and jelly."

"So do I!" Isabel exclaimed with a grin. "Never too old for peanut butter and jelly sandwiches."

"Marcia says they're bad for you."

"Well, maybe Marcia doesn't know that peanut butter contains the good fat, and as long as we don't make it three inches thick, I think we'll be fine. What do you want to drink? Tea? Soft drink? Milk? Whatever you want . . . or what I have. We can go shopping later for some of your favorite things."

"May I please have milk?" Jen asked in the most polite voice.

Isabel turned away from the cupboard and looked at the girl sitting so primly. "Okay, Jen, I do have one request, one thing I'd like to ask of you while we're staying together."

The girl sat up straighter and brought her hands back into that controlled clasp in her lap, like she was so used to being scolded.

"Jen, look at me, okay? You don't have to look down when I speak to you."

She waited for Jen to raise her face, and then smiled broadly. "Will you *please* stop being so polite? Relax, hon. We're in this for ten days, so we might as well make it as comfortable as possible. Not that I don't appreciate your excellent manners. It's just that we're friends now, right?"

Jennifer nodded.

"So that means we can be ourselves. Kick off our shoes and put our feet on the sofa. And you can have milk or any other thing you find in the kitchen. *Mi casa es su casa.*" Seeing a look of confusion, she translated. "It's Spanish, and it means my house is your house now. Do you understand? You're free here to be yourself."

"But I thought you were watching me. Marcia says that—"

"Marcia says a lot of things," Isabel interrupted, bringing out the peanut butter and closing the cupboard. "That doesn't mean everything she utters is the law." Then she realized she was undermining Jennifer's older sister and was treading on thin ice. "What I mean is that this is my house, and in my house I'm the boss and what I say goes. And I say here you're free to be yourself. Like right now . . . kick those new shoes off and put your feet up, if you want. I'm going to join you in a minute."

Isabel busied herself making sandwiches, but from the corner of her eye she saw Jennifer slowly taking off her leather penny loafers and slipping her feet up under her as she curled into a corner of the sofa.

Grinning, Isabel brought out the milk. Might as well have a glass herself. Calcium, and all that menopausal stuff. Though her behavior in the last few weeks had definitely not been typical of a woman her age. *Don't think about Joshua,* she told herself. That was a subject to gently ease into later.

When she was done, Isabel brought over a tray to the old coffee table in front of the sofa. "Here we go. Peanut butter and jelly. Grape jelly. Do you like that one?"

Jen nodded.

"Good," she answered, kicking off her flats and curling up on the opposite end of the sofa. She reached forward and handed Jennifer her plate and a napkin before taking her own. "How is it?" she asked as the girl began by taking a tiny bite.

Jennifer nodded and waited until she swallowed before saying, "Thank you."

"You're very welcome," Isabel muttered, not waiting until her mouth was empty. Then she swallowed and laughed, startling Jen. "Can you imagine Marcia talking with her mouth full?"

Jennifer grinned while chewing and shook her head.

Sorry, Marcia, she silently apologized, *but you seem to be my gateway into your sister, and I'm gonna use whatever I've got right now.* "So what do you think Marcia would do if she saw me like this?" And Isabel started smacking her lips together while saying in a prim voice, at least as prim as she could manage with a mouthful of peanut butter and jelly, "The proper way to eat is with your mouth closed, and never, ever, speak with your mouth full or you may look like Mister Ed, the talking horse, and—"

Jen was so surprised she burst out laughing and then started choking.

"Shit!" Isabel mumbled, putting her plate back on the table and rushing to pat Jen on the back. "I'm sorry," she said to the girl's red face. "Must have went down the wrong pipe, or something."

"You're . . . funny," Jen croaked out in a hoarse voice.

"Well funny while eating can be dangerous. My fault. Here, see if you can drink some milk." And she handed her the glass and watched Jen take a sip. "Are you okay now?"

Her face still red, Jen nodded.

Isabel went back to her side of the sofa. "Let's just eat then." She wondered when the last time Jennifer had played, really played. It was hard enough for most adults to remember, but something told her Jen's childhood hadn't been filled with much playtime outside of her imaginary friend.

Imaginary friends.

What were they . . . really? Fantasies, or maybe guardian angels who watched over us and sometimes made themselves known? There was a time, when Isabel had been about thirteen and she'd moved her bed to the wall with the windows on it . . . She remembered lying in bed, staring up at the ceiling, thinking of nothing in particular, lost in what her mother would have termed daydreaming. And then something bizarre had happened. Isabel had felt herself being turned to her side, easily, gently, just as the crash of Venetian blinds landed inches away from her side. She hadn't touched those heavy metal blinds in weeks, since they had been cleaned. What had made them just fall off the wall at that moment? Out of their brackets? And what had pushed her so calmly out of the way of them crashing down on top of her?

Something had been watching over her.

Joshua?

Turning her attention back to Jennifer, she saw the girl was eating again. "Would you like to take a walk later? We can bundle up and sit in the gazebo if you like. Sometimes the geese flying south stop over for a rest."

No answer.

"Or, we can sit and talk or watch television . . . whatever you want to do."

Jennifer finished her milk and put the glass back onto the tray.

"I like it . . . here," she murmured shyly.

Isabel grinned. "I'm glad. I like having you here. It can get a bit lonely living in this house all by myself. I think your visit will be good for both of us."

"I don't want to live with Marcia again. She thinks she's my mother, but she's not."

It was the most Jennifer had said in her presence, and Isabel was stunned, happily stunned—not by the words, but by the fact Jennifer was capable of intelligent and complete sentences strung together. Putting her plate back onto the tray, Isabel sighed slightly. "I understand how you feel, Jennifer. I really do. But I still think Marcia only wants what's best for you, or what she thinks is best for you."

"She doesn't know," Jen answered, looking troubled again.

"Maybe she doesn't, but I think that's what's in her heart."

"She's mean and bossy, and she's too loud. She hurts my ears sometimes."

Isabel bit the inside of her cheek. How to proceed? Trash Marcia for the sympathetic vote? This was the most Jen had volunteered, and she didn't want to stop the flow of a real conversation. "You know, Jen, Marcia was only a young girl herself when she thought she had to take over raising you. Young girls aren't as patient, sometimes, as adults, as mothers."

Jen was silent.

"Was your mother patient?"

The girl nodded.

"Mine wasn't," Isabel answered. "Not always. I think mothering must be very hard sometimes. My mother wanted everything done her way, or not at all. I guess she thought that was her way of controlling everything around her."

"Like Marcia."

"Maybe. Did you used to have good talks with your mother? Do you remember them?"

A nod.

"Were they special, just between the two of you?" Another nod.

"She gave you good advice then?"

There was a pause in the conversation as Jen simply blinked, as if wondering if she should proceed. Finally she took a deep breath. "She said it was better to not say anything at all than say something . . . mean. She told me to always remember that."

Major revelation. Perhaps in the fight-or-flight instinct, little five-year-old Jennifer had chosen to obey her mother, and her flight was to go within herself and shut out the rest of the world. How to bring her back out again would be the challenge.

"Well, that is good advice, Jen. Your mother must have been a very kind woman."

"She was."

Isabel nodded. "I bet if she had stayed with you longer, as you grew up, she would have also told you that there are times when you have to stand up for yourself and speak what's on your mind. Sometimes staying silent when our hearts are hurting only shoves the hurt down deeper inside of us until we don't know how to let it out."

"But she said to say nothing at all," Jen protested, as though she had been given the commandment from the mountain, and it would be sinful to disobey.

Isabel breathed softly, praying for guidance. "Maybe, just

maybe, she said that to you because you were a little girl and she was trying to teach you good manners. Or, perhaps, she knew she was going to have to leave you and she didn't want you to make Marcia's job of looking after you more difficult. I'm almost sure if she could speak to you now, she'd tell you that God gave you a voice to speak, to express yourself, even when you are upset. It's allowed. How else can you let someone else know they are trespassing? Do you know what that word means?"

Jen shook her head.

"It means when someone hurts you on purpose. They know it's wrong and they do it anyway."

"Marcia." Jen's mouth was now pursed with the first tinge of anger.

Isabel stared at the young woman seated next to her, unconsciously picking at the hem of her pink sweater as she bit into her sandwich again. Jennifer McMillan was definitely not autistic, maybe not even a slow learner. But she was filled with unexpressed anger at how her sister had been running her life. And now, it appeared, with this pregnancy, Jen had been given the opportunity to find her own voice.

This was not going to be easy, especially when Marcia returned.

Isabel knew her job was to help Jen find the voice she had stifled at five years old when she'd lost her mother. That voice, however, could mean Marcia's reign as older, wiser sister would be at an end. Could Marcia accept Jennifer as a young adult, no longer a slow learner, but someone whose views on her own life must be considered? "When is your birthday, Jen?"

"December eleventh."

Isabel blinked, counting the days. "Why that's next week!" Two days before Marcia returned.

Jen simply nodded.

Had Marcia completely forgotten about her sister's birthday in the excitement of a book tour? If Isabel hadn't asked, the day would have passed without even a card. "Well, we'll have to have a party!" she exclaimed. "What's your favorite cake? Chocolate? Or something more exotic?"

"I do like chocolate cake," Jen murmured.

"Then that's what you'll have," Isabel pronounced, her mind racing with plans. And by the time Marcia returned, Jennifer would be eighteen years old. A legal adult. She simply had to start acting like one. And the sooner the better.

"Jen, would you do me a favor and rinse these dishes, then put them into the dishwasher?" Isabel asked, rising from the sofa. "I have to go into my office for a few minutes."

Jennifer was blinking rapidly. "I . . . I don't . . ."

"You don't what?" Isabel asked gently, seeing the young woman was getting agitated.

"Marcia says I break dishes."

Isabel laughed. "Oh, c'mon . . . you won't break these. I know you won't. I'll show you how it's done."

Together they stood at the sink, and when Isabel had shown Jen how to rinse the dishes and then stack them in the dishwasher, she said, "Now I'll leave the rest to you. And stop worrying. These are old dishes. You're going to do fine. In fact, I think this will be your job while you're here, okay? I'll cook, and you do the dishes."

"I don't know. . . ." Jen's voice was still worried.

Who had stripped this girl of all self-confidence? It wasn't just Marcia. Maybe being given a label so young in life, no one had trusted her with chores and had kept her in a box of insecurity. Patting Jen's shoulder, Isabel said, "Well, I happen to know you'll be just fine. Take my word for it. I'll be back in a few minutes."

She left the kitchen and walked through the house to her office. Picking up the phone on her desk, she dialed the number she knew by heart.

"Cristine! How are you?" she asked her dear friend, glad she was home.

"Issy. Good to hear your voice. Haven't heard from you since our wild and crazy overnighter in the city."

Isabel grinned. "It was a little wild and crazy, especially at breakfast. Still haven't unpacked my goodie bag. It's in the corner of my closet."

Cristine laughed. "Just hope no one else ever finds it and wonders what kind of wild woman you are."

"God, I never thought of that!" Isabel whispered in a horrified voice. "I should get rid of it."

"At least wear the crotchless teddy once in a while for the hell of it. I would imagine it's very freeing."

"Right, especially if I cough hard. . . ." She could hear Cristine laughing. "Listen, I'd like to invite you over if you have the time. You and the baby I have a . . . a visitor, a young woman named Jennifer who's staying with me for ten days."

"Really?" Cristine's voice became serious. "She's staying with you?"

"I know. Sounds mysterious, but it's not. An old student of mine asked me to see her, and I volunteered letting her sister, Jen, stay with me while the older sister is on a book tour. I'll explain it better when I see you, but I just found out Jen's eighteenth birthday is next week, actually December eleventh, and I want to have a small party for her. Could you help me plan it?"

"I'd love to," Cristine answered. "What's a good time to come over?"

Isabel looked around her office. "Today. Tomorrow. Maybe tomorrow," she added, thinking she had to introduce Joshua to Jennifer first. "How about lunch here?"

"Sounds great. So one o'clock? That will give me time for Angelique's morning nap."

"Terrific. Thanks."

"One o'clock, then," Cristine said in a happy voice. "I can't wait to meet your new friend."

Isabel nodded. "Anything special I should cook for the baby?"

"She'll pick what she wants. You wouldn't believe how big she's getting."

"I can't wait to see her. Still as cuddly as a teddy bear?"

Cristine laughed again. "Oh, she's reaching out for her cuddles now. I'm going to have to teach her to be more discriminating as she gets older. Can't have her going up to strangers."

"Then I'll be in full cuddling mode tomorrow," Isabel answered. "And, Cristine, my guest is a little shy. No, a lot shy. I'm hoping that Angelique will help bring her out of it."

"If anyone can, this little charmer's the one." There was a pause. "Not that I'm bragging, of course."

Isabel grinned. "Of course you aren't. There really is something irresistible about your daughter."

"It's her father's genes, not mine."

"I'll argue that tomorrow," Isabel answered. "I should get back to the kitchen, where I have my guest washing dishes."

"Is she a guest or a slave?"

Isabel laughed. "Believe it or not, it's therapy."

"I love the way you can rationalize anything. See you tomorrow," Cristine said with a laugh, and hung up the phone.

Isabel replaced the receiver and stared at the papers on her desk. She really could rationalize almost anything. Except now. There was no way to rationalize what was happening to Jennifer, let alone herself. Yet she had to admit she was the perfect therapist to bring Jen to, someone whose own life was being altered by something unexplainable, something any other professional would term delusional. Was there some divine plan out there that had planted the seed in Marcia to call after all these years? Any other therapist would immediately have agreed with Marcia. She, on the other hand, had some personal experience with the unexplainable and mysterious side of so-called normal life.

She looked up to the ceiling and called out softly, *"Joshua! Are you there?"*

SHE FELT AN EXCITING SIZZLE OF ELECTRICAL ENERGY race over her skin, right before he appeared behind her and kissed her shoulder.

"I have been waiting for you to call out."

In spite of everything, Isabel smiled and leaned back against his chest as his arms came around her. "I've missed you," she whispered, turning around and smiling up at him. Good Lord, but he was looking at her with such tenderness that she had to stop herself from leaning into him and raising her face to be kissed. "Jennifer's here."

"I know," he answered, keeping her in his arms and lightly stroking her back. "I can feel her energy."

"You can? From in here, in the office?"

He nodded.

"So . . . ? What's your take on her, then?"

"My take?" he asked, a confused expression replacing the tender one.

"You know . . . what're your feelings? Are you picking up anything?"

"Simply a heaviness added to the energy already here." He nodded. "She is very troubled, frightened. I think she's afraid, even with you, to let down the wall she's built around herself."

Isabel was nodding. "Well, I think we should get started and you should meet her now. Get in her head."

"The Vulcan mind meld?" he asked with a grin.

She playfully slapped his shoulder as she moved out of his embrace. "It was a joke, but *yes*! Do whatever you have to, to find out the truth about this imaginary friend of hers . . . Manny."

"You say that name, Isabel, with a note of anger. Why is that?"

"Why is that?" she demanded in a whisper, her head jerking toward the back of the house. "Because whoever he is, if he's real, he had sex with that young woman and then left her to face the consequences alone, that's why!"

"And you are angry because . . . ?"

Isabel stared at him in disbelief. "I just told you! What kind of person does that? Especially to someone as confused and naïve as Jen? Do you have any idea how much trouble this has caused her?" She looked at the shelves and shelves of books on art, history, geography, psychology. What good were any of them now, in this bizarre situation? "And where is this Manny, hmm?" she added. "Out there in the ethers seducing some other naïve female who is no match for his powers? What about sticking around and dealing with the consequences? What about commitment, huh?"

"Are we still speaking about Jennifer?"

She blinked. "Of course we are. I wasn't . . ." Her words trailed off. She wasn't talking about herself, was she?

"You aren't naïve, Isabel. And, may I remind you, it was you who took our communication to a more intimate physical level and initiated sexual intercourse."

Even though he spoke the truth, she felt slapped. "I wasn't talking about myself," she insisted. "I knew what I was doing. I'm a mature woman and . . . I . . . and I don't know how this got turned around to be about me," she finished a bit too defensively.

"I simply don't want you to think you can judge another, for when your consciousness is expanding, as yours is now, what you judge you will experience. And quickly, much faster than in your past. It is truly in your best interests now to reserve judging anyone."

"I can't help being . . . upset, indignant even, that poor Jen has been left with this mess. I don't know how to stop that. It isn't like I can turn off a valve and suddenly become the Dalai Lama, all compassion and forgiveness. I'm not built like that."

Joshua smiled.

Smiled!

"Of course you are. If one of you can do it, all of you can. Why do you refuse to believe that you are capable of the extraordinary? Even the teacher you call Jesus told you whatever he did, whatever you perceived as miracles, you were capable of that and more. Those words are recorded and reprinted and read, but not believed. Most humans are programmed to hide their light and live in the shadows, repeating the same mistakes over and over and yet expecting a different result."

Isabel relaxed her lips and let the anger drop from her body. "We call that *insanity* in the therapy field."

"And that term, my love, is what I have been talking about and calling *programming* or *sleepwalking*. Humans have not just lost their way, they are losing their minds, giving away that power to others who already know how to manipulate energy. If you could see the chaotic electromagnetic field that surrounds this planet right now, you would understand. If humans could take back their minds they would see with an absolute clarity their truth unfold before them. Their confusion would end, and their purpose for being would be illuminated."

Isabel was shaking her head. "It's too big a job. There are over six billion people on this planet now. How can you really expect any kind of transition to a higher consciousness or dimension? Maybe in a couple hundred years or—"

"You don't have a couple hundred years, Isabel," Joshua interrupted, his expression very serious. "The planet is a living organism, and it is going to heal itself with or without the help of the humans who have created the dis-ease. The earth is alive and creative, and it doesn't have your fears, though your fears have contributed to the problem. And it is the fear that must be lightened and balanced, or this tiny planet in the corner of one universe in many universes will rid itself of the fear in a way that creates a rippling effect across all of creation. Again, we come back to cause and effect."

"I don't think I want to know about this," Isabel murmured, feeling very frightened. She didn't want to bear the weight of such a revelation. "I mean, what the hell can I do? Nothing . . . absolutely nothing."

"There you are mistaken. You can assist one being, one fearful being, and who knows who she will assist? You aren't the only one being asked to help. There are many across this planet who are being awakened. One by one, creating a different rippling effect, countering the fear, adding their light, they are tipping the scale back into balance."

"So all I have to do is help Jennifer?"

He reached out and stroked her hair, tenderly placing a strand behind her ear. "All you have to do is walk through whatever is presented to you each day without fear or judgment."

Isabel exhaled loudly as her shoulders sagged. "You ask a lot. It's so *big* . . . fear, worry, judgment. You want me to rewire my brain?"

"Yes. That is exactly what I am asking. Undo a bad habit. Learn a better one—one that actually does serve you and everyone you encounter."

She covered her face with her hands. "God, Joshua . . . you ask too much. I'm fifty years old. That's a lot of rewiring."

He pulled her hands down, and he was grinning. "I have great faith in you, Isabel. I know you intimately. I know your soul. And it is most beautiful, even what you term the fifty years of experience you have added to it. Now, come and introduce me to your new friend. She is standing by the door as we speak." And he looked to the doorway into the office and smiled.

Isabel stiffened with surprise and turned around. "Jen! I'm sorry. I didn't see you there." She walked over to the young woman who was now looking down again to the wooden floor beneath her feet. "I didn't expect to be gone for so long."

Okay, pull your act together, Isabel thought as she touched Jen's shoulder. Now was not the time to fall apart with the enormity of Joshua's request. "Jennifer, I'd like you to meet a very good friend of mine. His name is Joshua."

Isabel looked at Joshua and realized she didn't know his last name, or if he even had one. How could she love someone and not even know that information? Good God, she loved him! *She was falling in love with him?!* She quickly shook that thought out of her head, just as she recalled Joshua had called her "my love" earlier. *Concentrate on the now, Isabel!*

He came forward and held out his hand. "It is a pleasure to meet you, Jennifer."

She didn't say anything, and they all stood in silence as Joshua came closer and kept his hand out in greeting.

Isabel looked at Joshua's face for some direction, but he was staring at Jennifer with the most tender smile of compassion she had ever seen. Slowly, Jen raised her hand, and Joshua took it in his own. He shut his eyes for a moment, then closed the small distance between himself and Jennifer until he was still holding her hand and his other arm was around her shoulders.

Isabel watched in amazement as Jennifer's head naturally dropped to his chest and Joshua continued to hold her as swirling white lights encircled them for a moment, like a beautiful protective boundary she couldn't cross. In an instant, stronger than her awe, Isabel felt a pang of jealousy to see him holding the younger, prettier woman in his arms, communicating with her so intimately. She told herself to stop it. To try to be more like the Dalai Lama, or someone else with a purer heart, and hold no judgments. . . . But damn it, she was a woman, a woman newly awakened to love, and it felt like a knife thrust into her heart to see her man holding another woman.

Her man? What the hell was she thinking?! Could a normal man *do this*?

Isabel blinked as the lights began to disintegrate into swirling fairy dust, glimmering for a moment and then disappearing. She gulped and swallowed again, waiting for what would happen next.

Joshua, who had been in serious concentration, began to smile as he stroked Jennifer's long shining blond hair and released her from his embrace. "It is my honor to have met you, Jennifer," he whispered gently.

Lifting her head and looking into his eyes, Jen smiled back, knowingly, Isabel thought, as if the two of them shared a secret.

Mentally shaking herself, Isabel realized she simply had to get herself under control. This jealousy was irrational. So she cleared her throat, to remind them she was still in the room. Okay, enough of the Vulcan mind meld. She was beginning to wish she'd never suggested it. Talk about shortcuts backfiring.

"Shall we all sit down?" Joshua asked, smiling now at Isabel and looking a little confused.

Oh, she knew he was reading her *aura* again and had probably picked up on her negative thoughts of possessiveness, but really . . . what did he expect? She was human, after all, and not some enlightened being from out there in the universe who had evolved beyond such base feelings. And it was downright rude to exclude her like that! Making her feel like a voyeur intruding on such an intimate scene and . . .

damn it, she was going to have to stop this, stop acting so juvenile. Even Jennifer seemed more mature, sitting down on the sofa and looking up at Joshua with interest.

Isabel quickly took the seat beside Jen. Okay, so it was still a juvenile act, but a necessary one. Isabel didn't think she could concentrate if Joshua and Jen sat together and left her to a solitary chair. Joshua sat in her wing chair.

He smiled at them. "So you are staying with Isabel now, Jennifer?"

The young woman nodded.

"She is a wonderful woman, is she not?"

Isabel felt a little better as Jen again nodded.

"I'm sure the two of you will become very close friends. Do you have many friends?"

"No," Jen whispered, looking down.

"But you have one special friend, right, Jen?" Isabel asked.

Jennifer smiled. "Manny."

Isabel slowly let out her breath. There. The name was out now. "And Manny is the father of your baby?" She looked at Joshua, who simply nodded once. *Oh God . . .* Manny wasn't just an imaginary friend! It would have been so much easier if he were a guy they could find on the streets and force to take responsibility for his actions.

"Yes." Jennifer was staring at Joshua. "He's like you."

"Yes, he is," Joshua said, his smile directed solely now at Jennifer. "Have you tried to call out to him?"

"I did, but since Marcia took me away from the place I was living, he doesn't come."

"Would you like me to try to find him?" Joshua asked.

"Oh, please . . . *yes,*" Jen answered, tears beginning to fill her eyes.

Joshua stood up, and Isabel followed. "Then I will." He crossed the space between him and Jennifer and crouched before her, bring himself down to her level. Placing his hand on her cheek, he said in a sympathetic voice, "You have nothing to fear, Jennifer. Everything will turn out in the most appropriate way for you. Whatever happens . . ."

Isabel watched as Jen slowly tilted her head into Joshua's palm as her eyes closed. She had the most lovely expression on her face, as though filled with peace.

"And Isabel will be with you. You can trust her. She has your best interests in her heart."

Maybe he was so focused on Jen he couldn't read that snaking thread of jealousy weaving its way into her heart as she watched Joshua and Jen becoming so intimate again. Once more, she cleared her throat and forced a smile. "I'm sure Joshua will find Manny for you," she murmured. *Why was this ugly emotion of possessiveness rearing its head now?*

Joshua rose and tilted his face in a curious way as he looked at Isabel. "Will you walk me out?"

"Of course." She looked at Jen, still smiling peacefully. "I'll be back in a few minutes."

Jen seemed to be lost in her own pleasant thoughts, so Isabel headed out of the office with Joshua following. Turning in the foyer, she looked into his eyes. "So . . . you're off on your search."

He grinned. "My mission," he reminded her. "The one you gave me."

"And he's real, this Manny? I mean, as real as you."

"From what I could obtain, he came into Jennifer's life when her mother died. There is a deep connection between them."

"Then how could he just leave her like this? Especially now?"

Joshua sighed and pulled her into his arms. Above her head, he whispered, "There are many dimensions, and all beings are in a creative process to ascend to a higher, more expansive one. He came to Jennifer when she was a small child in a time of need, and perhaps he felt he had fulfilled his assignment with her."

She pulled back and looked into his eyes. "Do you mean *I'm* an assignment? After you finish with me, you're going to disappear? And how could this Manny ever think he's finished with Jen? She's *pregnant!*"

"Isabel, calm down," he said, stroking her back. "I can't remain in this physical world, this third dimension, indefinitely. Sometimes it's very difficult to maintain this body suit, especially after we achieve union. You know that; you've seen it for yourself. I would believe this entity Jennifer has named Manny would experience the same."

She pulled out of his arms. "So you are saying you're evolving too? You want me to evolve, and then you get to evolve to a higher dimension?"

"Basically, yes."

"So it's like . . . come down to this dimension, mess around with the females' heads, and then leave them? Like Jennifer? Pregnant?"

"Isabel," he said patiently, "you invited me in a very long time ago. I appear to you now as this . . . this man, for your benefit, not mine. Just as Manny would have become age-appropriate for Jennifer."

He was going to leave her. Not just now to search for Manny, but soon. He would accomplish his assignment, and then she'd never see him again while he was off evolving into a higher dimension. Hurt, angry, mostly hurt, Isabel straightened her shoulders and blinked furiously to stop any show of emotion from clouding her vision. "Well, you're not age-appropriate for me, Joshua. You're far too young, and perhaps you aren't as evolved as you think. Any real human man worth his salt wouldn't be so selfish as to do this to any woman and then leave her behind to clean up his mess."

"What mess?" he demanded. "Again I ask, are we talking about Jennifer now, or you? Because I certainly don't see your life as a mess."

Oh yeah? How about falling in love with someone or

something that isn't even human? How about having feelings I had so successfully buried being resurrected with a staggering force? She crossed her arms over her chest and tightly smiled, refusing to allow him to see how deeply she was hurt. "We are talking about Jennifer," she lied. "Now please find this Manny and bring him back here. There are a few things I'd like to say to him too."

"Isabel . . ." He moved closer to her, but her hand shot up like a crossing guard to stop him. "There is no need for this anger, this fear you have allowed to take over you."

"Always great advice, Joshua," she murmured, still holding her tight smile. "Maybe you might want to take some of mine. Find Manny, and we'll figure this mess out with Jennifer. And then I do believe you'll be free to leave, to *ascend* away from this mundane, fearful dimension. I got the message about women and balance. Your job is done. You'll have accomplished your assignment with me."

Joshua was shaking his head. "Why are you this emotional now? You are the one who asked me to leave, to assist Jennifer."

"I don't know why I'm emotional," she stated. Then she quickly added, "Yes, I do! I'm a woman, Joshua. *A real live breathing human woman.* I'm not some ascended being, free of emotions. I'm *me,* and I'm entitled to feel however I want."

His expression became sad. "Do you still want me to leave, or should I stay and we can discuss this further?"

"Leave. Go. You told Jennifer you would find Manny, so do it."

"I said I would try to find Manny. There are dimensions I cannot enter."

"Great!" she blurted out, not understanding why she so wanted to hurt him. "I guess you can only do what you can, then."

"I don't understand your anger."

"I don't either, so you'd better just go. *Leave!*"

He disintegrated before her eyes so quickly, all she could perceive was that swirling sparkling dust fading into nothingness.

His spontaneous departure left her feeling even worse, alone, deserted, as though something vital had been ripped away from her. She knew she had been irrational, childish, jealous, and a part of her was ashamed for what she'd said and the way she'd acted. Another part was furious. *Who the hell were these imaginary friends anyway, to come into a female's life, make her fall in love with them, and then leave to go off adventuring into the next dimension?* It wasn't right! It wasn't fair!

And she then remembered Jennifer waiting for her in the office. The poor kid was in even worse shape. Abandoned and pregnant. Blowing her breath out with force, Isabel ran her hands through her hair and walked back into the office.

Jennifer was still smiling as she waited patiently. "I like him," she said in a soft voice.

Isabel simply nodded as she sat in her usual chair. "He's going to try to find Manny for you."

"He will. I could feel the same things in him."

"You mean, like as in Manny?"

Jen nodded.

"What things?"

"Like love . . . and . . . and he loves you like my Manny loves me. That's why I'm here, I think."

"Why is that?" Isabel asked, ashamed at the relief that washed through her body with Jen's statement about love.

"Because you're like me."

"I am?"

Jen nodded. "Angels love us."

Isabel simply blinked. "Angels?" she finally asked, forcing herself to swallow.

"Angels . . . ," Jen breathed in a dreamy voice.

"I don't know, Jennifer, if Manny and Joshua are angels.

I think they are beings from . . . from a different time and place. And—"

"They're angels," Jen interrupted firmly. "Manny told me. That's what other people would call him. But he said those people had made up that name because they couldn't understand him."

"Oh . . ." Isabel bit the inside of her bottom lip. Had she just had a fight with an angel? What were the consequences of *that*? She didn't want to think about it.

"That's why I can't let Marcia take my baby away."

"Honey, I'm going to do everything I can to help Marcia understand you have a say in that decision."

Jen leaned forward, staring intently into Isabel's eyes. For the first time Isabel could see a force that wasn't afraid to hide. She was . . . changed, and a shiver ran up Isabel's back at the sudden transformation.

"She *can't* take my baby away."

It seemed that whatever Joshua had done when he'd held Jennifer had opened some gateway into her conscious mind. Jennifer appeared more cognizant, more together, with it in the present moment. And less afraid to speak, especially her mind.

"Would you let her take yours, Isabel?"

"I don't have any children,"

It was as if she had a secret. "Not yet."

"What? I'm not pregnant, Jennifer."

"Are you sure?" the younger woman asked, a smile creeping back into her expression.

"Yes, I'm sure. I'm too old to get pregnant. And I never could in the past when my husband was alive."

"I think you are."

Isabel grinned. "I'm not. Really." This was typical projection. She'd seen it many times. "Jen, just because you're pregnant, doesn't mean I am. Yes, we both . . . love extraordinary beings, but your situation is completely different than mine."

She'd had to force that word *love* out of her mouth. But why deny it here with Jen? She'd entered into Bizarro World when she'd taken her briefcase from Joshua backstage at that conference. The die had been cast. She was falling in love with someone who was going to leave her. Again. Why was she never the one to leave? Why was she the one left holding all the emotions? She was not going to allow it to happen, not again. This time she would be in control, and there would be no grieving. She simply had to stop this insanity now and avoid the later pain of abandonment. She would not fall in love again.

She simply couldn't survive it again.

"Joshua doesn't know yet, but I do."

"You do?" Isabel asked, lost in her own thoughts and confused by Jen's words. "What?"

"Our babies will be friends."

Isabel wanted to tell her to stop such ridiculous talk, but didn't want to hurt her feelings now that she was opening up so quickly. "Well, speaking of babies, I've invited my friend Cristine to come for a visit tomorrow. She has a baby. Angelique." Good diversion. "I think you'll like her. She loves to cuddle."

"A baby . . . ," Jennifer repeated, her eyes lighting up with excitement.

"What should we make for lunch?" Isabel asked to get off the baby fixation.

"Peanut butter and jelly sandwiches?"

Isabel grinned. "Maybe something that takes a little more effort. How about chicken salad? Do you like that?"

Jen nodded. "I will do the dishes."

"Okay, but I really need your help preparing the meal too. Why don't we go into the kitchen and see if we have everything? We can go to the store later and pick out a fabulous dessert."

Jennifer rose. "I'll help you, Isabel. You've helped me so much."

Standing, Isabel smiled. "Sometimes my friends call me Issy. I didn't like it in the beginning. I thought it sounded like a sissy, but now it feels like an endearment, a kind expression."

"I know what *endearment* means."

Startled a bit by Jen's statement, she said, "Good. I think you have a lot stored up there in your brain." She paused, then added, "You know you aren't a slow learner, don't you?"

Jen nodded. "It was easier to shut everyone out."

"And now?"

The younger woman smiled. "And now I have to be the best mother I can be."

Isabel simply stared at the transformed female in front of her.

What exactly had Joshua done to Jen?

Chapter

11

"SHE'S LOVELY."

"Yes, she is," Isabel answered, gazing at Jennifer sitting on the living room rug holding Angelique in her lap. The young woman was whispering to the baby, who, in turn, seemed fascinated by the interaction. All through lunch there had seemed to be a growing fondness between the two of them. "I'm telling you, Cristine, if you could have seen her a few days ago . . ."

"You said she's shy," Cristine murmured, sipping her herbal tea. "She certainly didn't seem shy at lunch. All those questions."

Isabel nodded. "She's very interested in pregnancy. Sorry if she was too personal."

"Not at all. Is she . . . ? I mean, I know it's none of my business, but she's positively radiant."

And that's when Isabel realized Jennifer *was* radiating some kind of inner beauty. She'd been so floored by the younger woman's startling transformation in coming out of her shell that she hadn't seen it until now. "I . . . ah . . . I can't say. Technically, she is a client." It was like a miracle to observe Jennifer speaking freely, interacting, and now even giggling with Angelique. How in the world was she going to explain it all to Marcia?

Cristine nodded. "Gotcha. Well, I'd say whatever she came to you for, you did it. She seems perfectly fine to me."

"I didn't do anything, not really." Isabel thought of Joshua. Too bad he wasn't sticking around. He could go about embracing people and all their troubles would disappear like melting snowflakes. She wasn't envious, not really, but it would be so much easier to mind-meld in search of the answers, rather than doing tedious root canals into the subconscious. Her way seemed almost primitive compared to his.

"Okay, so what about the party?" Cristine asked in a low voice. "How many?"

Blinking herself back into the conversation, Isabel shrugged. "I don't really know. Jen doesn't have any friends I could invite. Her sister is on the book tour. Do you think the Gang would be interested in coming?"

"Are you kidding? Chocolate cake? We could say it's a meeting."

"Okay, I'll call everyone."

"Let me do it," Cristine said. "You've got company. I think Claire's away on business, so I might not get to her for a few days, but I should have a head count by Friday."

"Then I'll make it into a dinner party. It's been a long time since I had a party here," Isabel murmured, looking around the large living room. "Years . . ."

"Since before Chuck passed away?"

Isabel nodded.

"You seem . . . I don't know . . . to have put a lot behind you, Isabel. You're different."

Isabel chuckled. "I am?"

Cristine nodded. "It's like you've turned a corner, or something."

"I turned fifty!" Isabel proclaimed, and laughed out loud. "It's one hell of a corner." She wasn't about to reveal the real reason she felt alive again was because she had thought she was falling in love with a being from another dimension. Had. Past tense. That simply couldn't continue.

Jennifer looked up from the baby. "You're fifty, Isabel?"

Isabel's laugh eased, and she nodded, realizing how loud she had been. "Did you think I was older? Because of the white hair?"

Shaking her head, Jennifer said, "I like your hair. It shines like a star sometimes. When you walk in the shadows, I sometimes think I can see sparkles around your head."

Neither Isabel nor Cristine spoke for a few moments, until Isabel forced a laugh to break the silence. "Did you hear that, Cristine? I want you to tell that to Tina and Kelly, and maybe they'll leave me alone about dyeing it."

Cristine leaned forward, seeming very interested. "Do you really, Jennifer? See sparkles around Isabel's head?"

Jen simply nodded and turned her attention back to Angelique, who at almost six months was trying to stand up as Jennifer held her under the arms.

"Maybe she's gifted," Cristine whispered. "Seeing your aura. There really is something about her. I can't put my finger on it, but it's almost like she's . . . holy."

"What?" Isabel demanded in a hushed voice.

Cristine was shaking her head. "Maybe that wasn't the right word. She's got that look, you know?"

"What look?" *Holy?* It sounded beyond odd, especially coming from Cristine.

"When I was a kid I was sent to Catholic school for two years, and the Catholics have these holy cards, pictures of saints. They collected them, like some kids collected baseball cards. Most of the paintings showed saints with this serene, almost angelic expression—even the ones with arrows sticking out of their chests. They were looking up to heaven with this holy look. You know what I mean, Isabel."

Isabel barely nodded.

I think they are beings from . . . from a different time and place. And—"

"They're angels," Jen interrupted firmly. "Manny told me. That's what other people would call him. But he said those people had made up that name because they couldn't understand him."

"Oh . . ." Isabel bit the inside of her bottom lip. Had she just had a fight with an angel? What were the consequences of *that*? She didn't want to think about it.

"That's why I can't let Marcia take my baby away."

"Honey, I'm going to do everything I can to help Marcia understand you have a say in that decision."

Jen leaned forward, staring intently into Isabel's eyes. For the first time Isabel could see a force that wasn't afraid to hide. She was . . . changed, and a shiver ran up Isabel's back at the sudden transformation.

"She *can't* take my baby away."

It seemed that whatever Joshua had done when he'd held Jennifer had opened some gateway into her conscious mind. Jennifer appeared more cognizant, more together, with it in the present moment. And less afraid to speak, especially her mind.

"Would you let her take yours, Isabel?"

"I don't have any children,"

It was as if she had a secret. "Not yet."

"What? I'm not pregnant, Jennifer."

"Are you sure?" the younger woman asked, a smile creeping back into her expression.

"Yes, I'm sure. I'm too old to get pregnant. And I never could in the past when my husband was alive."

"I think you are."

Isabel grinned. "I'm not. Really." This was typical projection. She'd seen it many times. "Jen, just because you're pregnant, doesn't mean I am. Yes, we both . . . love extraordinary beings, but your situation is completely different than mine."

She'd had to force that word *love* out of her mouth. But why deny it here with Jen? She'd entered into Bizarro World when she'd taken her briefcase from Joshua backstage at that conference. The die had been cast. She was falling in love with someone who was going to leave her. Again. Why was she never the one to leave? Why was she the one left holding all the emotions? She was not going to allow it to happen, not again. This time she would be in control, and there would be no grieving. She simply had to stop this insanity now and avoid the later pain of abandonment. She would not fall in love again.

She simply couldn't survive it again.

"Joshua doesn't know yet, but I do."

"You do?" Isabel asked, lost in her own thoughts and confused by Jen's words. "What?"

"Our babies will be friends."

Isabel wanted to tell her to stop such ridiculous talk, but didn't want to hurt her feelings now that she was opening up so quickly. "Well, speaking of babies, I've invited my friend Cristine to come for a visit tomorrow. She has a baby. Angelique." Good diversion. "I think you'll like her. She loves to cuddle."

"A baby . . . ," Jennifer repeated, her eyes lighting up with excitement.

"What should we make for lunch?" Isabel asked to get off the baby fixation.

"Peanut butter and jelly sandwiches?"

Isabel grinned. "Maybe something that takes a little more effort. How about chicken salad? Do you like that?"

Jen nodded. "I will do the dishes."

"Okay, but I really need your help preparing the meal too. Why don't we go into the kitchen and see if we have everything? We can go to the store later and pick out a fabulous dessert."

Jennifer rose. "I'll help you, Isabel. You've helped me so much."

Chapter

11

"SHE'S LOVELY."

"Yes, she is," Isabel answered, gazing at Jennifer sitting on the living room rug holding Angelique in her lap. The young woman was whispering to the baby, who, in turn, seemed fascinated by the interaction. All through lunch there had seemed to be a growing fondness between the two of them. "I'm telling you, Cristine, if you could have seen her a few days ago . . ."

"You said she's shy," Cristine murmured, sipping her herbal tea. "She certainly didn't seem shy at lunch. All those questions."

Isabel nodded. "She's very interested in pregnancy. Sorry if she was too personal."

"Not at all. Is she . . . ? I mean, I know it's none of my business, but she's positively radiant."

And that's when Isabel realized Jennifer *was* radiating some kind of inner beauty. She'd been so floored by the younger woman's startling transformation in coming out of her shell that she hadn't seen it until now. "I . . . ah . . . I can't say. Technically, she is a client." It was like a miracle to observe Jennifer speaking freely, interacting, and now even giggling with Angelique. How in the world was she going to explain it all to Marcia?

Standing, Isabel smiled. "Sometimes my friends call me Issy. I didn't like it in the beginning. I thought it sounded like a sissy, but now it feels like an endearment, a kind expression."

"I know what *endearment* means."

Startled a bit by Jen's statement, she said, "Good. I think you have a lot stored up there in your brain." She paused, then added, "You know you aren't a slow learner, don't you?"

Jen nodded. "It was easier to shut everyone out."

"And now?"

The younger woman smiled. "And now I have to be the best mother I can be."

Isabel simply stared at the transformed female in front of her.

What exactly had Joshua done to Jen?

Cristine nodded. "Gotcha. Well, I'd say whatever she came to you for, you did it. She seems perfectly fine to me."

"I didn't do anything, not really." Isabel thought of Joshua. Too bad he wasn't sticking around. He could go about embracing people and all their troubles would disappear like melting snowflakes. She wasn't envious, not really, but it would be so much easier to mind-meld in search of the answers, rather than doing tedious root canals into the subconscious. Her way seemed almost primitive compared to his.

"Okay, so what about the party?" Cristine asked in a low voice. "How many?"

Blinking herself back into the conversation, Isabel shrugged. "I don't really know. Jen doesn't have any friends I could invite. Her sister is on the book tour. Do you think the Gang would be interested in coming?"

"Are you kidding? Chocolate cake? We could say it's a meeting."

"Okay, I'll call everyone."

"Let me do it," Cristine said. "You've got company. I think Claire's away on business, so I might not get to her for a few days, but I should have a head count by Friday."

"Then I'll make it into a dinner party. It's been a long time since I had a party here," Isabel murmured, looking around the large living room. "Years . . ."

"Since before Chuck passed away?"

Isabel nodded.

"You seem . . . I don't know . . . to have put a lot behind you, Isabel. You're different."

Isabel chuckled. "I am?"

Cristine nodded. "It's like you've turned a corner, or something."

"I turned fifty!" Isabel proclaimed, and laughed out loud. "It's one hell of a corner." She wasn't about to reveal the real reason she felt alive again was because she had thought she was falling in love with a being from another dimension. Had. Past tense. That simply couldn't continue.

Jennifer looked up from the baby. "You're fifty, Isabel?"

Isabel's laugh eased, and she nodded, realizing how loud she had been. "Did you think I was older? Because of the white hair?"

Shaking her head, Jennifer said, "I like your hair. It shines like a star sometimes. When you walk in the shadows, I sometimes think I can see sparkles around your head."

Neither Isabel nor Cristine spoke for a few moments, until Isabel forced a laugh to break the silence. "Did you hear that, Cristine? I want you to tell that to Tina and Kelly, and maybe they'll leave me alone about dyeing it."

Cristine leaned forward, seeming very interested. "Do you really, Jennifer? See sparkles around Isabel's head?"

Jen simply nodded and turned her attention back to Angelique, who at almost six months was trying to stand up as Jennifer held her under the arms.

"Maybe she's gifted," Cristine whispered. "Seeing your aura. There really is something about her. I can't put my finger on it, but it's almost like she's . . . holy."

"What?" Isabel demanded in a hushed voice.

Cristine was shaking her head. "Maybe that wasn't the right word. She's got that look, you know?"

"What look?" *Holy?* It sounded beyond odd, especially coming from Cristine.

"When I was a kid I was sent to Catholic school for two years, and the Catholics have these holy cards, pictures of saints. They collected them, like some kids collected baseball cards. Most of the paintings showed saints with this serene, almost angelic expression—even the ones with arrows sticking out of their chests. They were looking up to heaven with this holy look. You know what I mean, Isabel."

Isabel barely nodded.

"Jennifer's got that," Cristine murmured, watching the subject of the conversation interact with her daughter. "She's . . . serene, or special in some way I can't put my finger on."

Isabel thought of Joshua's words. "Well, if Jennifer's special then so are you and Angelique, and me and every other human being on the planet."

"I know what you're saying," Cristine answered. "We're all one and all that. But sometimes there's those who are . . . blessed, you know? Like they've got it, while the rest of us are spinning our wheels trying to figure out which direction to go. I'd like Daniel to meet her."

Now that was the last thing Isabel wanted. "Maybe after the party. I thought it should be just us females." If anyone was special or gifted, it was Daniel. Until she figured out what was happening to Jennifer, she didn't want Daniel anywhere near her. In truth, she also wanted to protect her own privacy, for the man had a way of getting to the core of every issue. Like Joshua. "How is Daniel?"

Cristine smiled. "He's wonderful. Travels too much, I think, and he's exhausted when he comes home, but the next morning I'll wake up to find him out in the garden with the baby explaining to her the molecular structure of a fallen leaf."

"He's a great father," Isabel murmured. "It must be really draining to do his work." Cristine had explained many months before that Daniel did interventions, traveling from one family in crisis to another, dealing with all kinds of issues. She knew from colleagues how exhausting it could be to have nonstop sessions that didn't end until the client saw the light of day and admitted the problem. She certainly respected Daniel for dealing with addictions, abuse, incest—all of life's ugliness that is sometimes swept under the carpet and kept hidden. "I don't think I'd have the energy for it," Isabel added. "Maybe in focusing on learning challenges in children, I took the easy way."

"Your work is really important, Isabel. Just look, yesterday you called Jennifer *shy*. She certainly isn't shy now."

It was Joshua, not her, who had helped Jen. "It's that daughter of yours. Who could be shy around her?"

"Well, maybe," Cristine said with a grin. "Angelique does have a way of breaking the ice."

Isabel nodded.

"But I'm sure being here with you, Jennifer feels safe and can be herself. You underestimate yourself, Isabel. You always have."

Isabel hesitated, and then it was as if her instincts became sharper. She knew something was underneath Cristine's words. "Claire told you, didn't she? About the conference disaster."

"Big deal. So you were out of practice, that's all. Next time you'll wow them with—"

"There isn't going to be a next time," Isabel interrupted. "Claire should have added that to her gossip."

"Don't be upset with Claire. She loves you. We all love you, and we know your worth. It should be recognized and shared."

"Please . . ." Isabel was tired of the Gang's estimation of her abilities. Wanting to change the subject, she said, "So when are you going to put up your tree? Baby's first Christmas. Must be exciting."

Cristine's face immediately transformed. "Ever since Thanksgiving I've been fighting going out and getting a tree. I think this weekend. Daniel will be home, and it'll be a first for him too."

"A first?"

Cristine blinked rapidly. "The family thing."

Nodding, Isabel remembered all the years of getting a tree, searching for a huge one to fit the twelve-foot ceiling. She and Chuck had loved the holiday season.

"What about you?" Cristine asked. "Now that you've turned a corner, so to speak, think you'll put one up again?"

Blowing her breath out, Isabel shook her head. "I don't

know. Haven't done it in seven years. The mice probably have ruined everything in the attic. Besides, it's just me, and it's so much work."

"I know!" Cristine exclaimed. "Let's make this a birthday and tree-trimming party?" Not waiting for Isabel's answer, she called out, "Jennifer, how would you like it if your birthday party had a Christmas tree? We could all decorate it. Wouldn't that be fun?"

Jennifer's eyes lit with excitement. "I would like that."

Isabel sucked in her bottom lip. "That wasn't exactly fair," she muttered to Cristine.

"I know, but your time of playing Grinch is over, my friend," Cristine answered with a laugh. "Jennifer," she called out again, "what if everyone who comes brings something to decorate the tree? It won't be birthday presents exactly, because it would be for Isabel's tree."

Jen was nodding and smiling. "Then I would be able to do something nice for you, Isabel. I like that."

Talk about being boxed into a corner. "Thanks, Cristine, for your *great* idea."

"It's not your party," Cristine countered with a grin, knowing exactly what she was doing. "It's Jennifer's, and themed parties are really big now."

"And who are you all of a sudden? Martha Stewart?"

"Heaven forbid," Cristine said with a laugh. "I don't think there's a crafty bone in my body."

"Considering how you've maneuvered this party into something entirely your idea, I'd say you're pretty crafty."

Cristine playfully slapped Isabel's arm and stood up. "I'm clever, Issy. Much nicer way of putting it. And I think we've stayed long enough, and I've got things to do. Calls to make. Plans . . . Oh, this is gonna be fun!"

Isabel rose while shaking her head. "So I've been played once again by a member of the Yellow Brick Road Gang. Last time was a stunning disaster."

"Oh, stop it," Cristine said, walking over to Jennifer, who had stood up and was holding Angelique. "Will you just let that conference go? And as far as being played," she added while receiving her daughter into her arms, "I swear it just came to me while we were talking."

Isabel went to the foyer closet and brought out Cristine's coat and Angelique's pink one-piece snowsuit with attached gloves. "Right," Isabel muttered, holding out the bottom half of the snowsuit as Cristine tried to put Angelique's swinging chubby legs into it.

"May I put it on her?" Jennifer asked. "I need the practice."

Cristine glanced quickly at Isabel, who tried to keep her face impassive, then smiled at Jennifer. "Of course you can. It is easier if she's lying down."

Jennifer took the baby and the snowsuit to the sofa while Cristine again looked at Isabel.

"I can't say anything."

"No need to now," Cristine whispered, watching Jen naturally carry the baby on her hip while she spread out the snowsuit on the sofa cushion. "My God . . . seventeen and pregnant. Where's the father?"

Isabel simply shrugged.

Cristine exhaled, and her shoulders seemed to sag with the weight of the information. "I know you can't say anything, but however I can help . . . you only need to ask. We have the foundation too. Maybe we could set her up in her own apartment for a couple of years until she gets on her feet or—"

"Thanks," Isabel interrupted. "I'll keep that in mind. But there's the sister to consider."

. . . . Well, let's just make this a great party, okay? It's not an easy job. Mothering. It's the most rewarding job I've ever had, but seventeen? She's still a kid herself."

"Eighteen next week," Isabel reminded her. "And knowing the Gang, it'll be a fantastic party."

"Your job, and you have no choice now but to accept it, is to find the best tree and have it set up by Friday."

"Great," Isabel murmured, remembering she had a client on Friday afternoon so she'd have to get started on finding a tree tomorrow. And figure out a menu and clean the house . . . and she was already tired before she'd even begun. She'd been really tired lately, especially after she ate a meal. Maybe she should have her blood sugar checked. All those years of being a nurse had their advantages, but they could also make a person take the littlest symptom and self-diagnose into a troubling scenario.

"Here she is," Cristine declared, holding out her arms for her daughter. "All bundled up and ready to go. Thanks, Jennifer."

Jen handed over the baby, and Isabel could see she was sorry to see Angelique leave.

"She's . . . wonderful," Jennifer breathed. "You're lucky to have her."

"Yes, I am," Cristine agreed with a laugh as she kissed her daughter's fat cheek. Angelique turned her head and grinned back at her mother. "And I don't think there's one moment she forgets how precious she is, right, my little angel?"

The baby's eyes seemed to sparkle with good humor, and she bobbed her head up and down.

Everyone laughed.

Isabel closed the door on her friend, then turned back to Jennifer, who stood behind her.

"She is an angel."

Isabel smiled. "Yes, she is. An adorable one."

"A real angel. Like Manny and Joshua."

Isabel didn't say anything.

"Like my baby is."

A chill raced up Isabel's spine.

"And like yours."

Her brain seemed to short wire as an electrical current washed over her. "Jen. How many times do I have to tell you I'm not pregnant? You have to trust me on this. I would know."

Jennifer held her hands together in front of her and looked down to the floor, as though she'd been scolded. "I didn't know either," she whispered. "Until Manny told me and then they took that test. They took another one to be sure."

Shaking her head, Isabel crossed the distance between them and put her arm around Jennifer's shoulders. She led her back into the living room, saying, "I'm not upset with you. I'm just saying it isn't possible for me to be pregnant."

"I think I'm supposed to tell you, Isabel."

"Okay, you've told me," she said as the phone started ringing. "Excuse me," she added, leaving Jen and walking into her office. "I'll be right back."

Walking over to the desk, Isabel blew her breath out in frustration. Now she had to prove to Jennifer she wasn't pregnant to end that delusion? "Hello?"

"Isabel, it's Marcia. How is everything going?"

"Fine," she answered automatically. "Actually, better than fine. Jennifer is making remarkable progress."

"Really?" There was disbelief in Marcia's voice.

"Yes, really. I think you're going to be surprised." Not yet ready to elaborate, she changed the topic. "How's the tour?"

"Great. Fabulous. Exhausting, but exhilarating at the same time."

"Good for you, Marcia."

"Tomorrow I've been asked to be a guest on *America's Wake-up Call*. With Reggie and Carole Shelly. Do you know it? It's aired live in L.A. and syndicated nationally. It's going to be shown in Philly a few days later. Channel seven. Ten A.M., I think. Maybe Friday or Monday."

"We'll have to check the listings and watch it," Isabel answered, trying not to be judgmental. It wasn't working. So much for higher intentions. "Marcia, did you realize that Jennifer's birthday is in a few days?"

"Oh, that's right," Marcia said, mustering up sincerity. "I must have forgotten in the rush to leave. Don't worry. I'll send her flowers. But . . . Isabel . . . ?"

"Yes?" It sounded like another request was coming.

"The tour is going so well that my publisher's publicity rep is thinking about extending it for three more days to really saturate the Midwest. Would you have a problem with that?"

Isabel was silent as her stomach seemed to roll over in rebellion.

"I know it's a big favor. Huge, in fact."

Isabel wished she could wave a wand and get her old life back. No Joshua. No Marcia. No Jennifer. No problems or parties or favors. All she wanted was to crawl into bed and pull the covers over her head. "Fine, Marcia, but that's it. You have a situation here you need to deal with as soon as possible. The Jennifer you left is not the one you're coming home to next week."

"What do you mean?"

"I mean Jennifer is no longer withdrawn and—"

"Did she tell you who raped her?" Marcia interrupted. "Because that's the information I want."

"No, she didn't mention a rape. I haven't gone there yet," Isabel answered, not completely lying. Suddenly she thought she was giving out too much information. It was better for Jennifer to turn eighteen before Marcia returned and they had this discussion. "You know, Marcia, don't worry about any of this while you're on tour. We'll deal with it when you return. You want to be at your best when you're on television." Okay so maybe that was a wee bit of manipulation, but instinct was telling her to shut up about Jennifer.

"You're right," Marcia answered. "I simply have to focus.

I'm at the airport now. We're getting a plane for L.A. in an hour."

"Then I would find a place to sit down and relax. Maybe have a drink. I'm sure you'll be wonderful tomorrow."

"God, I hope so. You can't buy this kind of exposure. It's national television."

"Yes, I know. So break a leg, or whatever is the right thing to say. You'll have our support, and we'll be sure to watch when it airs here."

"Thanks, Isabel. I don't know how I could have done this without you."

You would have put your sister into a hospital, that's how, she thought, and then stopped herself from going there in her head. She tried to end the conversation on a more positive note. "Anyway, congratulations, Marcia."

"Thanks, Isabel. I'll check in with you later in the week and see what you think of the interview."

"And check up on your sister?"

"Well, of course. Give Jen my love."

"I will," she promised, and said good-bye.

Hanging up the phone, Isabel stood for a moment, feeling something between her shoulders. She looked over one and saw Jen standing at the doorway into the office.

"I . . . I just wanted to tell you that I put everything away and finished the dishes," she murmured. "I wasn't trying to spy on you."

Isabel let out her breath and smiled. "I know you weren't. That was Marcia."

"I heard you say her name."

"She said to give you her love."

Jen simply nodded.

"She's going to be on television tomorrow, and we can see it the next day. Won't that be something?"

"I don't want her to come back."

Isabel again pictured herself crawling into bed and pulling the covers over her head.

What had she gotten herself into?

§

Two mornings later, she and Jen were seated in front of the television watching the morning show. When the female host announced Marcia's name as a guest, Isabel glanced at Jen and saw an impassive expression. Even Isabel had to admit to a tight knot of excitement. It wasn't every day she watched someone she actually knew on TV.

They sat through a movie star promoting his next movie, which looked pretty amusing, and then a famous chef who cooked an Italian Christmas Eve dinner of fish, and finally, after a bit about money-saving tips on holiday shopping and a commercial break, Reggie Shelly asked his audience to welcome the author Marcia McMillan.

Marcia was already seated opposite her married hosts, and a copy of her book was on the small coffee table in front of them, facing the camera.

"Welcome, Marcia," Carole said with her big white smile.

"Thank you," Marcia answered, looking pretty good with tons of professionally applied pancake makeup. Her skin appeared flawless and tan. "And thank you for inviting me."

Isabel had to admit Marcia looked like a perfect author in her perfect red power suit. It even matched her nails. "She looks pretty good, don't you think, Jen?"

Jen simply shrugged, so Isabel turned her attention back to the screen.

"Well, let's get right to it since our time is limited. Now, if I'm correct," Carole continued, "your book, *Rescuing the*

American Family, is based on the premise that American women have left the rearing of their children to strangers while they go out and work."

"Yes, Carole, it's my belief that the increase in juvenile crime, both male and female, can be directly related to poor parenting skills, along with—"

"Are you married?" Carole interrupted, still smiling and showing her bright white teeth.

"Well, no, I'm not, but that really isn't pertinent to the subject, and—"

"Do you have any children?" Reggie asked, also smiling, looking almost sorry for Marcia. He must know his wife well and also knew what was coming.

Marcia seemed to realize that the interview wasn't going to go the way she had planned, and she fidgeted in her chair, pulling at the hem of her suit skirt. "No, I don't have children, but that doesn't mean I'm not qualified to write about issues relating directly to the choices of absentee parents."

"Absentee parents," Carole repeated, as though she was really thinking about the phrase. "I read through your book last night, Marcia, and I have to say there are more than a few of your observations that I take issue with. You mention parents working, but you state it's because they want to keep up appearances with the neighbors, because in America we now worship the climate of greed."

"I didn't write that exactly. I said that—"

"Did it ever occur to you that perhaps the mother *had* to go out to work to make ends meet? That the present economy, with exporting middle-class jobs overseas and demanding workers pay more and more for health insurance, might have something to do with it? And wouldn't the big corporations whose profits have soared while their workers' salaries have shrunk have something to do with that climate of greed?"

"Yes, but—"

"That the majority of those mothers' hearts break to leave

their children?" Carole wasn't giving Marcia a chance to rebut a thing. "What kind of research *did* you do if you left out the human side to the story? All your statistics don't show the face of loving parents struggling week by week to make ends meet. Instead, you blame parental greed, videos, television, and movies."

Marcia looked stunned and shell-shocked, staring at her hosts with a look of disbelief. It was as if she couldn't speak, let alone argue her side of the case.

To fill in the silence, Reggie asked, "What is your plan to rescue the American family?" .

Marcia simply stared at him, all the pancake makeup in the world not able to hide her terror. Isabel found herself biting her thumbnail, waiting for Marcia to come back to life. Even though she disagreed with Marcia's book, she was mentally urging Marcia to speak. It was too painful to watch her crumple on national television.

"Marcia," Carole murmured, reaching out to touch her sleeve. "You must have a plan. You wrote the book."

"Television . . . ," Marcia murmured, desperately trying to recover.

Isabel groaned, knowing she'd just handed them more ammunition.

"Television? You blame the ruination of the family on television?" Carole demanded.

"Not all television," Marcia hurried to add. "But so much of it is unfit for children."

"Like "Teletubbies"? Don't you have the same publisher as Pat Robertson? Isn't this, perhaps, another attempt by the far right to make the American public feel guilty? Or don't you believe in the Constitution, the separation of church and state?"

Marcia blinked. "I don't have anything to do with Pat Robertson," she said in her defense, her voice shaking.

"Except have the same publisher and share his outrageous views," Reggie added, looking like he was trying to even out the criticism. "But that's what free speech is about, isn't it? Whether it's Pat Robertson saying the people in a little town in Pennsylvania had better not call out to God in a natural disaster because their school board voted down Creationists, or it's you, free to tell us a plan for saving the family, or even if it's . . . Reggie and Carole, putting you on the hot seat. Thanks for being a good sport, Marcia." He then turned to the camera and grinned. "And any way you call it, it's a great day for America when you watch *America's Wake-up Call,* and we'll be back to tell you about Monday's show right after these words from our sponsors. Don't turn that dial."

The last shot before the commercial showed Marcia looking like she was about to cry.

"Now that was mean," Isabel said, sitting back on the kitchen sofa and staring at a commercial about diapers. "They didn't have to blindside her."

"Marcia thinks she knows everything, but she doesn't."

She glanced at Jen, remembering her saying that days ago. "But didn't you feel sorry for her?"

Jennifer shrugged, then nodded. "Now she knows how it feels to lose her voice."

She then remembered Joshua's warning about being judgmental. What did she know? Somehow, would this serve Marcia in the end? Would she get the message or the lesson?

There's gotta be an easier way than humiliation on national TV.

Chapter

12

"HAPPY BIRTHDAY, DEAR JENNIFERRRRRR . . . HAPPY birthday to you!"

Applause followed the traditional singing, and Tina called out, "Blow out the candles!"

"Wait!" Kelly declared. "First make your wish!"

"Right, right," Paula murmured. "The wish first."

"Make it a good one," Claire said, holding up a champagne flute filled with fruit juice. "Eighteen's a big birthday."

"Oh, to be eighteen again," Paula moaned as Jennifer closed her eyes and concentrated on her wish.

"She'd better hurry, or the top of that cake is going to be all wax," Cristine whispered.

Isabel simply smiled, pleased that the dinner party had turned out so well. All her friends had immediately accepted Jen into their tight circle. The birthday girl seemed to have that effect lately on everyone, from grocery clerks to the man selling Christmas trees. Jen had simply asked if the huge tree could be delivered, and the man hadn't been able to resist. Didn't even charge for the delivery. She seemed to be radiating some kind of contagious happiness.

"Okay," Jennifer said, opening her eyes and bending over the cake. In one long breath, she blew out all eighteen candles.

Everyone applauded again, and Jen looked very pleased with herself and those around her. "First slice is for Jen," Isabel declared, handing over the knife.

Still smiling, Jen blinked a few times and then accepted the knife. She neatly cut herself a slice and placed it on the top plate next to the cake. "Should I cut a piece for everyone?" she asked Isabel, who was standing next to her. It was as though she didn't know the correct procedure.

"Absolutely," Isabel declared. "I don't think there's a person here who's going to refuse chocolate cake, especially with Morelli's butter cream icing."

"Oh, Morelli's," Claire groaned. "God, they make the best cakes. I'll have to add a half hour at the gym, but I don't care. Gimme a slice."

While Jen was busy with handing out birthday cake, Isabel slipped into the living room and again looked at the Christmas tree, now adorned with white lights. It almost got her into the spirit of the season, especially with Nat King Cole, Aaron Neville, and others singing in the background on a continuous loop. She looked behind her to the piano, to the pictures of Chuck. How he'd loved the Christmas season. He'd been like a little kid, with enough enthusiasm to make up for being childless at a time when children are at the center of the holiday. But that was the past, she told herself, seeing all the birthday presents wrapped and under the tree. A season of memories long gone. How many times did she have to remind herself not to time travel back there?

"Here's your cake," Claire announced, handing over a plate as she came into the living room.

Isabel accepted it and smiled. "Thanks. Is it as good as I think?"

"Mmm. Better," Claire answered, smacking her lips in appreciation. "And dinner was fabulous. Who knew you could cook a traditional English holiday meal?"

"It's from the Calloways I married into. At Christmas they

were strict English traditionalists. It seemed easier just to join them and accept their way."

Nodding, Claire asked, "So what are you doing in here by yourself?"

Shaking her head, Isabel grinned as she picked up the fork. "Taking a moment for myself. Trying not to travel back in time."

"Chuck?"

Isabel shrugged as she tasted the cake. She swallowed, then said, "Haven't had a tree in here for years."

"Well, you got yourself a beauty. How tall is it?"

"I think it's about ten feet. Thank heavens the man who delivered it also set it up, or we would have been struggling with it tonight."

"Well, bless his soul for saving us from that. They do come in handy sometimes."

Isabel grinned at her friend. "A little cynical, are we?"

"I wouldn't call myself cynical. Practical. There are times a man can come in handy; I won't deny it." She leaned in closer to Isabel and whispered, "Like your little tryst with the gorgeous singer. Seems to have done wonders for you."

"Madness, that's what it was," Isabel claimed. "And I don't know about it doing wonders for me. I'm so tired lately."

"Then let's get this trimming party finished and we can leave."

Isabel shook her head. "No. Let Jen enjoy the night. I don't know if she's ever had a party like this before."

"You're kidding!"

"I don't know."

"You know, Cristine said Jennifer was a client of yours, she didn't elaborate and—"

"And neither can I," Isabel interrupted. "So don't ask me questions."

"Well, I just wanted to say that I can't imagine someone so . . . I don't know . . . so glowing and joyful as Jennifer not having friends. You'd think she would have been the center of any social occasion. And I should know, because I usually try to make sure I am. But I can't compete with whatever mojo that girl's got going for her."

Isabel laughed. "Jen's changed since she's been here. And that's all I'm going to say."

"Okay, so tell me when's the last time you saw the exotic younger man who rang your bell so exquisitely?"

"Oh, for God's sake," Isabel replied, moving back toward the dining room. "That isn't even an issue any longer. Hey, everyone," she called out, "let's open the presents under the tree."

Even though she had successfully eluded the question and was smiling at all her guests filing into the living room, she could feel Claire's penetrating stare, as though her friend didn't believe a word she'd said.

Sometimes, that woman's intuition was just unnerving.

And where was Joshua? How long before he returned?

Though she would never admit it aloud, she was starting to feel like she'd been abandoned along with Jennifer.

Jen sat at the base of the tree and began opening her presents of decorations. Glass ornaments of every color and style made their way onto the branches of the mountain pine. There was a step ladder set up for the taller branches. Isabel sat back and watched it all unfold before her and had to grin when she realized she'd never had such a Christmas tree before. There was no rhyme or reason to any of it. Cristine's ornaments were tasteful white satin. Kelly's were bright in colors of red and green and blue. Paula's were geared more for the family, with painted Santas and snowmen and reindeers. Tina's were wacky, modern spirals of glass in shades of pink and lime green. Claire's were drums and horns, big and brass and standing out.

Her friends. Her wonderful loud, brassy, colorful, wacky, compassionate, and fragile friends had made Christmas happen for her once again. Tears crept into Isabel's eyes, and she sniffled as she took it all in: the laughter, the arguing over ornament positioning, the admiration of another's choice.

God, she was blessed to have them around her.

Especially now, when her world was tilting out of her control.

Everyone stayed for another hour, and then, as if some silent communication passed between them, they all stood up to leave at the same time. They kissed Jen and Isabel and left the house singing Christmas carols. Cristine took something from her large shoulder bag and handed it to Jennifer and then joined the others while Isabel and Jen stood out on the porch, shivering, waving good-bye.

"Thank you, Isabel."

She looked at Jen and grinned. "You had a good time?"

"I had a *great* time," she said, hugging Cristine's present to her chest as she continued to wave.

"We'd better get inside," Isabel said, moving toward the door. "It's freezing out here!"

"I want to wait until they all drive away," Jen answered, still waving.

"I'm sure they appreciate that, but they wouldn't want you to get sick."

"They didn't even know me, and they were so nice to me."

"That's the Yellow Brick Road Gang," Isabel said. "They really are a terrific bunch. Now, c'mon," she said as Claire's car backed out of the driveway. "Let's get inside."

She put her arm around Jen's shoulders and led her through the door.

"I hope I see them again."

"I'm sure you will," Isabel reassured her, holding her hands up to her mouth and blowing on her cold fingers to warm them. "And I see Cristine gave you a present. Are you going to open it?"

Jennifer nodded and delicately pulled on the colorful

ribbon. The wrapping paper came away easily, and they both stared down to the cover of a book.

MOTHERHOOD
Everything you ever wanted to know about pregnancy, birth, and delivery
Written by mothers for new mothers

"What a nice present," Isabel said. "Now you can have all your questions answered."

Jen was holding the book as though it were something precious. "Cristine is a very good woman, isn't she?"

Isabel nodded. "She is. She's very thoughtful of others. I think all of my friends are good women in their own way."

"How long have you known them?" Jen asked, leafing through the book.

"Gosh, I think it's about eight or nine years now. It seems we've all known one another forever, in one another's lives, helping one another where we can. We started out as a book club."

"What were all of you reading?"

Isabel thought for a moment as she walked into the living room and began to pick up glasses and empty coffee cups. "I believe it was *The Celestine Prophecy,* or it might have been *Conversations with God.* We were searching for some answers, you might say."

"Did you find them?" Jen asked, putting her book on the sofa and helping Isabel clean the room.

"You could say that. We were into everything then—New Age stuff mostly, though we'd research different paths of faith. But we like to say we sort of came full circle eventually and realized all the answers were within ourselves." Isabel put everything onto a silver tray and added, "We just had to pay attention."

"Are you?"

Isabel looked up to see Jen holding empty ornament boxes and staring at her.

"Am I what?"

"Are you paying attention?"

"I think so. I hope so. Why?"

"I just saw in that book that fatigue is one of the signs of being pregnant. *Fatigue* means "tired," doesn't it?"

Isabel sighed, her lower back beginning to ache. It had been a long day. It had been a long week and a longer month. "It does, but that doesn't mean it applies to me. Jen, we've been over this. I'm too old to get pregnant, and my husband and I tried for many years. I can't have babies, never could."

"I think Joshua is the father. Like Manny is the father of my baby."

Isabel bit her bottom lip so she wouldn't yell, but that damn tingling sensation raced up her spine again and washed over her brain. Shaking her head, she answered, "Look, tomorrow I'll go get a pregnancy test at the drugstore, all right? Will that satisfy you?"

Jennifer was now clutching the boxes and looking worried. "Please don't be mad at me, Isabel. I'm just trying to let you know what I know."

"I'm not mad at you, Jen. I'm simply tired and . . ." Her words trailed off. Why give any more explanations that might be misconstrued?

"I'll clean up everything," Jen said. "You go to bed."

"I'm not going to leave you with this mess."

Jen smiled softly. "I want to do it. It will make me feel better to help you for a change. You've already done so much for me. . . . You've given me back my voice, Isabel. Maybe everybody isn't going to like everything I say now, but you taught me that God gave me a voice to speak. And I'm going to speak now."

Isabel softened. "Well, you are legally an adult today, so

it's only right you say what's on your mind. Just no more talk about me and pregnancy tonight, okay?"

"Okay. But I do think you should go to bed. I can take care of cleaning the house. And then I want to stay up and read. Can I make myself a cup of that herbal tea?"

"Honey, you can do anything you want."

"You trust me?"

Isabel smiled. "I trust you. You've come such a long way, Jen, in so short a time. Do whatever you want, and whatever you don't finish leave for the morning. It's been a long day for you too." She walked over to the younger woman and kissed her cheek. "Happy birthday, Jen. I wish for you everything good in life."

Jennifer grinned shyly. "Thanks, Issy. I feel like I can call you Issy now, because your friends do and we're friends."

"Yes, we are," Isabel stated. "And that's why I can say leave all this and we'll do it in the morning. I am tired."

Jen nodded. "I'll be up soon. You go to bed."

Unable to argue any longer, Isabel patted Jen's shoulder and headed for the staircase. "Good night, Jen. It was a great party. I thoroughly enjoyed it."

"Me too, and thanks again."

Isabel simply nodded and began walking up the stairs.

It was then she realized Marcia hadn't sent flowers or called or anything. She had ignored her sister's eighteenth birthday. Another name to add to the MIA list.

So where *was* Joshua?

§

The next afternoon Isabel was waiting for her client as she kept Jennifer company in the kitchen. Jen was poring over a cookbook and asking questions.

"So I just put the herbs over the pork roast and then add the potatoes later?"

"Well, you should actually rub the herbs over the roast with a little bit of olive oil," Isabel said, straining her head to look out the side window. No sign of Linda Winston and her son, Terry. They were late. From what she'd gathered from the phone interview with the mother, Terry was classified dyslexic and also ADD, attention deficit disorder. He was scheduled to attend an alternative school after the Christmas holiday, because he'd never seemed to catch onto the concept of reading. He was working in a first-grade workbook, although by his age he should be at a fifth-grade level. He'd had special teachers and private tutors, but had never made much progress.

Isabel had been uncomfortable with the mother's negative report and had asked her about Terry, her son, the boy. He wasn't a real discipline problem, not at home or at school, though it was hard to capture his attention. He was liked by his peers, and he could do fifth-grade math. And Terry was a pretty good football player. Seeing she had areas of successes to work with, Isabel had agreed to see the boy and his mother.

Hearing a car pull up, Isabel again looked out the window and saw her clients had arrived. "Okay, Jen, I'm going to be in my office. Remember, you can't come in or disturb me while I'm with a client. It wouldn't be fair to them."

"I won't disturb you, Isabel," Jen said from the kitchen counter, wearing jeans and a pullover sweater and looking pretty absorbed in her task at hand. "I think I can do this and make dinner."

"You go for it," Isabel said, straightening her blouse over the waistband of her brown slacks. Too much food and cake, she told herself as she left the kitchen and walked to the front of her house. And was it just last week that Jen had been frightened to do the dishes on her own? Remarkable progress. Yet how in the world was she going to explain it to Marcia, *whenever* Marcia resurfaced?

Compartmentalize, she told herself. Put Jen and Marcia and Joshua and Manny and everything else that was pulling at her for attention . . . put it all into a closet to take out later. Right now she had a client.

She answered the door and saw a well-dressed woman and an adorable ten-year-old boy standing on her porch. Linda was dressed in a tailored red coat and black slacks, and blond-haired Terry was wearing a football jacket with jeans and white sneakers. His hands were stuffed into the pockets, and he didn't make eye contact.

"Linda?" Isabel asked, holding out her hand.

"Hi," she answered, and shook Isabel's hand. "I'm so sorry we're late. It took me forever to get him ready, and then the traffic, and I was afraid I was getting lost and—"

"It doesn't matter now," Isabel interrupted with a smile. "Come in and we can all get to know each other. Hi, Terry."

Terry didn't respond, and Linda looked even more apologetic. As they came into the house, Isabel figured Linda was a good mother who had probably been apologizing to a lot of people: teachers, family members, friends, doctors, clerks in stores. "Why don't I hang up your coats?"

Linda first removed Terry's and handed it over, and then began unbuttoning her own. "This is a lovely house," she said, and then saw her son drift into the living room. "Terry, come back here."

"It's okay," Isabel murmured, taking Linda's coat and figuring Terry was just exploring. But they would have to direct him into the office, so she hung up the coat and followed Linda into the living room.

"Terry, put that down! Don't touch that ornament! It's glass! It can break! Come back here," she chanted, following him out of the living room and into the dining room. "Terry, please come back. We have an appointment."

Isabel watched Linda chase after her inquisitive son. If Terry had ADD, he was exhibiting classic signs. Isabel followed, not yet disturbed until she saw Terry heading for the swinging kitchen door. "Oh, dear . . . ," she muttered, now hurrying. The last thing she wanted was for Jen and Terry to collide.

When she entered the kitchen, she heard Linda apologizing for her son again. This time to Jennifer. Jen smiled at the boy and then bent down and whispered something into his ear while touching his shoulder. Terry smiled and nodded.

"Okay, I think he's ready now," Jen said shyly, smiling at Isabel.

"Ah . . . thanks, Jen," Isabel said, not knowing what was happening. She forced a smile and said to Linda and Terry, "Shall we go into the office now?"

"Absolutely," Linda answered, taking her son's hand and leading him out of the kitchen.

When they were alone, Isabel whispered, "What did you say to him, Jen?"

Jennifer grinned. "I said he should listen to you because you are going to help him. And when he was done he could come back here for a piece of cake. Is that all right, Isabel?"

"Sure," she said, though until Jennifer she had always made it a strict rule not to get personally involved with her clients. "Thanks. I'll send him back when we're done."

She left the kitchen and followed the Winstons into her office, asking Terry to sit in the reclining leather chair. He immediately began fooling with the release on the side, falling back and then straightening into a sitting position again. Linda sat down on the sofa and then scolded her son to behave.

"Have you ever been hypnotized before, Terry?"

"No, he hasn't," Linda answered. "This is the first time, and I'm desperate. If the school doesn't see some change by the end of the semester, he'll be going to a different school in the new year."

"I know you're concerned, Linda," Isabel said, sitting down in her usual chair. "But I'd really like to speak with Terry now. If you could hold all comments and questions until the end of the session, I promise we'll get to them, okay?"

"Okay. . . . So, I just sit here?"

Isabel grinned. "You're allowed to relax too."

"Relax . . . ," Linda murmured wistfully. "That would be nice."

Isabel turned back to Terry, who she could see was itching to lower his hand to the release button again. "Hi, Terry. I'm Isabel. We didn't exactly meet earlier." No response. "Are there any questions you want to ask me before we begin?"

He looked over at her. "Are you going to make me bark like a dog?"

Isabel grinned as she heard Linda sigh with embarrassment. "Why would I want to do that to you?"

Terry shrugged. "You can make me do stupid stuff and I won't remember."

"Well, first of all, I'm not going to make you do anything stupid, or allow you to feel stupid, because that's not who you truly are, right?"

He shrugged.

"I've heard you can do fifth-grade math, and that must mean long division and decimals and multiplication. You can't be stupid and do that, can you?"

Terry still didn't trust her, but he shook his head.

"Okay, so we've established you aren't stupid and that I'm not going to allow you to feel stupid around me, so what was the next thing? Oh, right, you won't remember anything here. That's not true, Terry. You will remember everything that happens here, and you won't do or say anything that you won't be able to remember anytime you want."

He didn't respond, but she could see his shoulders had relaxed a tiny bit.

"So how do you feel about going to a new school, Terry?"

His mouth tightened. "Don't want to."

Isabel nodded. "Can't blame you. You've probably got friends at your present school you would miss."

He nodded, just a little.

"Do you want to give this a try and see what happens? You never know . . . it might just work. Really, Terry, when you think about it, you've got nothing to lose by trying, and maybe a lot to gain."

" 'kay."

"Good," Isabel answered, standing behind him and clicking on a recording device. If the induction worked, she'd make a copy and give it to Linda to take home with them. "Can you relax? Just sit quietly and listen to my voice . . . ," she said, sitting back down in front of him. "We're going to do this together, you and I. Can you feel your toes, Terry? Can you feel the muscles in your toes?"

"Yeah?"

"Can you feel them relaxing?"

"Nope."

"Can you try to feel them relaxing?"

He shook his head.

"Okay, then just listen to me and pretend they are. Feel your toes, the muscles in your toes . . ." And she went through the entire induction while Terry didn't even close his eyes, just fidgeted and picked at the leather seam on the edge of the arm. Isabel glanced at Linda. Her head was hanging down to her chest. Her eyes were closed. Clearly she was an easier subject than her fidgety son.

Then it was as if some window opened in her mind, and she remembered Linda telling her of Terry's love of football. He'd even worn the jacket today.

"I know, Terry. Close your eyes for a minute and see if you can watch this imaginary game of football where you're the big hero. Go ahead. It'll be fun."

He closed his eyes.

Isabel searched her mind for facts about football. This had been Chuck's area of expertise, not hers. But then again, she'd always liked the opening kickoff.

"Okay, Terry, I want you to see yourself way back on your own ten-yard line, ready to receive the ball. You're waiting. You know the ball is going to come right at you. I want you to see the kick and the ball soaring through the air, all the way back to you on the ten-yard line. Here it comes. Catch it! Now start running toward the goal line. Go ahead . . . you can do it. You pass the fifteen-yard line feeling powerful, the twenty-yard line and then the twenty-five-yard line, feeling strong, confident, and relaxed. Keep going—keep running past any obstacles, any other player. There you are on the thirty-yard line, dodging and outrunning everyone. You are so confident and relaxed with each line you pass. You can feel your success, and you keep going, figuring out the way as you pass the fifty-yard line and really push hard toward the goal. With each line you pass you feel even more confident, more relaxed, more calm that you're going to succeed. There's the other team's ten-yard line, and you're so relaxed now and confident. The five-yard line, even more relaxed . . . three . . . calm, peaceful, sure of your success, and one!"

Isabel put energy into her voice as she cheered his *touchdown* into a deep state of hypnosis. She watched Terry raise his fist in victory, a smile on his face. His eyes remained closed as he continued to watch his visualization. Then, suddenly, his arm fell to his lap, his head dropped forward to his chest, and finally, Terry was in hypnosis.

Isabel exhaled in relief. "Terry, I want you to stay in your football uniform. You're so good at the game, and you have such a good mind because you have to think quickly to outplay the other team. It stands to reason that if you are such an excellent player, you must also have an excellent mind. You can take that love you have for football and carry it to other areas of your school. You must like your school, because you play for them. See yourself reaching a goal in your math and reading classes, passing a test with good grades. And you are going to be as skilled at passing tests as you already are at passing a football. Everything will make sense to you again. Do you remember the first time you thought you couldn't read?"

He barely nodded.

"Was it in first grade?"

Another nod.

"I want you, Terry, in your football uniform, to go up to that little boy that was yourself in first grade. Introduce him to this competent, successful, intelligent football player of today. Can you see him?"

A nod.

"Good. See how much you've changed during the years from then until now. See how much bigger you are, how you even think differently. What if that little boy was also wearing his first football uniform? Put it on him. Would you be able to fit into that uniform now? Of course it wouldn't fit. It would be much too small. You couldn't protect yourself with outgrown equipment from that time, could you?"

Terry slowly shook his head.

"Maybe, just maybe, Terry, you're also unable to protect yourself with outgrown ways of learning and behavior, things you first started when you were little. Do they seem to help you now? There's no reason to be scared anymore of the reading workbook. That was then, when you were little. And now, well . . . those ways don't meet your current needs of a ten-year-old who is so skilled in math and football and has good friends and family. Maybe now that you aren't that scared little boy anymore you can focus more completely on the work at hand."

She paused, letting him think about that. "The crisis is over, Terry. Every time you're stumped at reading now, you'll picture yourself ready to receive the answers as easily as you did the football. You know all the information every teacher in reading ever gave you is stored in your brilliant mind. It's all there for you, so you can now retrieve it easily and quickly when it's required."

She let him absorb her words for a few moments. "Now, I want you to say good-bye to that six-year-old little boy. He's always with you, but now you can take care of him because you're older and smarter and stronger, okay?"

He nodded.

"Good. Now when I count to three you're going to take off the uniform and hang it up in your locker as you begin to wake up. One, hanging up the uniform. Two, coming awake, feeling confident and calm and knowing everything you need is stored inside you, and three . . . awake, taking a deep breath and opening your eyes."

Terry opened his eyes and then blinked a few times as he oriented himself. "That was cool."

"Yeah, I know," Isabel whispered, getting up and turning off the recorder. "How do you feel?"

He stretched his arms. "Okay. Can I have that cake now?"

"Absolutely."

"Hey, look at my mom. . . ."

Linda still had her eyes closed.

Isabel giggled with Terry. "You go on back into the kitchen and see if Jen is still there. I'm going to gently wake up your mom."

Terry slid off the chair and slowly, quietly walked out of the office.

Isabel grinned as she brought the thin recording device to her desk. Poor Linda . . . she must be mentally and physically exhausted. "Linda," she called out in a little louder voice. "On the count of three you will awaken refreshed and calm, feeling like you've spent a weekend at a spa. One, waking up. Two, feeling every cell in your body is refreshed and . . . three . . . awake and aware of your surroundings."

She was still grinning as Linda blinked, realized what she'd done, and covered her mouth. "I'm . . . so sorry," she murmured. "I must have fallen asleep."

"Don't apologize. It's perfectly fine. How do you feel?"

Linda sat up straighter and moved her head, as though checking herself. "I feel great, like I've just had eight hours of uninterrupted sleep." And then she laughed. "How embarrassing."

"It's not embarrassing. Actually, it's a compliment to me."

"Where's Terry?"

"In the kitchen eating his cake, I think." Isabel plugged in the recorder to her computer. "I'm making you a CD and I'd like you to play this for Terry as he falls asleep. Every night. I don't think he's going to object. Don't worry if he falls asleep; his subconscious is going to absorb it."

"Is it about the football?"

Isabel nodded, and within moments she had burned her session with Terry. "It's the same induction." She put the CD into a clear plastic case. "It will be an extra twenty dollars for the CD. I hope that's okay?"

Linda got up from the sofa and sat in the chair opposite the desk. "That's fine. I would have paid a hundred dollars to a masseur to feel that relaxed. Let alone if it did anything for Terry. Should I make another appointment now? We only have until the end of the year to get him reading."

"Why don't we see how he does this week? He might surprise you."

"If he falls asleep listening to the tape it will surprise me." Linda brought out her wallet. "How much do I owe you?"

Isabel had a good feeling about Terry. He might be one of the ones who made it out of the system.

After Terry and his mother left, Isabel was gathering up the cake dishes when she said, "Jen, that roast smells wonderful. You really have come such a long way."

Smiling, Jen took the dishes from her and began rinsing them in the sink. "It's all because of you, Isabel. I think I was meant to come here at this time."

They looked at each other, and a silent communication passed between them.

"Fine," Isabel said. "I'll go to the drugstore and get it."

"Now?"

Shrugging, Isabel walked over to the back door and grabbed her winter jacket off a hook. "Why not? Let's just get it over with." She simply couldn't believe she was going to do this!

At least it would put an end to the pregnancy talk once and for all.

Chapter

13

STANDING IN HER BATHROOM, HOLDING THE TESTER, Isabel felt embarrassed for herself. How in the world had she gotten into a situation where she'd have to buy one of these things at her age and then prove to an eighteen-year-old girl that she wasn't pregnant?

How much more bizarre *could* her world become?

She placed the tester on the side of the box and walked into her bedroom. The bed looked so inviting, but it was already made, and she was reluctant to mess it up to lie down for such a short time. Why *was* she so tired lately? It didn't make sense. She couldn't even blame it on Joshua, because it appeared that he was gone. She didn't even know if he would return.

What if he found this Manny character and the two of them just decided that human beings, especially female human beings, were too emotional, too clingy, and so they had given their messages and they both were moving on to a higher dimension? What if Jen truly was abandoned?

And what if I'm no better off than the girl downstairs and am left holding these damn emotions again?

She sat on the edge of the bed and looked down to the hardwood floor. If it ended now, if she never saw Joshua again, would it have been worth it? To experience that kind of desire and passion again? A part of her, the very human part of her, knew it had been incredible to feel so alive again, even if it had been just endorphins. But then there was her mind, fragile enough in the last month, so scared of loss, and she didn't think she could survive another period of grief.

What had she thought was going to happen? Joshua was going to remain with her, make love to her, solve all the riddles and problems in her life? Teach her how to heal others, like he did with touch? That he would *marry* her? That was the kind of fantasy for a much younger woman's mind. She should have known better. Males, even males that are from another dimension, are a tough lot when it comes to commitment. And did she really want someone invading her life anymore? She had been fine until the group had convinced her to go to that conference. She'd had a pretty good life, despite what they had thought. She had come to a place where living alone was all right, sometimes downright enjoyable—never having to please another, pick up their socks, watch an afternoon of sports or the History Channel. She made decisions without consulting anyone. Her days and nights were her own. She could walk around all day in a flannel nightgown and not give a damn. She could have cereal for dinner if she didn't feel like cooking.

Why would she want to give that up for sex?

That sneaky voice inside whispered it was more than sex, far more.

She was starting to fall in love again.

Hell, she could admit it to herself, if not to anyone else.

She did love him.

Who could resist someone who knew everything about you and yet thought you were wonderful? What woman could resist those smoky, exotic eyes? His endearing and compassionate smile? His tenderness? The magic of his touch? The heat of his passion? The desire to please her in . . .

Knock it off, she mentally commanded.

He's gone, and now you've got to prove to Jen that you aren't pregnant from the whole insane encounter. Talk about a departure from reality!

Pushing herself up with a sigh, she left the bedroom and entered her bathroom. For a moment she thought she had read the directions incorrectly. It was supposed to have a straight line, a negative sign. She picked up the tester and turned over the box.

Positive. Pregnant.

Isabel simply blinked, looking from the tester to the box.

What had gone wrong? She'd done the simple test according to the directions.

She took the tester to the bathroom window. Maybe her eyes were going. Age. She'd been lucky not to have worn reading glasses before this, and she'd certainly take the reading glasses over the flat-out ridiculous possibility of pregnancy.

Looking at the little sign box in the receding afternoon light, Isabel swore she saw a positive sign, a plus sign, a damn add sign, which could only mean the test was defective.

It had to be.

She didn't have any symptoms. No morning sickness. No breast tenderness. Nothing that would indicate . . . and then she remembered thinking she might have had a touch of the flu. And all the tiredness.

Her stomach turned, and she clasped her hand to her mouth, breathing in deeply through her nose. *This is wrong. It can't be.* She'd buy another test. Do it all over again. Really, she should write the manufacturer and complain. She knew she wasn't pregnant, but what about a younger woman where a mistaken result could mean so much more? She'd just have to go back to the drugstore and buy another, maybe two, and different brands.

What was she going to tell Jen?

She wrapped the tester in tissues and stuck it into the pocket of her jeans. She'd just say it hadn't worked right and she had to get another. It was the truth.

Isabel drove to a different drugstore and threw the tester out in the waste bin by the front door. She bought two more kits and drove home in a state of urgency. She refused to let her mind go into a dark and scary place. It had just been her bad luck to have picked up a malfunctioning kit, that's all.

Once more standing in her bathroom, holding the alarm clock from her night table, Isabel tried deep-breathing exercises. *Stay calm,* she told herself. *You are not going to be sick. It's just nerves. You couldn't get pregnant during a twenty-year marriage, and God only knows how hard you tried. You simply got a bad kit that had slipped through quality control.*

She continued to talk to herself, this time aloud as she sat on the toilet seat. "Feel your toes. . . . Feel the muscles in your toes. . . ." Damn, all she could feel was rigid with tension. She got up and began pacing back and forth in the bathroom, which only gave her six feet each way. "You're doing this to yourself," she whispered, peeking at both testers on the sink. "You're causing all this stress for nothing."

And she was talking to herself. Aloud.

Sitting once more on the toilet seat, she covered her face with her hands and exhaled loudly. "Just stay calm," she repeated. "Calm . . . soothing, peaceful, relaxing waves are washing over you and . . . *hell!*" It was excruciating to wait for the minutes to tick by so slowly, and no amount of positive visualization was going to make them pass faster or calm her down.

"Screw it!" she muttered, and picked up one of the testers.

It was turning pink.

She grabbed the box. Pink equaled positive.

Her heart was slamming against her rib cage as she stretched and looked at the other tester. The word PREGNANT was beginning to appear, while the NOT PREGNANT space was pure white. Clear.

She held them both in her hands as she sat back down and

watched, second by second, remaining minute by minute, as the messages became clearer and clearer.

It felt like her brain stopped functioning as she dropped the testers into the sink and walked back into her bedroom. She didn't give a damn about messing up the bed as she slowly slipped out of her shoes and pulled back the comforter. Crawling into bed, she lay down on her side and stared out to her bedroom.

It couldn't be true. She was too old.

This just didn't happen in the life of a fifty-year-old woman! A single, unmarried fifty-year-old woman!

But it did, because she'd had sex with a being from another dimension. Sex she had initiated and then craved over and over again. This was it, then. Karma. Three pregnancy tests couldn't be wrong. She was a fifty-year-old widow who'd gotten herself pregnant with . . . Oh dear God . . . she was like those hysterical women who said they'd been abducted and impregnated! Who was going to believe her?

She would be the crazy one, the kook, and she had tried so hard for so long to be sane. . . . She'd known her family was crazy from an early age. She had watched her parents fighting, the ugliness that went on behind closed doors, and then had seen them act completely different in public, like the happily married couple everyone had expected. Pretense and appearances were everything, and her parents lived for pretending. They would have their "sundowners" way before the sun began receding, and within a few hours they'd verbally attack the other with relish. Her mother could be in the middle of an ugly criticism, yet if the phone rang she would change with lightning speed into the gracious homemaker to answer it. On too many occasions she had seen her parents shred each other and then attend a party at the country club, acting as though they were the model for marriage. Crazy. It was more important to them what others thought than what they thought of each other, or even of themselves. So she had fought pretense all her life, knowing that beneath the polite exterior were hidden emotions that were the key to healing. And now . . . now, she was the one who was worried what others might think of her. Pregnant. Fifty. Unmarried. Younger man, or *being from another dimension?!*

This was too hard!

It was then she realized that she wasn't even considering terminating it. Could she? She was fifty. It was a health risk at any age, but carrying full term at fifty was a serious challenge. She clutched the edge of the pillow, wondering how her life had gotten so out of control. . . .

"Issy? Isabel?"

Oh, God. She forced herself to look toward the doorway. Standing there was Jen, looking worried.

"Are you sick, Isabel?"

She couldn't make her mouth work and watched as Jen came into the room and stood by the side of the bed.

Staring down at her, Jen added, "I was worried. You ran out of the house so fast and then came up here and . . . don't you feel well?"

"I . . ." She tried to speak, but her throat felt as though someone had their hands around it, choking off her speech. She simply couldn't say it out loud and make it real. Real? Three pregnancy tests don't make it real?

"You what?" Jen prompted, bending down and touching her hand. "You *are* pregnant, aren't you?"

Isabel looked up at the younger woman. How had they switched places so fast? Now she was the withdrawn one, and Jen . . . Jen, whose hand was warm and soothing, had become the sane, rational one who gave comfort?

"Should I call someone? Cristine?"

"No!" she croaked out in terror. "Don't tell anyone."

"Why not? I think you need your friends now. I . . . I don't know what to do!" Jen stood straight up and began wringing her hands. "Both of us pregnant and scared. We need some help, Isabel!"

Isabel forced herself to lean up on her elbow. "Jen, this has just been a shock, that's all. Of course I'm scared. I'm stunned and terrified. I didn't believe it was possible."

"I tried to tell you. I knew it when I looked into your eyes."

"*How* did you know it?"

Shrugging, Jen said, "It just came to me. I was looking at you, and I thought it. I heard it."

"You heard it?"

"A tiny voice inside said, 'She's pregnant.' Your baby is special too."

"Jen, please," Isabel begged. "Don't talk about it like that now. I don't know what I'm going to do."

"What do you mean?"

"I mean," Isabel said, plopping her head back onto the pillow, "that being pregnant at my age is . . . well, dangerous. Do you realize I would be almost seventy before this child went to college? I don't know that I can go through with it." But even as the words left her lips she thought they sounded hollow, like she was playing for time until she accepted reality.

Jen sat on the edge of the mattress and stroked her shoulder. "Isabel, I have a very good feeling about your baby."

The more Jen stroked her shoulder, the more she could feel the tension leave her body. She had that same gentle energy Joshua had when he wanted to calm her down. Threads of soothing energy raced across her shoulders, and Isabel sighed. Then she startled Jen by sitting straight up. "And where are *they,* huh?" she demanded, sudden anger surging through her. "How dare they do this to us and then disappear?" Maybe the anger was what she needed, because she pushed past Jen and stood up. Running her fingers through her hair, she added, "They don't have the right to turn our lives upside down and then evolve right on out of them. It isn't right! It isn't fair!"

"They'll be back, Isabel. Manny said he'd come back."

"Really? When? 'Cause I don't see either one of them showing up, Jen. Maybe we should just face it. We're alone in this . . . insanity. They have their way with us and then evolve into some far dimension and leave us holding the bag!"

"The bag? We're going to have babies, Isabel. Isn't that wonderful?"

Isabel stopped pacing and looked at her. "Wonderful? Your sister doesn't think it's wonderful. My friends are going to think I've had a nervous breakdown and—"

"Why do you care what others think?" Jen interrupted.

Isabel stared into Jen's calm blue eyes. What *had* happened to Jen since Joshua touched her? She was so mature now, so sure of herself, that Isabel was beginning to feel like the client and Jen was now the voice of reason. "You're right. I shouldn't care. But I do care that you and I have been abandoned. Doesn't it bother you?"

"I miss Manny terribly, but he said he would come back, and I know he will. Joshua will find him."

"Joshua's had enough time to find him, Jen. Hasn't it even occurred to you that they may not be coming back?"

Jen simply shook her head slowly.

"You have more faith than I do," Isabel muttered. "Far more."

"Joshua will come back, Isabel."

"How do you know that? They've done what they came here to do. Delivered their messages *and* their seed. How could I have been so stupid?"

Jen started smiling. "You aren't stupid. You're in love."

That statement stopped her cold. "I'm not in love," she protested.

"I think you are, Isabel. I saw how you and Joshua were together when I first met him, before you knew I was at the office door. I think you love him, and I know he loves you."

"How do you know that?" God, she felt like a teenager asking for reassurances.

"I could feel it, and I could see it in his eyes when he looked at you."

"Well, none of that matters because he's gone. I don't think they're coming back, Jen." Even thinking it made her stomach clench in dread. She would be facing this all alone.

"Isabel, you are special. And your baby is special. Just as mine is."

Isabel sighed deeply. "And you want to know what Joshua says to that? Either we're all special, or none of us are."

Jen's grin widened. "Exactly. We are all special."

Shaking her head, Isabel walked into the bathroom and looked at the two testers. Yep . . . positive. Pregnant. "I feel so special," she muttered, grabbing them up and throwing them into the trash basket by the sink.

She had to make a plan, but first she had to make a decision.

Isabel bit her bottom lip, thinking. She should call Kate Abrams. Kate specialized in women with high-risk pregnancies. God . . . how could she face her friend with *this* situation? She touched her belly, realizing now it hadn't been too much food or cake. She was gaining weight for an entirely different reason. And then she stopped herself.

Shouldn't she have had other symptoms, besides brief bouts of dizziness? And she couldn't be more than a month pregnant. Why would she have gained weight already? It didn't make sense.

Knowing that the longer she put it off, the bigger and scarier it was going to become, Isabel knew she had to become proactive. She had to call Kate right away and make an appointment. Should she make one for Jen? No, let Kate deal with one bizarre pregnancy at a time.

And where *was* Marcia? The woman should have at least called.

She couldn't worry about Marcia now. She had enough to worry about for herself.

A baby.

Her mind couldn't wrap around it.

For so long she had yearned for this, prayed for this, gone through a barrage of testing and needles and drugs and disappointments to achieve this. And now it had happened. Like this . . . It took a being from another dimension.

She sniffled down her emotion.

Too bad he was years too late.

Chapter

14

ISABEL LEFT KATE ABRAMS' OFFICE AND WAS ON autopilot as she got in her car. She simply sat behind the wheel and stared out the windshield to others wrapped in winter coats walking in and out of the tall building.

It couldn't be true.

Not only had she had to go through an embarrassing interview, admitting she was pregnant, but after Kate's examination she was told she was at least three months pregnant! Which was flat-out impossible!

Three months ago she had been sane, living her solitary life and going about her business as she pleased. Three months ago she had been seven years celibate. She hadn't known anyone like Joshua could possibly exist. Three months ago her life had been her own: predictable, but with some semblance of normality!

Three months pregnant!

Now decisions were critical. Kate had said she wasn't the first fifty-year-old to have walked into her office and that there was no reason, with careful monitoring, why she couldn't successfully carry to full term. Isabel had tried to listen to Kate after the exam, but she was in such shock that it was like those Charlie Brown specials when the teacher is talking. All Isabel heard was gibberish, and nothing made sense.

Shivering in the cold, Isabel started the car and turned on the heat, only to be hit with a blast of cold air that broke through her shock. Where could she go? What should she do?

She didn't want to go home, not with Jen there waiting with her serene smiles, so sure now of herself and her pregnancy. The only one, besides Jen, who know about Joshua was Claire. God . . . Claire. She could just picture Claire's astonishment. At least Paula would be sympathetic. But Claire was pragmatic and practical. She needed practical now. She'd spent enough time in fantasyland with Joshua.

Now having a destination, Isabel put the car into reverse and headed toward Claire's. Maybe she wouldn't be home. She could call her on the cell, but Isabel thought if she was home it would be a sign; if not she could postpone telling anyone in the group until she knew what she was going to do. Either way, she was moving, and she knew she had to go forward, no matter what her decision.

Fifteen minutes later, Isabel saw Claire's BMW parked in her driveway. Claire's house was a sprawling white contemporary with sharp angles and lots of glass windows. The landscaping, even in winter, was impeccable, with garden beds of heavily mulched evergreens and two spirals of junipers in big heavy pots on either side of the double front doors. Isabel parked behind Claire and took a deep breath as she got out of the car. Practical. Realistic. No-nonsense. That's what she needed now.

Pulling her coat tighter around her, Isabel walked up to the entryway. Claire had hung two simple pine wreaths on each door. No bows, no ornaments. Just simple and clean. To the point, with no fussiness. Like Claire, Isabel thought, and rang the bell. Within moments, the door opened and Claire, dressed in jeans and a pale yellow cashmere sweater, looked back at her with surprise.

"Issy! What are you doing here?"

"Am I interrupting anything? I can come back later."

"Get in here," Claire ordered, hunching her shoulders against the cold air. "It's bitter out there."

"Thanks," Isabel murmured, walking into the square foyer with its slate flooring.

"Let me have your coat," Claire directed, holding out her hands. "There's a fire going in the living room. I was working on foundation business from home and decided today was the perfect afternoon to light one."

She handed over her long coat and wrapped her arms around her waist. "I won't stay long. I just need to talk to you."

Claire hung up her coat in a closet and turned around. "What's wrong? Not that I'm not glad to see your face outside my door, but—"

"I just need a voice of reason," Isabel interrupted, walking past a modern sculpture in black marble as she headed for the fireplace. She heard a laugh behind her.

"Now that's funny," Claire said, following her. "*You're* supposed to be the voice of reason."

"The key words in that sentence, Claire, are *supposed to be*. I've come to you for that."

"Damn, Issy. Now you're frightening me. What's up?"

Isabel walked through the spacious living room, past the deep brown antiqued leather sofa with its nail-head trim, to the black marble fireplace. Sitting down on its wide hearth, she smiled at Claire as the heat from the fire warmed her back. "Do you have any tea? Herbal tea?"

"So you're gonna drag this out?" Claire answered with a grin as she headed for the kitchen.

"I just want to thaw out first," Isabel called back, noticing on the big glass coffee table the papers that Claire had been working on for the foundation. Sighing deeply, she looked around the living room decorated in browns and blacks and creams. Everything had a clean line to it. Everything had its functional place. Just like Claire. Her life was orderly, normal, uncluttered with insanity.

She'd come to the right place.

The heat from the fire seemed to crawl up her back, tickling her skin with pleasure, and Isabel felt her muscles relaxing. Now if she could just find the courage to tell Claire the truth. Would Claire cart her off to a hospital for intensive therapy? If they'd switched places, Isabel knew she would have considered it.

"Okay, so until the water boils, do you want to tell me what this is all about? Is it Jennifer?"

"No. Well, not really."

"The boyfriend? Is he back in the picture?"

"There is no boyfriend, Claire. I'm not eighteen."

"Fine. Is the gorgeous, exotic singer back in the picture?"

"Not in the way you mean. . . ." Her words trailed off. How could she possible explain this?

"Issy, we're good friends. Don't make me play twenty questions with you. Just say it."

She looked at Claire, waiting so patiently with a compassionate expression. Maybe she could trust her. "I'm . . . well, you see, I'm pregnant."

Claire blinked. Her jaw dropped. Then she laughed. "C'-mon, Issy. It's funny, I agree, but just tell me."

"I just *did*. Don't you think I know how laughable it is? I'm pregnant, Claire. At my age . . ." She felt tears burning her eyes.

Claire didn't say anything—just continued to stare in disbelief. It was the whistle of the teapot that seemed to bring her back to life. "All right. Okay. Just hold that thought until I get back!" And she ran into the kitchen to silence the annoying sound. "Well, maybe not *that* last thought!" she yelled.

There, Isabel thought. She'd said it aloud. She'd made it real.

She was pregnant. With Joshua's child. It didn't matter what Kate Abrams said about being three months along. She was carrying his child, so nothing about this pregnancy could be considered normal. Joshua wasn't normal. And now she was carrying a fetus whose father was from another dimension! How could she possibly tell Claire *that*?

Sniffling as Claire came back into the room with two mugs filled with tea, Isabel tried to grin. "Bet you didn't expect that, huh?"

Claire placed a mug in front of her and then sat opposite her on the sofa. "Geez, Issy, I didn't mean to laugh. I mean all those years with Chuck . . . you said you couldn't have children and . . . and now . . . ?"

"Right," Isabel murmured. "Now it appears I can. Now that I'm fifty. Now that I'm a widow. Now that my whole life is turned upside down and inside out."

"It's his—the singer's?"

"He's not a singer. His name is Joshua."

"Joshua what?"

Isabel's lips began to quiver. "I still don't know."

"God, so you're pregnant with this Joshua's child, and you don't know his last name."

"You make it sound so cheap, and it wasn't like that, Claire."

"I know, I know," Claire answered quickly. "I didn't mean it like that. I was just trying to get the facts straight. Are you sure, Issy? It couldn't be . . . like a missed period or one of those hysterical pregnancies? What about menopause?"

Isabel shook her head and chuckled at Claire's naïveté. "First of all, Claire, I'm a registered nurse. I understand the body. And I've seen Kate Abrams. I'm pregnant."

"Oh."

"Yeah. Oh. I am an honest-to-God pregnant, unmarried, fifty-year-old woman. It does sound laughable. You're right."

"Oh, Issy, I didn't mean to laugh, but—"

"But it's the very last thing you thought would have come out my mouth, right?"

Claire looked uncomfortable. "Well . . . kinda."

"It's okay, Claire. It's the last thing I thought would have happened to me."

Claire sat up straighter. "So where's this Joshua?"

"I don't know," Isabel answered. It was the truth.

"Does he live in Philly? Should we go back to that bar and see if we can find him?"

"He doesn't live in Philadelphia."

"Where does he live, then?"

Isabel sniffed and picked up a square cocktail napkin from the stack on the coffee table. "I don't know."

Claire leaned in over her mug. "Issy, I don't mean to appear insensitive, but what *do* you know about him?"

Isabel wanted to cry, a full-blown sob session, but she swallowed down the burning lump in her throat. "Claire, I never thought it might be a forever thing."

Lie. She knew it as soon as the words left her mouth. Of course she had let her head wander into forever, sharing a timeless love. What a fool she had been.

"Okay, so all this might be moot anyway. Are you planning on having this baby? I mean, look at the circumstances. Even the church looks the other way when the mother's life is endangered."

"Oh, Claire . . ." Isabel couldn't hold back the tears any longer. "I . . . I don't know what to do," she cried, wiping at her eyes and her nose. "That's why I . . . came to you."

Claire immediately got up and sat next to Isabel on the hearth. She wrapped her arm around her shoulders. "Damn, Issy . . . who would have ever thought we'd be having this conversation."

Isabel simply nodded, grabbing another cocktail napkin and blowing her nose. She hung her head and sighed. Claire was stroking her back, which felt wonderful with the heat of the fire, but it couldn't dispel the hanging question. "What should I do?" she whispered.

"Honey, I don't know. This has to be your decision. What did Kate Abrams say?"

"She said I'm not the first fifty-year-old to walk through her office doors, and if I choose to go on with it, I won't be the first to successfully carry to full term. She thinks it's entirely doable. I just don't know." She lifted her head and looked, unseeing, out to the living room. "Claire, I'd be almost seventy before a child went to college. What kind of life is that for a kid?"

"I don't know," Claire murmured. "But you're so young at heart, Issy, and you've wanted a child for so long."

"I wanted a child with Chuck, not with some . . ." She didn't know how to finish her sentence.

"Not some gorgeous, healthy, alive male who thought you were a hot piece of tail?"

"Oh God . . ."

Claire laughed, "Well, is that not the truth?"

Isabel shook her head. "I don't know what the truth is anymore. Joshua . . . he's not like anyone I've ever met."

"Not like Chuck, you mean?"

"No. I didn't mean that. In some ways he's a lot like Chuck, but Joshua's different."

"How different?"

"He's very spiritual, but intelligent and . . ."

"And?" Claire prompted.

"And . . ." How could she say this? How could Claire believe her if she did? Not wanting to be thought of as crazy, she said, "And he's a free spirit. He wouldn't want to be held too long in one place. I don't think he could manage it, so it appears I'm on my own in this." No lies yet. "I just have to figure out what I'm going to do."

Claire clucked her tongue in disapproval. "All well and good to be a free spirit; just use a fucking condom then."

Isabel cringed. "I didn't think it was possible, Claire. Why would I think I needed protection?"

"I guess you're right. It's just that it galls the shit out of me that men get to spread their seed wherever they please and then move on. This whole marriage and commitment thing is a conspiracy against women, to keep them in their place and dependent. Why should you have to carry the accountability of this alone? Let alone the financial responsibility? He can't get away with this, Isabel. He should at least pay child support and establish a college fund."

"So you think I should . . . have this baby?" Isabel asked in a tiny voice.

"I don't know what you *should* do, Issy. But you'd better figure out what you want to do. And quickly. Which way are you leaning?"

Isabel felt like crying again. "I don't know. I'm right in the middle of the road."

"Okay, so what's on either side of the road?"

Taking a deep breath, trying to calm down and be practical, she answered, "On one side is a baby, a child, someone I've waited for and wanted all my adult life; but I managed to put that behind me with Chuck's death. On the other side of the road is raising that child alone, keeping my health, growing old and not being a good parent, leaving the child before I've prepared it for life. It's terrifying."

Claire picked up the mug and handed it to Isabel. "Here, drink your tea." She stood up and grabbed her own mug, then sat back down. "Okay, so the way I see it is you want the baby, but you're afraid of the future. One is real and the other isn't—not yet, anyway. Aren't you the one who taught all of us in the group about living in the present? Not time traveling out of our lives into the past, which is over, or the future, which hasn't yet been created?"

"I'm so good at it when it's about someone else." She turned her head and stared at Claire, who was now blowing on her tea. "But what if something happens to me? I'm old, Claire! How fair would that be to a child?"

"First of all, you are not old! Fifty of today is not your mother's fifty. You don't even look fifty—not even with that white hair. Fifty is the new forty; just ask any baby boomer who's still as active and vibrant as a thirty-year-old. Look, I can see you're scared, Issy, and I understand it. Believe me, I do. You're trying to be responsible." She smiled compassionately. "Nothing is going to happen to you while I'm around. And if you should get hit by a car, or something totally out of the blue happens, well, it could have happened to Paula too, remember? She was in that accident and could have died. She would have been leaving five kids. You don't know the future, Issy. You know that."

Remembering Paula's accident, Isabel shrugged. "At least Paula's got a husband who could have taken over."

Claire nudged her shoulder. "Hey! You've got the group. That's five independent, strong, loving women, and if it makes you feel better, make me the legal guardian if, God forbid, you get hit by a bus. I'll finish what you started."

Isabel started crying again. "You . . . you'd do that?"

Claire chuckled. "Of course I would. It would probably be my best shot at motherhood anyway. And I promise I won't use foul language in front of the kid. Or at least until he or she is in college. And then all bets are off and I get to tell them how they're fucking up their life by smoking weed all night in the dorm and missing classes."

Isabel laughed in spite of herself. "Ah, that was you, Claire."

Claire grinned. "And somebody did take me aside and told me just that. Straightened me right out too."

Sniffling, Isabel smiled. "There's a reason I love you, Claire Hutchinson, and it has nothing to do with your colorful way of expressing yourself."

"No shit?"

Isabel shook her head. "No shit. It has everything to do with your heart of gold. You are one phenomenal woman."

Claire placed her arm over Issy's shoulders and sighed. "Too bad you aren't a man. I'd marry ya."

Isabel laughed. "At least marriage would make me respectable again."

"To hell with what anyone thinks."

"C'mon, Claire, eighteen and unmarried isn't even a big deal anymore. Fifty, unmarried, and pregnant is juicy gossip."

"You're right," Claire whispered. "Promise you won't tell anybody else in the group unless I'm there. I don't want to miss their expressions."

"I should call a meeting and announce it." Isabel almost grinned, imagining it. "Be prepared to revive Kelly. She might just faint."

"Nah . . . Kelly will be shocked, but then she'll give you the down and dirty about raising a child alone." Claire paused. "We've got to find that girl a man who won't break her heart."

"Is there one out there like that?"

"Wow, now that's cynical," Claire stated with a laugh. "And I didn't even have to say 'Come over to the dark side, Issy.'"

She grinned back at her dear friend. "It does sound cynical, I know, but even Chuck, a good man and a good husband, broke my heart when he left me. Why *do* we put ourselves through it, Claire?"

Silence filled the warm room as both women stared off into space.

Finally, Claire murmured, "Because maybe if we're lucky or blessed or something, we get to experience real love with another human being and express ourselves through that."

"And it's heavenly," Isabel added wistfully. "We get glimpses of heaven, and we want more."

Claire nodded. "Yeah . . . that's the problem. We want more, and we think we can have it. Why else would women put up with their crap?"

"I don't know," Isabel whispered. "Maybe the big payoff is children."

"Or security." Claire sighed. "That's why it's so important to be an independent woman, at least financially. Then you get to choose your life. It's freedom."

"It really is a form of freedom, isn't it?" Isabel asked. "With security, you can make choices for yourself that are in your best interests. Like Cristine. Even though she and Daniel are together, she chose not to marry."

"Yeah, so . . . now we'll have *two* out-of-wedlock babies?"

"What a word," Isabel said. "Wedlock. If you think about it, it sounds like prison."

"You haven't answered me. Have we possibly settled this earth-shattering dilemma you walked in the door with?"

Isabel swallowed.

Then she nodded.

And took a deep breath.

"I'm going to have a baby," she whispered.

Claire exhaled and tilted her head to Isabel's shoulder. "I get to be a godmother again. But please . . . let's call a meeting tomorrow. I don't know if I can contain myself if I speak to anyone before that."

"You have to, Claire."

"Make it an emergency meeting, then. I'll call everyone. We can have it here."

"No. I want it to be in my house."

"Fine. Then an emergency meeting of the Yellow Brick Road Gang is called for tomorrow night." She raised her head and giggled. "I can't wait to see their faces!"

Isabel put her mug back onto the coffee table. She then turned to Claire and said, "And no calling Cristine before I've backed out of your driveway."

"Are you questioning my integrity, Isabel Calloway?" Claire asked in an falsely arch voice.

Claire grinned. "Not at all, Claire. I just know how juicy

this is. And I'm going to need your support when they all fall apart on me. You're usually the tough one, so at least the worst is over."

"You can be pretty tough too at these emergency meetings. I watched you with Cristine when Charlie left. Glad I wasn't in the hot seat on that one."

"Promise me."

Claire sighed again. "Okay, okay. I promise. No leaks when I call them."

"Good. Now I should let you get back to your work."

Claire's eye's widened. "Like you think I could work after this?"

"I'm sorry," Isabel said with sincerity. "I didn't mean to upset your whole day, though I can see I have."

"Don't you be sorry," Claire said with a smile. "We're going to have a baby again in the group. God, I hope it's more sane than the last time with Cristine. Do you remember how we all acted?"

Isabel nodded. And she hadn't even told Claire the truth about Joshua. Nothing about this pregnancy was going to be sane. She just knew it.

"God, Issy, our last emergency meeting was to coax you out of the shadows. I remember I said something like, 'Nobody expects you to become a wild and crazy woman.'" Claire laughed. "You should be wearing that purple hat when you tell them the news."

A wild and crazy woman.

That was exactly what she had become.

Chapter

15

ALL OF THE GANG WERE WEARING THEIR SPARKLY RED high heels and, except for Isabel, drinking red wine. They were gathered at the large dining room table, eating dessert after a meal of eggplant parmigiana, angel hair pasta, and a spinach salad.

"Dinner was fabulous. *Now* are you going to tell us what this emergency meeting is about?" Tina asked, not for the first time.

"Yeah, Issy. You've got me worried," Paula added.

"I told you I would tell you when dinner was over," Isabel stated. "So be patient. Let's enjoy this fruit tart. And, Paula," she added with a smile, "don't be worried."

They all fell into silence until Tina, obviously wanting to fill the space with conversation, said, "Okay, so this big deal now about saying 'Merry Christmas' or 'Happy holidays' is flat-out absurd." Digging into her fruit tart, she continued, "I mean, do these fanatics understand the English language? *Holiday means* 'holy day.' What's the fuss about, except to bring more attention to their agenda?"

Claire snorted and shook her head. "I actually had some woman hand me a piece of paper outside Genuardi's that stated this is one nation under God and we must take back

Christmas. I only wanted a half gallon of two percent milk, and I got a lecture."

Kelly laughed. "*You* stood outside a food store and listened to a lecture?"

Grinning, Claire answered, "I handed it right back and told her I was an American and I believed in the Constitution and the separation of church and state and that she might be interested to know this country was founded by people looking to get away from people like her."

"What did she do?" Paula asked.

"Nothing. And I didn't wait for her to answer. I went into the store and got my milk."

"You know it's funny when you think about it," Cristine said, then sipped her wine. "All this fuss, and yet most biblical scholars will say that Jesus was born in September, about six months after Passover, not in winter."

"Right. It's highly unlikely that shepherds would be tending sheep at night during a cold winter in Judea," Claire agreed. "This tart is fabulous."

"Imagine how that woman would feel," Paula began, "if she knew that Christmas has pagan origins. In ancient Babylon the feast of the son of Isis, the goddess of nature, was celebrated on December twenty-fifth. Eating, partying, and gift giving were traditional."

"It sounds like Christmas," Jen murmured shyly.

Paula smiled at their young guest. "Yes, it does, doesn't it? Especially the part about it being a feast for the son of a goddess. Then there was Rome. They called it *the winter solstice*. The whole season was called *the birthday of the unconquered sun*. That's sun with a *u*."

Cristine, sitting next to Jen, said, "Leave it to Paula, the anthropologist, to have the facts."

"What's an anthropologist?" Jen asked.

"Someone who studies people and their cultures," Isabel answered.

"Here's one for you, Jen," Paula said, twirling her wine-glass. "You know the Mummers Parade in Philly every New Year's Day?"

Jen nodded.

"That began in ancient Rome during the winter solstice."

"No kidding," Kelly said in amazement.

"Seriously. The mummers were groups of costumed singers and dancers who traveled from house to house during the solstice festival season entertaining their neighbors. I guess they were the first carolers."

"How about that?" Tina asked with a grin. "I never knew that."

Truly into her element now, Paula obviously took pleasure in enlightening her friends. "And in northern Europe," she continued, "the pagans had their own winter solstice cele-bration they called *Yule*. Yule was a symbol of the sun god, Mithras, who was said to be born on the shortest day of the year. Huge Yule logs were burned in honor of the sun. The word *Yule* means 'wheel,' the symbol for the sun. Mistletoe was considered a sacred plant, and kissing under it began as a fertility ritual. Holly berries were thought to be food for the gods."

"So how did all this become part of a Christian holiday?" Kelly asked.

"I think it was around the year 350 that Pope Julius the first declared that Christ's birth would be celebrated December twenty-fifth. I guess he was trying to make conversion to Christianity as painless as possible to the pagans. But any scholar will tell you that essentially most Christmas traditions celebrated today have their origins in the pagan religion."

"Damn," Claire muttered. "I wish I'd had this info when I went to get milk."

"The woman was lucky you didn't," Tina declared. "I could just see you giving her a totally different lecture."

"They annoy the hell out of me," Claire said. "I don't care

if it's politically incorrect to say that. They do! The arrogance in attempting to hijack this country is sickening. And how many of them actually practice true Christianity of love and nonjudgment?"

"I'm sure there are many who do, Claire," Isabel said. "But they don't make the papers or fill a sound bite on television."

"They probably feel the same way I do when I listen to the news," Tina said. "I hear about a crime, and I silently pray that the suspect isn't a person of color. Real Christians must feel the same way about the fanatics. They must cringe."

"Well, I wish more of the real ones would start speaking up and drown out the fanatics," Claire added, pushing her chair back and standing up. "And I think we should all make our way into the living room. Jen, we'll give you a hand in the kitchen later, okay?"

"Just leave everything," Isabel said as the others rose from the table. She looked at Claire and wished she could silence her. Claire simply shrugged, as though saying enough time had been wasted. The purpose of the meeting was about to be revealed.

"I'll do the dishes, Isabel," Jen said, gathering up the dessert plates. "I don't mind."

"No. We'll all help you," Tina said, picking up her wineglass and bringing it with her. "Maybe you could just get it started."

"Jen, it's too much," Isabel said.

Jen smiled. "Have your meeting, Issy. If I need help I'll let you know."

Isabel nodded, remembering when Jen had come to her and was afraid to wash a few plates after their peanut butter and jelly sandwiches. How she had changed.

"Okay," Claire said in a loud voice. "Get in here, Isabel, so we can call this meeting to order."

"I'm coming," she answered, thinking she would rather be in the kitchen with Jen. She'd wash dishes for an army rather than be the focus of this meeting.

"Get in here, woman," Tina called out. "And end this suspense."

Isabel walked into the living room and saw her dear friends seated on the sofa and chairs, looking up at her with expectation. How could she begin? Tell them about Joshua? She'd practiced this in her head a dozen times; each time it had sounded as ludicrous as it was in reality.

She took a deep breath. "All right. First, thank you all for coming on such short notice. I know how busy everyone is . . . Christmas right around the corner—"

"Get to the point, Issy," Kelly interrupted. "Now the suspense is getting to me too."

Isabel could feel the burning at her eyes, the tightness of her throat. If she didn't say it soon, she was going to embarrass herself even more by falling apart.

"There's no other way to say this—"

"Oh God, Issy, you aren't sick, are you?" Cristine demanded, sitting up straight in the chair. "I know what you said earlier, but—"

"I'm pregnant."

Claire turned to the group to catch their expressions.

Stunned, jaw-dropping disbelief would be a good description.

"Well?" Claire demanded of the group. "Is this not a surprise?"

"You *knew*?" Tina demanded of Claire.

"Just . . . like since yesterday," she answered, looking a bit defensive.

Cristine was shaking her head. "Shut up you two. Isabel? You're really *pregnant*?"

She swallowed deeply. "I know it's a shock. You can't imagine how I feel."

"Who's the father?" Kelly demanded, still blinking in disbelief.

"Right," Paula agreed. "I didn't even know you were seeing

someone. Did anyone know this?" Paula looked around at the group.

All shook their heads, save Claire, who acted like she didn't know anything more. "So who's the father, Isabel?"

"His name is Joshua. You all saw him the night of my birthday in that karaoke bar. He was—"

"*Ohmygod!*" Kelly nearly screamed. "That gorgeous guy who sang?"

It seemed the women inhaled as one in shock and awe.

"I *knew* he was singing to one of us," Tina exclaimed, slapping her pant leg.

"Isabel, why didn't you invite him over and introduce him?" Paula asked, sounding hurt.

She shook her head. "I . . . I really didn't think I'd ever see him again."

"Wait, wait . . . ," Kelly said, holding up her hand. "So this means you've been sleeping with the gorgeous singer guy."

"His name is Joshua and . . . well, yes." She was so embarrassed, revealing her personal life like this. But Isabel also knew she was going to need support, and these women would be like Amazon warriors in protecting her.

Cristine threw back her head and laughed. "Good for you, Issy. He's gorgeous."

"So exotic," Paula added. "How did you meet him?"

"At the conference."

"And you didn't want to go!" Tina stated.

Did she wish she had stayed home? Isabel wasn't sure.

"Wait a minute," Claire said. "We're forgetting something here in our admiration of Joshua's many fine attributes."

Everyone looked at her.

"He also got her pregnant. Issy's *pregnant,* you guys!"

Kelly was shaking her head. "I know!"

"How do you feel about it?" Cristine asked.

Isabel laughed nervously. "To be honest? Terrified. I feel like I'm too old for this!"

"You're not too old," Paula protested. "Women in Europe have children into their fifties. I remember reading about a woman who was sixty-four, who carried her daughter's child for her."

Claire grinned. "Bless you, Paula, for your retention of obscure facts."

"They'll probably do a caesarean," Kelly said. "Less stress on you and the baby to not go through labor."

"Look guys," Isabel said, coming farther into the room and sitting on her coffee table. "I know how insane this sounds. Me. At fifty. Unmarried and—"

"Forget unmarried," Tina interrupted. "Nobody is going to judge you today. You probably didn't think you could even get pregnant."

"I didn't!"

Cristine was nodding. "I know it's a shock, Issy. But have you thought it all out? Are you ready for this? Take my word for it: Your life is never going to be yours again."

"I know," Isabel murmured. "I've already seen Kate Abrams, and she said she wasn't worried. I've tried to think of everything, both sides of the coin. I know it's not going to be easy. I know I'm starting at this far too late in the game. But I also know that I've wanted a child since I married Chuck. I tried to accept being childless while I was married, and then, after Chuck, I was resigned to it. And now . . . well, to be honest, if I don't travel out into the future . . . it's like I'm being blessed with this miracle. Like the universe is telling me it's never too late."

"It isn't too late, Issy," Tina agreed. "And you'll have us. Whatever you need."

Isabel smiled and sniffed. "Thanks. I knew I could depend on the Gang for—"

"Hold on," Cristine interrupted. "What about this Joshua? Is he no longer in the picture?"

"I don't know. I don't think so, though. He doesn't know

about this. Like I told Claire, he's a free spirit and probably wouldn't want to be tied down."

"Tied down?" Kelly asked, a note of anger in her voice. "*Tied down?* This guy got you pregnant—and okay, okay, I realize you didn't think you'd need protection, but he is the father. Not only do you deserve to tell him, he deserves to know. Raising a child alone, Issy, is hard work. And the child deserves to have the father in its life in some way if possible."

"In an ideal situation I would agree with you, Kelly. But this isn't ideal. He's far too young for me and . . . and I don't think he could stick around to raise a child."

"First of all," Tina began, "he wasn't too young for you to sleep with him. Sorry, Issy, but that's the truth, isn't it? And sticking around to raise his own child? He needs to know there is going to *be* a child to make that decision. You have to tell him."

"She doesn't know where he is," Claire said.

"So what's his last name?" Paula asked. "We could start on the internet."

Everyone was looking at her, expecting an answer.

Isabel's throat was so tight she could barely breathe.

"She doesn't know his last name," Claire whispered, saving Isabel from saying it.

They all tried not to show their surprise, but failed, and the silence was painful.

"Look, no judging here," Claire stated to the Gang. "Which one of us wouldn't have been swept off our feet by that man? You saw him at the bar. Every single one of us at that table was hoping he was singing to us. Only it was Issy. And you know what? I'm glad it was her. I'm thrilled she came out of mourning and years of celibacy, and I'm jealous as all hell that it was the gorgeous singer, but overjoyed that if she waited seven years for sex it was with him. You tell me if you were wearing her shoes, which one of you could have resisted that man?"

"But she's pregnant," Paula whispered. "I'm glad for her too, but now there's a consequence. A child."

"Don't you think I've tried to look at this from every side?" Isabel demanded. "If you think I haven't beaten myself up over this, you're mistaken. I know how foolish I must look, and you guys love me. Imagine going out in public . . ." She couldn't hold back the tears any longer.

Cristine reached out and took Isabel's hands. "You hold your head up high, Isabel Calloway. And if anyone dares to say anything to you, you tell them what you told us. It's a miracle. A blessed event. And don't you let anyone tell you differently."

Sniffling, Isabel nodded.

Claire cleared her throat. "Okay, so from what Isabel told me yesterday, her biggest fear is her age. That something might happen to her and the child will be left alone. I told her she has us, right?"

Everyone nodded.

"Right," Claire answered for the group. "And if she should get hit by a bus, God forbid, then she's going to make me this child's guardian and I'll take over. So there's nothing to worry about on that end either."

"You?" Paula asked, unable to keep the surprise out of her voice.

"Yes, me," Claire stated. "Why? Do you have a problem with that?"

"Well . . ." Paula looked uncomfortable.

Tina laughed. "Face it, Claire, you aren't the most maternal woman in the room."

Claire's jaw dropped. "I can be maternal!"

Everyone else joined the laughter.

"Well, it's nice to see what the group thinks of me," Claire said, sounding hurt.

"I have great faith in Claire," Isabel said, smiling at her friend. "If the time ever came she would step up to the plate beautifully."

"Thank you, Isabel," Claire answered, glaring at the rest of the women. "I am *so* maternal," she reiterated to them.

They all laughed at her childish response, even Isabel. "Hey, is anyone going to say congratulations to me?"

In a better mood, the group crowded around her, kissing her cheek, hugging her, making plans for a baby shower, and Isabel felt uplifted by their support.

Maybe she could do this after all.

She had the Yellow Brick Road Gang behind her, and no one could ask for a more united front. And then she thought of Jen, in the kitchen alone.

Alone. Her heart went out to the younger woman.

"C'mon," she said, standing up. "Let's help poor Jen with the dishes."

They all stood up and made their way into the kitchen, still talking about baby showers.

"Issy, I have all of Angelique's newborn things to give you."

"I have Conor's crib," Paula said. "It's a little worn after five kids, but we could paint it or—"

"Thanks," Isabel said, gathering up the cloth napkins from the dining room table. "But I've waited a long time for this to happen. And now that I've accepted it, I have some dreaming to do. But thanks anyway. I'll let you know if I need anything."

"She's right," Cristine said, heading for the kitchen. "I wanted everything to be my choice too. Go ahead and dream, Issy. You deserve it."

And in that moment, Isabel felt the first swelling of peace in days.

She was going to have this baby.

A baby!

Later that night Isabel was in bed . . . dreaming. She placed her hand on her lower abdomen and sighed. "Welcome, little one," she whispered into the darkened room. "I promise I'll try to be the best mother I can."

There was that old wives' tale of waiting until you were past the first trimester before buying anything or dreaming of the future. She couldn't wait. And anyway Kate Abrams had said she was heading into the second trimester, so dreaming was allowed. She pictured herself showing, growing bigger. In her day maternity outfits had been unattractive tents. Now pregnant women proudly showed off their bellies, wearing clothes that outlined their changing figures. What did they call it now? The bump?

She grinned. Maybe this could be fun. She worked at home, so she would be with the baby all day. When clients came, she'd hire a sitter. And she couldn't wait to begin redecorating the bedroom closest to hers and transforming it into a nursery.

A boy or a girl?

She honestly didn't care. Closing her eyes, she prayed, *Please, please, let my baby be healthy.* She would start those prenatal vitamins tomorrow, and she would start walking. Maybe Jen would join her.

Thinking about Jen, Isabel wondered where Marcia was. If she didn't hear from her soon, she was going to call her publisher. She'd already tried her house phone several times. The woman couldn't just disappear like this. Jen was going to need Marcia's support, and the sooner they reconciled the better for all involved.

And Joshua . . .

Where are you?

Was he ever coming back? And if he did, what reaction would he have to her news?

It wasn't that she wanted to tie him down, not really. Just because her nature leaned toward marriage and commitment, that didn't mean his reaction was going to match hers. He wanted to evolve to a higher dimension. That meant he wasn't hanging around.

So she was going to do this alone. No man. No husband. Just her and a child.

"I will make it up to you," she whispered. "We'll have a good life. . . ."

But a part of her wished with all her heart that Joshua would want to play some role in the life of their child. That is, if she ever got the chance to tell him he was going to be a father.

She opened her eyes and looked out the bedroom window to the dark sky.

Where are you . . . ?

Chapter

16

ISABEL DROVE INTO STANTON WITH HER HANDS GRIP-
ping the steering wheel. She was filled with a mixture of
worry and anger. After days of waiting for Marcia to make
an appearance—even a phone call would have sufficed—
Isabel had called Marcia's publisher and found out Marcia
had been home for three days. Three days and not a word!

She got the address from Jen, who had an identity card in
her purse, and decided it was time to confront Marcia about
her behavior. How dare she leave her sister like this, without
even a phone call? And talk about taking advantage of a favor. Not that Isabel minded sharing her home with Jen. She
didn't. It was like a younger cousin visiting, and Jen couldn't
be more helpful, but there were unresolved issues to be dealt
with, and ignoring every phone message wasn't the answer.
Jen couldn't remain with her indefinitely. There was a baby
coming, and Jen needed to become independent. She'd taken
Jen grocery shopping, something the younger woman had
never done. That had shown her how much else needed to be
done. There were things like getting a driver's permit and
then driving lessons, or even teaching her how to use public
transportation. And what about getting a GED, to finish her
education? These were things Marcia was going to have to
help her sister accomplish.

Slowing down in front of the brick colonial home, Isabel sighed. How she hated confrontation, but something had to be done. She parked her car in the empty driveway in front of the garage and got out into the bitter cold. Shivering, she walked up to the front door and saw a light on in the house. She rang the bell and waited.

Nothing.

She rang it again. And again.

Finally she pounded on the door. "Marcia," she yelled out. "I know you're home. I called your publisher. Now either answer the door, or I'm calling the police to break it down!"

Really! Did she think she could hide out forever? Angry, Isabel again pounded on the door. And then she heard the sound of the metal deadlock turning. Slowly, the door opened, and Isabel's jaw dropped as she saw Marcia standing before her in a stained bathrobe. Her once-perfect hair was greasy and tangled, as though it hadn't been brushed in days. "Are you all right?" Isabel asked, concern now replacing anger.

"Isabel . . . ," Marcia nearly slurred, slowly blinking as though she'd just awakened. "Hi," she added, raising her fingers and showing red nail polish that had chipped away.

"Marcia, why didn't you call when you returned? Are you sick?"

Marcia laughed and turned around, leaving the door open to the cold. "Sick. That's it. I'm sick," she answered, her words again sounding not quite right.

Isabel entered the house and closed the door behind her. "What is it? The flu?" She then noticed the living room was littered with newspapers, and the coffee table held empty glasses, a pizza box, and an empty bottle of Bombay gin.

Marcia was walking through the dining room into the kitchen, as though she'd been expecting Isabel all along. "I'm sick of it all!" she yelled back.

Isabel pushed newspapers to the side and sat down on the

sofa. Obviously, Marcia had been having one hell of a pity party, she thought, sighing as she waited for Marcia to join her.

Marcia walked back into the living room, her furry slippers slapping the floor, a glass in one hand and clutching her robe together with the other. "Did you hear me? I'm sick of it all, Isabel. I followed all the rules. I did everything right and look at me! *Look at me!* I'm ruined!"

"You are not ruined, Marcia," Isabel said firmly while unbuttoning her coat. "You're drunk and feeling sorry for yourself."

"Who has a better right?" Marcia demanded, plopping down on the edge of the sofa and bringing her glass to her mouth.

"Plenty of people do, Marcia. People who are homeless, who are in jail, who have life-threatening diseases." She paused, trying to control her annoyance. "Do you want me to go on? I can start with Africa and mothers watching their babies starve to death in their arms, or young girls who are raped by men with AIDS because they believe the myth that sex with a virgin is a cure."

"Okay, okay," Marcia moaned. "I get it."

"I don't think you really do," Isabel answered. "You're devastated, holed up in this house, drinking and letting yourself become a wreck. Why?"

Marcia snorted. "Why? You must have seen it. Even my publisher said it was a disaster. I froze."

Isabel nodded and sighed. "Yeah, you did freeze. But it's not the end of the world, Marcia. One bad TV interview. Big deal. That was last week. Who even remembers it?"

"My publisher and any other person who was watching. They attacked me!" she cried and began to sniffle.

"They did blindside you," Isabel agreed. "But you did put yourself out there with that book."

"They were cruel. That bitch!" Marcia's tears ran down her cheeks. "She set me up."

Isabel sighed again, praying for patience. "Wipe your tears, Marcia. I hate to be the one to tell you, but you simply aren't that important. It happened. It's over. No one's bringing it up again, except you. You're doing this to yourself. And have you given any thought at all to Jennifer?"

"I've given my life to my sister," Marcia stated while wiping her cheek on the sleeve of her robe. "I deserve a few days to myself to recover."

Isabel laughed. "*This*"—and she held her hand out to the littered coffee table—"is recovery? C'mon, Marcia, you'd be the first therapist on record to use Bombay Blue Sapphire as a tool of recovery. You're wallowing in a pity party."

"I have a right!" Marcia insisted.

"Okay, so you've done it. Now get over it and take a shower. Your sister is waiting."

Marcia was shaking her head. "Oh, it's so easy for you, isn't it, Isabel? Always the one with the answers. Do you know I envied you once?" She held her glass of water out and pointed to her with it. "You had it all. A great career. A handsome, loving husband. A beautiful home. People seemed to gravitate to you at all the conferences, like they just wanted to be near you. I thought I could do it too, but how was I supposed to make it happen when I've been taking care of my sister since I was fifteen years old? I'm still living in my parents' house, for God's sake! How was I supposed to find a man to marry me *and* take on my sister, who was like a living ghost? No man wants that responsibility."

She put her glass down on the table and ran her hands over her face. "And then I get my shot, my one chance at making a name for myself, and I blow it on national TV. Do you even know what it's like to be a failure?" she asked, her eyes wide with misery. "To know your chance is over? To have the brass ring in your fingertips and watch it slip away? I'm thirty-three years old, and the clock is ticking."

"You're still a young woman, Marcia. Thirty-three is prime time. And I agree you had to grow up fast and assume mature responsibilities, but believe me, the universe really does give us second chances."

"Easy for you to say. You've had it all. But then you went into hiding when your husband died. You could have been something, Isabel, and you threw it away. You took years to get back in the game, so who are you to deny me a couple of days?"

Isabel unclenched her jaw. "Losing a husband of twenty years and being humbled on television aren't exactly the same thing, Marcia."

"National television. It went out all over the country."

"I'm not going to sit here and debate this with someone whose ego has been bruised. I'm just waiting to see if you're even interested enough in your sister to ask how she is."

Marcia sat up higher and straightened the front of her robe. "How is Jen?" she asked with a false smile.

"Why don't you get a shower and come see for yourself?"

Marcia shook her head. "I don't want a shower, and I don't want to get dressed. I don't want to come to your house, and I don't want Jen and all her problems to come crashing in on me again. Not now."

Isabel was stunned. "Then when, Marcia? You can't simply drop your sister at my house and think she's going to disappear."

Marcia didn't answer her.

"And you can't sit here and drink yourself into oblivion and escape reality. For God's sake, Marcia, take some responsibility for this mess. You wrote that book attacking working mothers. Did you think they were all going to shut up and let you get away with it? Carole Shelly, who is obviously a working mother, was probably speaking for the hundreds of thousands of women who are forced to leave their children and go outside the home to work in order to pay bills and keep their kids in schools. Do you think any of them actually enjoy leaving their children to others?"

Marcia sighed and shook her head. "This society of greed, of getting ahead and buying kids tennis shoes that cost over a hundred dollars and—"

"No woman left her children to buy hundred-dollar shoes," Isabel interrupted. "So before you launch into your prepared speech, be glad you didn't include that one on television. *Get over it,* Marcia. You're still a young woman. While you're here medicating your life away with alcohol, it's passing you by." She stood up and began buttoning her coat. "And I'm not going to waste any more time listening to your sad story. We've all got sad stories to tell. You're young. You're healthy. And when you aren't drinking and having a pity party, you're an intelligent woman. You can pull your life together with ease. So do it, Marcia. And then come see your sister."

She walked to the door and opened it. "You'll be surprised at the progress Jen's made. She's not the same girl you brought to my house. She's a fine young woman who deserves some support."

About to leave, she heard Marcia ask, "Did she see it?"

"The television show?"

Marcia nodded.

"She saw it. We watched it together."

"Did she say anything?"

Isabel sighed. "She said, 'Now Marcia knows how it feels to lose her voice.'"

Marcia simply stared at her as she closed the door.

§

Isabel opened the front door to her own home and heard Jen laughing. Curious, she didn't even hang up her coat, but walked through the living room toward the back of the house and the voices coming from the kitchen. It sounded like a male voice. Low and deep.

Her hand was actually shaking as she pushed the door into the kitchen.

Please, please . . . let it be him.

She stood, her mouth open, watching Jen wrap her arms around a thin young man with platinum hair. He appeared to be in his early twenties and had a dazzling smile as he took Jen into his arms and kissed her forehead.

It was then they noticed her at the door.

"Isabel! He's here!" she said, holding the man's hand and pulling him with her. "This is Manny. My Manny." Jen was near bursting with pride.

"How . . ." She had to swallow to bring moisture back into her mouth. "Hello," she whispered, staring into the man's magnetic friendly eyes.

"Isabel." He said her name like it was an endearment, filled with warmth and happiness. "I am honored to be in your presence."

"You . . . you're Manny?" she asked, looking around the kitchen for anyone else.

Joshua wasn't there.

He nodded. "That is what Jen calls me. I am known as Emmanuel."

"Emmanuel," Isabel repeated, trying to keep it together. " 'God with us.' I should have figured that out."

Manny smiled. "Thank you for helping Jennifer. Under your care she is truly blossoming."

Isabel nodded and bit her bottom lip. She had to ask it. Feeling like a teenager, she mustered up her courage. "Is Joshua here?"

"No, just Manny came," Jen answered, looking up at her beloved with happiness. "But Joshua did find him."

"Good," she murmured, attempting to keep her voice steady

and not give in to the overwhelming feeling of disappointment. "Well, I should leave you two alone. I imagine you have a lot to discuss."

"Manny said he's going to be with me during the pregnancy, Isabel. Isn't that wonderful?"

She would not cry. Not now. Plastering a big smile on her face, she said, "That's great, Jen. I'm so happy for you."

Jennifer was literally beaming with happiness.

"I'm just going to hang up my coat," she said, wanting to get away from the couple before she burst into tears. "Welcome, Emmanuel. I . . . ah, I'll speak with you both later, all right?"

She pushed herself out of the kitchen and began unbuttoning her coat. Not long ago, she had wanted Manny to answer all her questions about leaving Jen alone to deal with everything. Now she was walking in Jen's shoes. Alone. Left. Pregnant. Thank God she had the group for support.

Hanging up her coat, she heard Jen laugh again, and the sound of it only made her more upset. God, she didn't resent Jen's happiness. If anyone deserved it, it was Jen, but where was Joshua, and why was he staying away? Maybe he'd had it with her quarreling, as though she knew better what was best for everyone. They'd argued when she'd sent him away. But she hadn't known she was pregnant at the time, and as far as knowing what was best for anyone . . . what a laugh.

She wished their last time together hadn't been so disagreeable. Why would he want to come back? He'd accomplished his mission, with her and in finding Manny, and now he was ascending to a higher dimension. He'd told her that was his intention. Why hadn't she wanted to believe him?

She walked up the stairs, needing more than anything to lie down and forget her confrontation with Marcia, her disappointment at Joshua's absence. She simply had to get herself under control and surrender to what is, not what she wanted. How long would it take her to accept the the present and stop yearning for something beyond her reach?

She was tired of fixing lives when her own was in such a mess.

Maybe it was time to focus on herself . . . and her baby.

The phone rang, and Isabel hurried into her bedroom to answer it. She picked up the receiver and sat on the bed. "Hello?"

"Isabel?"

"Yes?"

"Hi, this is Linda Winston. My son Terry and I came to see you and—"

"Of course," Isabel interrupted, not wanting the woman to think she'd been forgotten. "How are you? How's Terry doing?"

"Actually he's doing great. He's reading on a fourth-grade level. It's like a miracle—like he's had everything inside of him waiting to come out."

"That's wonderful," Isabel said with a smile, picturing the cute boy in his football jacket. "Good for him."

"The reason I'm calling you, besides to thank you for saving my son, is because my sister-in-law is the talent coordinator for *A.M. Philly*. Do you ever watch it?"

"Sometimes," Isabel said cautiously.

"Well, she's so impressed with Terry's progress in such a short time that she wants to put together a show on children with learning challenges. We both think you'd be perfect for showing an alternative method of helping them—one that really works without medication."

Linda was waiting for a reaction, yet with lightning speed Isabel pictured Marcia being attacked and freezing on television. "I don't know, Linda. It's very flattering, but I'd like to think about it."

"Can I have my sister-in-law call you? Her name is Mary Ellen Fenerty."

Isabel didn't know a polite way out. "Sure. But could you give me a few days? I have a lot going on right now."

"Absolutely. Sometime in the next few days, then?"

"That would be fine."

"Great. And thank you again, Isabel. You seem to have unlocked something in Terry, and he's almost at grade level and gets to stay in his school. Words can't thank you enough for what you've done for our family."

Isabel's smile was tight. "You're very welcome, but it was Terry who did it for himself. I simply showed him there was a path to follow. It was his choice whether or not to take the steps. Please tell him congratulations for me. Tell him it looks like he's made the winning touchdown in the Super Bowl."

Linda laughed. "I will. He'll like that."

"Well, thank you for calling, Linda."

"No, thank you, Isabel. And I'll tell Mary Ellen to call you soon."

She said good-bye, hung up the phone, and stared at it.

Karma. Now that was fast.

Here she'd been judging Marcia, and the opportunity to walk in her shoes had presented itself. First Jen and now Marcia.

She looked up to the ceiling of her bedroom.

"I want my own shoes back!" she called out, feeling like her life had been taken over by outsiders.

She slipped out of her shoes and then stood up to pull back the comforter. Snuggling under it, Isabel stared out her bedroom window to the barren branches of a tree and felt her eyes burn with tears.

She didn't want to go on television and expose herself, especially her pregnant self. She didn't want to debate a medical doctor who thought giving kids pills to make them acceptable to the school system was standard procedure. She didn't want to judge anyone anymore about anything.

Karma. The more she thought about it, the more it seemed that not judging another was simply self-protection. If she didn't want to walk in that person's shoes, she had better learn to keep her thoughts to herself.

After all, she'd lost Joshua because of it.

And that did her in. After a difficult day, all she wanted to do was sleep away whatever remained of the evening. She didn't want to confront Manny about any plans. She didn't want to see Marcia show up at her door. She didn't want to hear Jen's well-deserved squeals of joy. And she didn't want to think about appearing on television.

She just wanted her old, simple, predictable life back.

But her old life was now forever gone—she was going to have a baby.

Alone.

Sniffling, she realized Marcia's pity party—to just wallow in the unfairness of life—now looked very appealing. When was she going to stop judging, thinking she knew best? Jen's simple faith in Manny had never wavered, while Isabel had judged Manny and Joshua both. And Marcia too. And now she was judging the judging. It was an endless loop of confusion that seemed to have landed her in a position to finally understand what Joshua had tried to tell her before he left.

If you judge another, you will be given the opportunity to walk in their shoes.

Bloody damn karma!

Chapter

17

AT FIVE-THIRTY IN THE MORNING ISABEL WOKE UP TO go to the bathroom. She'd slept right through the night. Groggy and hungry, she splashed water on her face and then looked at herself in the mirror. Sleep had done wonders, she thought, leaning in closer. Even in the harsh bathroom lights, she looked refreshed, maybe even . . . younger?

She dried her face and looked again. The fine lines around her eyes seemed to have filled out. Her skin seemed tighter, more vibrant.

Well . . .

Must be the hormones kicking in again. And then she looked down to her belly, which was, surprisingly, rubbing up against the sink.

There it was.

The bump. Appearing overnight as a definite swelling.

In awe, Isabel ran her hands over her abdomen. It was like she really was in her second trimester. This was too fast, too sudden. None of this was normal. How could she go about her life if she kept expanding at this rate? She'd be huge. . . .

And then her heart seemed to skip a beat as she thought about Cristine. She remembered walking into Cristine's home and being shocked by how quickly her friend's pregnancy was progressing. She even remembered thinking Cristine's baby had to have been Charlie's, Cristine's old partner.

Cristine.

What if . . . ? It was too incredible to think that Cristine and Daniel might be like her and Joshua, or Jen and Manny. But there was definitely something almost ethereal about Daniel. Like Joshua. Like Jen's Manny. And it would completely explain the confusion over Cristine's pregnancy. A sizzle of electricity ran up her spine, and Isabel couldn't help feeling as though she was on to something.

She needed to see her friend and tell her the whole truth about Joshua. Maybe, just maybe, if Cristine didn't think she was crazy, she would have some answers.

Now that she had a plan, Isabel headed for the shower and turned on the water. She would take scones to Cristine, and then she would come clean, about everything. She needed to trust someone now that she was all alone in this, and Cristine might just be the one to help her understand what was happening to her body and also to her heart.

It took every shred of patience to wait until eight o'clock, but Isabel busied herself baking scones, something she hadn't done since Chuck's death. With every kneading of dough, Isabel sent out a wish for Cristine to understand her and not call out the men in white coats.

That was always her fear. Having worked with mental patients for years before opening her own practice, Isabel knew how easily one could be labeled. How many times had she thought the only difference between herself and some of the patients was that she had the keys to get out? People were terribly frightened if one left the herd of conformity. How many times had she seen experiments where people who knew the right answer said the wrong answer just to conform with those who'd answered first? Very few wanted to be the odd one out, and so people tended to betray themselves for the security of being part of the herd. Well, she'd definitely left the herd, that's for sure. And she might as well be wearing a sign saying ODD ONE OUT. There was nothing sane or normal about her situation, and her pregnancy wasn't conforming to any known medical research. *The New England Journal of Medicine* would laugh at the very idea of accelerated pregnancy.

But maybe Cristine wouldn't.

She knocked on her friend's door at precisely eight o'clock while admiring Cristine's Christmas decorations and hoping she wasn't waking the household. Waiting by the front door, Isabel felt nervous but knew she was doing the right thing. She had to trust someone. Nothing about Cristine's pregnancy had been normal, and Cristine had always been evasive when speaking about Daniel. Why hadn't she questioned it more before now? Had she secretly thought that Cristine must have known Daniel before Charlie left?

With no more time to contemplate answers, Isabel plastered a smile on her face as the front door opened.

"Issy!" Cristine exclaimed, surprised by her appearance. "This is unexpected."

"I know I should have called," Isabel quickly said. "Did I wake you?"

Cristine shook her head and opened the door wider. "Come in out of the cold."

Isabel walked into the foyer and held out her basket. "I baked scones and thought maybe we could have a chat if you aren't busy with Angelique."

"Let's go into the kitchen," Cristine said, running her hand through her tousled hair and then drawing her silk robe tighter around her. "The baby isn't awake yet, so we'll have to be quiet."

"I can do quiet," Isabel whispered, following her friend into the kitchen. She perched on a stool by the counter and placed the basket of scones before her. "I'm sorry to come unannounced like this, Cris, but I need to speak to you."

"Are you all right?" Cristine asked, pulling out another mug from the cabinet. "It's not the pregnancy, is it?" She looked over her shoulder to gauge Isabel's expression.

"In a way, it is," Isabel murmured, watching Cristine pour coffee into the extra mug.

"What's wrong?"

"Well, you see . . . the thing is . . ."

Cristine turned around and faced her friend. "Just say it. Are you spotting?"

Isabel shook her head. "I went to see Kate Abrams, and she said I'm in my second trimester, which isn't really possible medically, considering I haven't known Joshua for four months."

Cristine's eyes widened. "And . . . ?"

"And I remember you when you were first pregnant with Angelique, and because your pregnancy was so . . . well, unusual, we all thought Charlie must have been the father, because you'd said Daniel came into your life after Charlie left."

"Daniel *is* Angelique's father," Cristine said with emphasis.

"I know that. We all do now. But there's something about Daniel that reminds me of Joshua."

Cristine straightened her shoulders. "Really? And what is that?"

Isabel took a deep breath. "He's unusual, isn't he? Sometimes, I swear I can see lights around him and . . . well . . . I saw those same lights around Joshua. Please don't think I'm crazy, Cristine, but Joshua . . . he's not like any of us. He's . . ." She was so afraid to just say it.

"From another dimension?" Cristine asked in a frightened whisper, clutching the coffee mug to her chest.

"*Yes!*" Isabel pronounced in relief. "Daniel. Is he . . . ?"

Cristine simply nodded as the two women stared at each other in disbelief.

"I thought I was all alone in this," Cristine finally said in an awed voice. "And now to find out you too, Issy . . . your Joshua is like Daniel. It's . . . *amazing*."

"Not just us, Cristine," Isabel said in a hushed voice, filled with emotion. "Jen too. You're right; she is pregnant. The father's name is Emmanuel, another dimension traveler. What the *hell* is going on?"

Cristine leaned on the counter, as though she needed support. "Ohmygod . . . Jen?"

Nodding, fighting to keep her emotions under control, Isabel said, "How ironic is it that Marcia brings her sister to me, telling me Jen has been raped, and then I find out that Jen's pregnant by what she calls her imaginary friend? I mean, I'm probably the only therapist in this country who wouldn't have labeled her delusional, because I had just met my own!"

"What has Joshua told you? I mean, Daniel said that I'm not the only one, but—"

Isabel burst into tears of relief before Cristine could finish her sentence. She wasn't crazy. She wasn't alone. Immediately she felt herself being enfolded in Cristine's arms.

"I know, I know," Cristine murmured with sympathy. "I felt the same way. It all seems bizarre, doesn't it? Totally overwhelming."

Isabel nodded, reaching in her coat pocket for a crumpled tissue. She blew her nose hard as Cristine stroked her back in circles of comfort. "He's gone," she wailed. "We had a big fight, and I sent him to look for Jen's Manny. He hasn't come back."

"He will, he will," Cristine whispered. "He'll find this Manny, and then—"

"Manny showed up yesterday," Isabel interrupted, dabbing at her eyes. "But not Joshua."

Cristine bit her bottom lip. "Okay, so . . . take off your coat," she said, as though the thought had just popped into her head and would fix anything. "And we'll have a cup of coffee, decaf, and figure this thing out."

Isabel slipped out of her coat, and Cristine folded it and put it on the other stool.

"Look at me, Cris," Isabel demanded, standing up and holding her blouse tight around her belly. "How can I be this big in a month? I can't even zip my jeans anymore. Nothing is making any sense to me."

"I know," Cristine said, staring first at Isabel's stomach and then up to her face. "Look, everything will speed up now for you. You . . . your baby . . . you're both vibrating at a higher rate than others. The father isn't a being from this dimension. You have to accept that as your new normal. You'll only drive yourself crazy if you don't. Believe me, Issy, I almost did exactly that."

"How did you accept *any* of this?" Isabel demanded, fighting not to cry again. "I can't believe you just said the father isn't from this dimension! Like who would ever even think those words would come out of your mouth? Or anyone's mouth, for that matter?"

Cristine smiled sympathetically. "I know how you're feeling. Completely overwhelmed. I didn't accept it easily either, I'll tell you that. Daniel had to be very patient with me. But it's so worth it, Issy. It's been the biggest blessing in my life. And I can't imagine it now without Daniel or Angelique in it."

Isabel sat back on the stool and picked up the warm coffee mug. Staring down into the dark liquid, she murmured, "You have Daniel to help you get through it. I've driven away Joshua." She lifted her head and looked at her friend. "I am so scared, Cristine. How can I explain any of this to anyone? I can't go back to see Kate Abrams. She'll never believe me."

"That's why I didn't go back," Cristine said, walking around the counter to get her cup of coffee. "So many times I wanted to tell the group, but I was scared too. It is unexplainable, if you aren't in the midst of it, I'll give you that."

"But I'm a high-risk pregnancy. Women my age are going

through menopause, waiting for grandchildren, not having babies of their own!"

"So? You're an RN. Take your own blood pressure every week. Check your blood sugar levels. What more would Kate do?"

"She'd do an ultrasound, to make sure it's normal."

Cristine reached across the counter and clasped Isabel's hand. "Honey, I'll tell you again, nothing in your life is ever going to be like the old normal again. You have to accept that, or you'll drive yourself nuts."

Isabel withdrew her hand and held her forehead as she leaned on the counter. "But I so wanted normal."

Cristine chuckled. "So did I. But I got a miracle instead. Just like you."

Isabel looked up. "So I'm not crazy?"

Shaking her head, Cristine came back and sat next to Isabel. "It's as though you're walking in two worlds, on a tightrope, trying to maintain your balance. Nothing is as you expect, and your equilibrium is way off. But little by little you find your place of balance. Like Daniel couldn't stay with me for long periods of time. He couldn't maintain his human form for over six or seven hours. I resented that at first, but now it's getting better. He's up to eight or nine hours now, so sometimes we actually get to spend the entire day together or I wake up in his arms. It's doable, Isabel. And I would rather have eight hours with Daniel than twenty-four with anyone else."

Was she really having this bizarre conversation with her dear friend? Cristine was talking about all this like it wasn't insane. "What about Angelique?" Isabel asked hesitantly, trying to keep her worry under control. "Is she . . . ?"

"Like Daniel?" Cristine asked, supplying the question.

Isabel nodded.

"She's like Daniel. And she's also like me. She has . . . gifts, though."

"What kind of gifts? She doesn't disappear on you, does she? I couldn't handle that!"

Cristine laughed. "No, she doesn't disappear on me. Her gifts seem to be in healing others. Like this little girl who had leukemia. Even while Angelique was still inside me, this girl swears she helped her go into remission."

"My God . . ." Isabel was stunned.

"I know. And I was beginning a cold a few weeks ago. I was miserable with sneezing and a runny nose and could only breathe through my mouth. Angelique cured me. She ran her tiny hands over my forehead and sinuses. I thought she was just being playful or sweet, and didn't want her to catch it; but within minutes I could breathe through my nose again, and I haven't sneezed since. You have to be prepared for anything, Issy. Your child will definitely be gifted in some way. Daniel says that's what is happening now. It's time for the females to help balance out the darkness surrounding this planet."

Isabel nodded. "That's what Joshua said too, but I thought he meant like women getting more involved with politics. Electing a female president. I didn't think it would be by having babies! This is like being in the middle of some bad science fiction movie!"

Cristine smiled. "Issy, may I ask you something?"

Isabel shrugged. "Why not? You now know my darkest secret."

"Okay, you and Joshua . . . did he force you in any way?"

Isabel cringed, then shook her head. "No. The truth is I'm pregnant because I initiated sex. God . . . now *that* is my darkest secret!"

Cristine laughed. "Okay, you willingly had sex, so don't be embarrassed. And don't forget I saw your Joshua. Claire's right. I don't know who could resist him."

"Claire!" Isabel covered her mouth in horror. "What are we going to do about her?"

Nodding, Cristine said, "She will be a problem. You don't know how many times I've wanted to tell her, to tell all of you, but . . ."

"But who'd believe you, right?'

"Right."

"If it hadn't happened to you, you'd think the person was delusional and in need of medication."

"I didn't want to take that chance," Cristine said, and sipped her coffee. "I just don't think the group is ready to accept that two of their members are in love with beings from a different dimension."

Isabel almost spit out her coffee. "Who said anything about being in love?"

"Oh, get off it, Issy. You can tell just by looking at you. Pregnancy agrees with you, by the way. You look fabulous. Maybe younger too. So how could you not be in love?"

"I was in heat, not love. Love takes some time to develop or—"

"Or," Cristine interrupted, "it can happen in an instant. What do you think those songs about looks across a crowded dance floor are about? It's something inside of you that you just *know*. In a timeless moment you know you are meant to be with that someone, and there's no logical reasoning behind it."

Isabel sighed. "Well, it's an arguable point in my case since Joshua is gone. I followed my body, instead of my head, and that's why I'm sitting in your kitchen having this insane discussion."

Smiling with compassion, Cristine said, "I think you followed your heart, Issy."

"Why do you insist that love is involved? It was lust, pure and simple."

"Are you saying that you didn't even *think* you might be falling in love with him?"

Isabel paused, unwilling to admit the truth.

"I'm right, then. You do love him."

"C'mon, Cristine. How many women confuse love with just being horny? After all, it had been over seven years since I'd been with a man." She then laughed. "And Joshua isn't even technically a human man. He can disappear in a swirl of lights anytime he wants. Which he did . . . obviously not wanting to be in my presence again."

"Do you want me to have Daniel try and find him?"

Isabel quickly turned to her friend. "No! Promise me you won't tell Daniel about this. If Joshua comes back, it has to be because he wants to, not because I've sent someone out looking for him to drag him back."

Cristine nodded. "Okay." She sighed deeply. "So do we break into the scones now? Because I have a feeling the baby is awake and waiting for me to get her."

"I'm not hungry," Isabel said, sliding off the stool. "I should get going."

"Stay, Issy," Cristine pleaded. "We can spend the day together."

She shook her head. "Thanks, but now that I know the truth I want some time to think about it." She reached around Cristine and picked up her coat. Smiling, she added, "I can't tell you how relieved I am that I'm not alone in this insanity, Cris."

Cristine took Isabel's coat and held it open for her to slide her arms into it. "It's not insanity, Issy. It's your new normal, and it's a miracle. All those years, and you're going to have a baby now."

With her coat on, Isabel turned to her friend. "You know it was Jen who told me I was pregnant. I thought she was transferring onto me, but she kept it up, and so I bought three pregnancy tests to prove her wrong."

"Three?" Cristine asked with a laugh.

Isabel nodded. "I thought the first one had to be defective, so I went out and bought two others. I couldn't see how it was possible. In truth, I still don't. I keep thinking I'm going to wake up from this dream."

"Makes you question reality, doesn't it?"

Isabel nodded.

"So which is real? What we've been taught to believe? Or what we're experiencing right now?"

"I don't know," Isabel murmured, turning toward the front of the house.

Behind her, she heard Cristine singing in a low voice:

"Row, row, row your boat, gently down the stream. Merrily, merrily, merrily, merrily . . . life is but a dream."

She couldn't get that nursery rhyme out of her head as she drove home. Was life a dream we made up each morning when we awoke? It was called daydreaming. We thought about our day, what we wanted to create in it, and went about trying to achieve it. From brushing our teeth to mergers of large corporations . . . Did we daydream our reality into being? She knew the importance of the subconscious. She'd spent her adult life trying to help others gain access to it. Was that the secret?

Our thoughts really do create our reality?

Had she been so fearful Joshua would leave her that she'd created the circumstances to make it happen?

She had no more time to think about it as she turned into her driveway and saw a red Jaguar parked in her usual space. As she turned off the ignition she could see a woman opening the door.

Marcia.

Isabel sighed. This she didn't need. Not now.

Resigned to once more being pulled into others' problems, Isabel opened the car door and got out. "Morning," she called out.

Marcia didn't look quite so bad as yesterday. Obviously, she had taken a shower and washed her hair. There was little makeup, though, and there was also a firmness about her posture. "Good morning, Isabel," Marcia said as they both walked closer to each other. "I rang the doorbell, but no one answered."

"As you can see I wasn't home."

"You just left Jen?"

Isabel smiled, not willing to be baited into an argument. "Jennifer is quite able to take care of herself, Marcia. Perhaps she didn't open the door because she wasn't awake yet. I left a little before eight, and she was still sleeping."

"Well, it's going on ten now, and I'm here to pick her up."

"Why don't you come in and have a cup of coffee? There are things we need to discuss."

"Fine," Marcia answered in a short voice, obviously not pleased by the situation.

Isabel unlocked the back door and found Jen, dressed in jeans and a white blouse, in the kitchen making breakfast. The aroma of pancakes filled the room.

"Good morning, Jen. Marcia's here," Isabel said before the woman actually walked into the kitchen.

Jen seemed to freeze, the spatula held upright before her.

"She's *cooking?* Alone?" Marcia demanded of Isabel. "How could you leave her like this?"

"Hold on, Marcia," Isabel said, sliding out of her coat and hanging it on the hook by the door. "I told you the Jen you left is not the one you're picking up. She's been cooking for some time now."

Jen turned around and looked at her sister. "Hello, Marcia."

Marcia seemed startled by the direct, normal salutation. "Jen?"

No one said anything for a few awkward moments, and so Isabel asked, "Would you like a cup of coffee, Marcia? I'm afraid it's decaffinated."

"Yes," Marcia murmured. "Sure. Thanks. . . ."

"Why don't you take off your coat and sit down at the table?"

Jen was already busy pouring the coffee, and so Isabel took Marcia's coat and hung it up next to her own. Jen placed the coffee cup on the table, and Marcia sat down in front of it.

Neither sister spoke to the other.

Isabel poured herself a half a cup, added sugar and cream, and brought it to the table. She sat down on the other side of Marcia and left the opposite space for Jen to join them. "As you can see, Marcia, Jen is perfectly fine in the kitchen. She pores over cookbooks and tries recipes I wouldn't even dare attempt."

"I can't believe it!" Marcia whispered, staring at her sister, who was turning over a pancake in the skillet. "She's so . . . confident."

"Please don't speak about me like I'm not even in the room, Marcia," Jen said in a low voice, placing another pancake on the stack she had already prepared. She brought the plate to the table and then opened a cupboard and took out three plates. Opening a drawer, she grabbed three forks and knives, then began to arrange three place settings on the table.

"How long . . . ?" Marcia asked Isabel, who was secretly so proud of Jennifer that she wanted to hug her.

Talk about taking back your power. Isabel knew she couldn't have arranged a better display if she'd tried, as Jen went into the drawer and took out three cloth napkins and folded them neatly before placing them at each setting.

"Jen was interested in cooking almost immediately," Isabel said in answer to Marcia's question. "Weren't you, Jen? Remember we started with peanut butter and jelly sandwiches?"

Smiling, Jen nodded, and she placed a tin of maple syrup on the table beside the butter. She sat down next to Isabel and began to butter her pancakes.

"Well, dig in," Isabel told Marcia. She then turned to Jen and grinned. "I'm starved. I made scones for Cristine this morning, but I didn't get to eat yet. Thanks for breakfast, Jen."

"You're welcome, Isabel." She looked up to her sister. "Aren't you going to eat?"

"Didn't you hear me ring the bell?" Marcia asked, still looking at her sister as though she'd just met a stranger.

"I heard you. It wasn't my place to answer the door," Jen said, cutting into her pancakes. "Besides, I knew you were coming today, and I wanted to wait until Isabel was here before seeing you."

"Jen . . . when did you start speaking like this?" Marcia demanded in a shocked tone.

Jen smiled. "Since I got my voice back."

Marcia stared at her sister in silence.

Jen continued to eat her breakfast as though nothing extraordinary was happening. Isabel cleared her throat. "Marcia, why don't you taste the pancakes. They're very good."

"Thank you, Isabel," Jen said with a smile.

Even Isabel wasn't sure how this reunion was going to go. It seemed Jennifer was the only one who did.

"I'm not hungry," Marcia said, pushing the empty plate away from her. "But I would like some answers, now that you've decided to finally grace us with your voice, Jen."

Jennifer swallowed and put her fork down. "And what is it you would like to know?"

"I want the name of the person who raped you."

Isabel put her fork down and was about to say something when Jen surprised her by holding up her hand, as though to say *I'll take care of this.*

"First of all, Marcia, I can see how you would have come to that conclusion, but I wasn't raped."

"You had to have been . . ." Marcia seemed to suddenly

understand Jen's implication, and her jaw dropped along with the rest of her sentence.

Jen shook her head. "No. I'm in love."

"Love?" Marcia exclaimed in disbelief. "What could you possibly know about love?"

"For so long, Marcia, you've misunderstood me. You thought I was slow, that I couldn't understand what was happening around me. That I couldn't comprehend. I understood everything. I learned everything presented to me. I *chose* to shut down after our mother died because I thought she was the only one who could understand me. I was wrong. There were others; I just didn't know they existed then."

"Others? What are you talking about?"

Isabel sat in fascinated silence, marveling at how well Jen was handling everything.

"Our mother was . . . special," Jen began gently. "I'm not saying this to hurt you, but she and I had a special understanding between us. I knew what she was thinking. We would play games while you were in school. She would think of something, and I would find it. I don't know how I knew. But I did. And she would laugh when I brought back a belt or a picture. She told me I was going to help others one day, but I didn't believe her because I couldn't help her when she needed me. I knew she was getting weaker, but nothing I did seemed to help. When she died, I shut down in my grief. That's what Manny told me, and now I see it too. I was frightened because—"

"Hold up," Marcia said, raising her hand. "Manny? Who is Manny?"

"I am," a voice said as the kitchen door swung open. "I am Emmanuel. The father of Jennifer's child." He stood next to the table and smiled endearingly at Jen and then at her sister. "And you must be Marcia." He held out his hand. "It is a pleasure to finally meet in person."

Isabel's jaw dropped.

And she wasn't alone.

Marcia was slack-jawed as she stared up at the young handsome man in jeans holding his hand out to her.

Chapter

18

MARCIA TURNED HER HEAD. "ISABEL?" SHE ASKED, AS though Isabel could explain the strange man holding out his hand.

Isabel swallowed, as surprised as Marcia. "This is Emmanuel. Don't be rude, Marcia. Shake his hand."

Marcia hesitantly held out her hand. Manny closed his other hand over hers and smiled warmly.

"Please don't allow your fear to cloud your thinking, Marcia. I mean you no harm."

Marcia pulled her hand away and glared at Isabel, as though Isabel had allowed a stranger into their lives. She turned back to Emmanuel. "I don't fear you. I don't even know you."

Manny smiled and placed his hand on Jen's shoulder. "As I just said, I am the father of Jennifer's child. And could it be your fears are simply the unknown?"

Marcia was nervously biting at her bottom lip. "Then do you know you can be arrested? My sister was only seventeen when you took advantage of her."

"Marcia!" Jen shook her head. "How many times do you have to hear it? I love Manny. And he loves me. No one took advantage of anyone. I *love* him!" She paused, taking a deep breath. "Why can't you understand that?"

Marcia pushed back her chair. "Get your things, Jen. We're leaving."

"No, we're not," Jen answered. "You don't get to order me around any longer."

Marcia, in the midst of standing, froze. Slowly, she sank back to her seat and stared at her sister.

"Things have changed, Marcia," Jen said in a warmer voice. "You don't have to take care of me anymore. I'm eighteen now. I'm an adult. And I'd like to use some of the money Dad left in trust for me to get a place of my own."

"You . . . you know about the trust fund?" Marcia asked in shock.

Isabel felt like she was watching a fascinating tennis match as she looked from one sister to the other—and it seemed like the underdog had just scored big-time.

Jen smiled slightly. "I really wasn't slow. I heard everything everyone said around me. I learned the lessons when I sat in classrooms. I just didn't participate, so everyone assumed I couldn't learn. Like Isabel said, I have it all stored in my subconscious, and little by little I'm able to gain access to it. So yes, I heard you speaking to a man named Robert Andrews many times about my trust. You also have one, right?"

Marcia simply nodded, too taken a back to speak.

"So I was thinking I could get an apartment on my own now."

"Do you think you're ready for that?" Isabel asked.

"Manny has a friend who is going to let me stay with her until I find a place. We talked about it last night, and it's all arranged."

"Who's this friend?" Marcia asked Emmanuel in a suspicious voice.

"Her name is Grace," Manny answered smoothly. "She has a large house, and Jennifer is welcome to stay as long as—"

"For God's sake, Jen!" Marcia interrupted. "He knows

about your trust fund! How can you believe him? He'd tell
you anything to get his hands on your money!"

Isabel put her hand over her mouth as she watched Manny
throw back his head and laugh.

"Marcia, please rest your fears on that matter. I don't need
money. Jennifer does, but I don't."

Marcia glared up at him. "Oh yeah? And why not? Don't
tell me—you're independently wealthy?"

Manny looked at Marcia with affection. "I am independent when it comes to the use of money, and wealth can be
measured in many things besides the paper you pretend rep-
resents something."

"What is he talking about?" Marcia demanded of Isabel.

Isabel's eyes widened, and she looked up to Manny.
"Maybe he means when America dropped the gold standard.
That we print more money than we actually have."

"What I mean, ladies, is your true wealth is measured by
the intangible: Health. Happiness. Love. Laughter. How many
moments of joy have you stored up, Marcia? I hope they
equal what is in your bank balance."

Marcia stared at Manny and then near glared at Isabel.
"Who *is* this guy?"

"He told you," Jen answered. "He loves me, and he's the
father of my child."

Marcia was breathing heavily, trying to control her anger.
"So you . . . you're going to have this baby? When you can
barely take care of yourself?"

"I can take care of myself," Jen stated calmly. "And I can
take care of our baby, now that Manny is with me."

"Do you *know* anything about babies? How much trouble
they are? How much work they take? You're a child yourself."

"I'm not anymore, Marcia. I'm prepared to work hard. I'll
learn everything I can before my baby is born. Manny says
that Grace will help me get a GED—that's the right term,
isn't it, Isabel? What we talked about?"

Isabel nodded.

"And I'd like to take driving lessons too. I want to buy a car."

"You're going way too fast," Marcia said, shaking her head. "Tell her, Isabel. Tell her she should come home with me and take this one step at a time."

Isabel felt all attention directed at her. "Well . . . really, Marcia, I think she is taking it one step at a time. I know all of this is a shock to you. I tried to tell you Jen had made great progress. It seems to me that she and Manny have thought this out. My only question is, who is this Grace?"

"Grace Mulvey," Manny said, his hand now on Jen's shoulder. "She is an old friend."

An old friend? How long had Manny been making *friends*? "How old?" Isabel asked, not really comfortable with the thought of Jen moving in with a woman who had been intimate with Emmanuel.

"You might say she is in her sixties," he answered. "She is a gifted woman who never lost her abilities."

"What? A mind reader?" Marcia demanded in a sarcastic voice. "What does she do? Tell fortunes? C'mon, Isabel, you can see why I can't allow this!"

"Hold on," Isabel said, lifting her hand to Marcia. "What do you mean 'gifted'? How?"

"She is in service to humanity. A healer, if you will. Not unlike you, Isabel. Whereas you use the mind to heal, Grace uses the soul, through holistic practices."

"Where is this house?" Isabel asked.

"In Philadelphia," Jen answered.

"In Philly?" Marcia demanded. "The murder rate is climbing every month and—"

"What part of Philadelphia?" Isabel interrupted, not willing to listen to Marcia's argument yet.

Manny closed his eyes for a moment and said, "It is called Chestnut Hill."

"Now that's very nice," Isabel said to Marcia. "Huge, lovely homes with lots of grounds."

"Look, all this is beside the point, which is, Jen is not ready to go out on her own yet!"

"Marcia," Jen said calmly, "I love you. And I thank you for taking care of me all those years, but I am ready. I have to do this. And you can't stop me. I have a right to live my life . . . and so do you."

Marcia looked ready to continue the fight. Manny, who was standing at the head of the table, left one hand on Jen's shoulder and touched Marcia's shoulder with the other. "It's time to let go. For both of you."

And Isabel watched in fascination as Jen and Marcia looked into each other's eyes for a timeless moment, neither one speaking, until tears formed. Marcia hung her head and covered her face as she began to cry in full force. Manny left his hand on her shoulder and said in a soothing voice, "You are allowed to let go now, Marcia. Let go of the years of worry and responsibility. Make new choices for yourself. You did the best you could. Everyone knows that. Now it's time for you to reap your rewards."

Isabel's eyes filled with emotion, and Manny smiled at her with that same magnetism she had seen so often in Joshua. He tilted his head toward the dining room, and Isabel nodded as she quietly rose from her chair.

Jen also rose, patting Manny on the arm as she took his place next to her sister. With her arm around Marcia's shoulders, Jen held her sister to her chest and rocked her, stroking her hair.

As she left the kitchen, Isabel heard Jen whisper, "Marcia . . . thank you for everything. . . ."

Isabel wiped her eyes as she turned in the dining room and looked up to Manny.

"He's waiting for you, you know."

Her chest muscles tightened. "Joshua?"

Manny nodded.

"Where?" she asked in a breathless voice.

"Wherever you want," he answered with a tender smile of understanding. "He's waiting for you to call out to him again. To invite him back into your life."

"You mean . . . ?"

"He's waiting, Isabel, for your permission to reenter your life."

She quickly hugged Manny and ran for the stairs. Taking two at a time, she hurried into her bedroom and stared at her bed, her closet. She'd waited this long. She could wait a little longer for him. Smiling with excitement, she pulled open a dresser drawer and reached in. She withdrew something exquisitely soft and beautiful. Years and years ago, she'd bought this black silk nightgown and kimono robe to surprise Chuck on her birthday. She'd never worn it. Never had the chance. But now . . . now it was perfect. Soft, yet sexy. It didn't matter if her belly was outlined. Just her luck to have saved it all these years, and now showing a pregnant bump was in style.

Almost reverently, she laid it out on her bed while catching the faint aroma of lavender that scented her drawers. She'd take a long bath. Lots of oils. Drench herself in enough delicious flavors that he'd be tempted to inhale her. Giggling, she thought about lighting candles all over the bedroom, playing romantic music. Bowls of fruit and a bottle of red wine . . . for him.

Now, if she could just get everyone to leave.

Wait . . . wait! Did he already know she was pregnant?

Isabel rushed down the stairs to find Marcia putting on her coat, while Manny held Jen's luggage. Everyone was dressed to leave.

"Where are you all going?" she asked with surprise, even though she wanted them gone.

Jen turned around and smiled. "I was going to come up

and say good-bye. I packed last night. Marcia is going to drive us to Grace's home."

Isabel exhaled in relief, seeing Marcia smile slightly and shrug.

"She's got a mind of her own now," she murmured.

Grinning, Isabel said, "And thank God for that, right?"

"Thank you," Jen answered, "for everything, Isabel. It's all going to be okay now."

"I'm so happy for you, Jen," she said, hugging the young, confident woman. "We'll have to stay in touch, okay?"

Jen kissed her cheek and nodded. "We'll visit. All of us. We're a family now."

Smiling, Isabel blinked, not knowing how to respond. Instead, she looked at Manny. "May I speak with you for a moment?"

"Certainly. Excuse me, ladies."

Isabel felt him following her back into the dining room. She turned around and said, "I need to know if Joshua knows I'm pregnant."

Manny's eyes lit with pleasure. "So *that* is why you are beaming with an inner light of such intensity."

Isabel's shoulders dropped in relief. "So he doesn't know."

"He will be pleased. Don't worry."

"I hope you're right. Take care of Jen, Manny. She's a wonderful young woman who trusts you with her life."

"I will. You will see, Isabel. For Jen was correct in saying we are family now."

"Really?" she asked. "I don't get it."

Emmanuel kissed her forehead and whispered, "Ask Joshua to explain it."

And then he joined the others, and Isabel saw them to the back door. She watched from her window as they got into Marcia's car. *They* looked like a family. She didn't know how she was supposed to fit into it.

Family. For years she had tried to find peace with her own. And now another was beginning. . . .

No time to think about it now, she told herself as Marcia backed out of the driveway. She had to clean the house. Go shopping for fruit and wine. Take a nap, then a bath. So much to prepare . . .

"Just be patient, my love," she called out, gathering up the plates on the table and taking them to the sink.

She wanted it to be perfect.

The perfect reunion.

§

She was running her hand up from her ankle, smoothing lotion onto her leg, when she noticed the drop of blood on the white bathroom tile. Staring at it, Isabel felt herself go weak with terror. She sank onto the toilet seat, willing her heartbeat to slow down.

Breathe, she told herself. *Maybe you cut your leg while shaving.*

She turned her legs around, checking the backs of her calves. Nothing. No cuts.

Oh God, oh God . . . please no.

She sat, unwilling to rise and find the source. Everything in her was saying it was too good to be true. Pregnant at her age. What were the chances? Every warning she'd ever heard about pregnancy ran through her head. She felt frozen in fear and blamed herself. Since five-thirty she'd been on the go. Good intentions to take a nap had been thrown out the window as she prepared for a perfect reunion. She should have been taking care of herself instead of trying to control everything.

Realizing she couldn't sit there all evening, she inhaled and stood up while pulling on the roll of toilet paper. She stared at the streak of pink and wanted to cry her denial. Instead, she flushed the evidence down the toilet, grabbed a clean washcloth from the linen closet, and went into her bedroom to find a pair of panties.

Because she'd thought she was in menopause, she didn't keep anything in the house for such a situation. Folding the washcloth, she stuck it in her underwear and sat down on the bed. She dialed Kate Abrams' office, left a message with Kate's service, and waited, staring at the grain in the old hardwood floorboards. Maybe the old wives' tales were right. Never talk about the pregnancy too soon. Don't make plans. Don't hope. Don't feel as though a miracle has happened. . . .

She touched her belly and whispered, "Please stay. I promise I'll take better care of myself."

The phone rang, and Isabel was so startled she jumped in fright. "Hello?"

"Isabel? Kate Abrams here. What's up?"

"I'm staining, Kate. Just started."

"Is it tissue? Clots? Or just blood."

Isabel briefly closed her eyes in gratitude. "Just blood. No tissue or clots."

"Okay, well that's good. It isn't rare, Isabel, especially for someone your age. Stay off your feet for a few days. No lifting. Vacuuming. That kind of thing. Just be sensible."

"Right," Isabel answered, feeling guilty that she'd cleaned the house and vacuumed.

"You're a smart woman, Isabel. Just take care of yourself now. It should stop. Call me in a few days, or if there's any change."

"I will," Isabel promised.

"And *rest*!"

"Yes ma'am," Isabel said. "Thanks, Kate."

"Anytime."

She hung up the phone and allowed herself to fully exhale. She had to take care of herself. She couldn't afford to take on anyone else's problems now. "You stay put, little one," she whispered, dialing another number.

"Hello?"

"Claire. It's Isabel."

"Hey, lady . . . how's the pregnant momma doing?"

"Well, truth is, I'm spotting."

"Oh no . . ."

"I just called Kate, and she said I need to rest, to put my feet up."

"Gotcha. What can I do? Want me to pick you up some food?"

"Actually, would you mind picking me up some pads? I got rid of everything a few years ago and have a washcloth in my pants now."

Claire chuckled. "Talk about frontier woman. Sure, Issy. What else?"

"Nothing, really. Oh, and the house is locked and I shouldn't take the stairs for a few days, so would you mind getting the extra key?"

"Where is it?"

"Go to the gazebo and unscrew the first finial on the left-hand side as you step inside. Chuck made a spot for the key underneath it."

"Smart move," Claire said. "So what about dinner?"

"It's okay," Isabel answered. "I really don't need anything else."

"I made chicken soup . . . from scratch."

"*You* did?"

"Now why is everyone so surprised that I actually have homemaking talents?"

"Maybe because you have a cleaning service once a week and eat out almost every night."

"I'm lazy," Claire admitted with a laugh. "That's not true either. I can clean and cook; I just don't like knowing I have to do it."

"Just the pads, Claire, and I would be most grateful."

"Are you sure, Issy? Do you want company? I can stay with you if you're . . . well, worried or anything."

Isabel's heart warmed, and she smiled. "Thanks, Claire, but I'm sure I'll be fine if I follow Kate's orders for a few days."

"Okay. I should be there in about twenty minutes."

"Thank you so much."

She hung up the phone and wrapped her arms around herself. She would be fine. She had to be fine. And her baby would stay put. Reaching out, she grabbed the nightgown off the comforter and slipped it over her head. Then the kimono robe. She only lifted a few inches off the mattress to pull them both down her body.

Shifting her legs onto the bed, she plumped a few pillows behind her and lay back. All the candles were unlit. The wine was still corked on the dresser, next to a silver tray of glasses and fruit. So much for plans. When would she ever learn?

Even though in her head she was still young, her body was telling her a different story. She needed to be careful now, and all thoughts of a romantic reunion with Joshua disappeared in her new reality. Now the baby had to be her focus.

She closed her eyes, trying to let the stress drain from her body. Positive thoughts. She knew the importance of not entertaining negativity, so she tried to imagine herself holding her baby, the happiness she would feel, the love washing through her. . . .

One, she thought, giving an autosuggestion to relax her lower body.

Two. Her torso relaxed, along with her shoulders and arms.

Three. Her head and mind.

She walked up the ten stairs in her mind, going deeper and deeper into relaxation with each step. When she reached the top, she opened the doors and entered her sanctuary, a beautiful garden with a path that led over a small wooden bridge.

In her mind, Isabel stopped at the bridge. She wouldn't let herself cross it until she took all her worries and tossed them over the side.

I'm too old for this.

I might die for this.

I won't be a good mother,

I might be alone in this.

I may not get the chance to prove I can be a good mother.

My body is rejecting this baby.

She imagined herself stripping each worrying thought off her like a spandex slip, clingy and tight. She pulled and pulled until it was separate from her, and then she opened her hands and allowed it to fall, carried away in the rushing water below. It was as if she could breathe deeper, more easily. Expanding her lungs, Isabel slowly left the bridge and walked toward the small cottage. In her mind she saw it covered in old wisteria vines, with urns and containers of flowers scattered around. She opened the door and sat in the rocking chair before the fire. Staring into the flames, she felt a deep sense of peace and closed her eyes.

Here she was safe. Here nothing could harm her. Here there were no expectations, no plans, no disappointments. . . .

"Isabel! *Isabel!*"

Chapter

19

STARTLED, SHE OPENED HER EYES AS THE HEAT OF fear so quickly filled her chest.

"Damn, woman, you scared the hell out of me!" Claire exclaimed, plopping on the bottom of the bed and exhaling so forcefully her shoulders sagged. "Didn't you hear me calling you from the stairs?"

Isabel shook her head. "I . . . I'm sorry, Claire. I must have fallen asleep."

Claire shook her head. "You could sleep for America in the Olympics, then. Do not do that to me again!"

Calming herself, Isabel smiled as she pushed herself upright. "I promise. I got up at five-thirty today, and I guess I was exhausted."

"Where's Jen? I forgot to ask about her on the phone."

"She left today. Marcia finally showed up."

Claire nodded, bringing the plastic bag up onto the bed. "Here's your pads."

"Thanks. I really appreciate you going out of your way like this."

"Oh, knock it off, Issy. You're like my sister. And family does this stuff. Besides, that baby had better stay right where it is so Auntie Claire can buy herself a new outfit for the christening. Have you even thought of names yet?"

Isabel grinned. "No, not yet. I'm trying to stay positive, though, so any suggestions would be appreciated."

Claire looked up to the ceiling. "I suppose Claire is out. It means 'brilliant, shining light,' you know."

"No, I didn't."

"Thought you'd find that interesting," she said with a laugh. "Seriously, start thinking of names. Make this baby real, Issy. You know how powerful your thoughts are. You taught us that."

"I know you're right. I guess I had more fear about this than I was realizing."

Claire's eyebrows raised. "And why are we dressed like a femme fatale? Pretty sexy getup you got going there, Miss Isabel."

Isabel felt her cheeks flush with embarrassment as she pulled the edges of her robe tighter around her.

"And look at the setting!" Claire said, pointing to the dresser. "Wine. Fruit. Candles. *Lots* of candles . . ." She turned her head back to Isabel. "Were we expecting someone?"

"We weren't," Isabel said. "I was. Or at least I was hoping I was."

"And now?"

Sighing, Isabel said, "Now I just want to get comfortable and sleep. And maybe try tomorrow for visitors."

"Best-laid plans, huh?"

"No kidding!" Isabel agreed. "I really have to think of myself first now."

"So no sex?"

Isabel's eyes widened, and she laughed. "Sex is definitely out of the question."

"Sheesh, for how long?"

"I don't know. The way I'm feeling right now, until after the baby is born."

"So I take it Joshua is back in the picture?"

Isabel hesitated. "I hope so."

"Let me talk to the man."

Holding up her hand, Isabel grinned. "Let *me* talk to the man first and prepare him for you."

"Why does everyone think the worst of me, like I'm the ogre of the group? I can be very sweet."

"Claire, you're not the ogre. You're the protector, the beautiful Amazon warrior of the group who will coming charging into any situation to rescue any of us. And we all love you for that."

"But . . . there's a *but* coming. I can feel it."

Smiling, Isabel said, "No *but*s about it. Just sometimes we need to handle things ourselves or we might never learn the lesson involved. Then we'd have to repeat it."

"Like Kelly. How many times have I fixed her up with decent men and she finds fault with all of them? I mean, if you really want a man, at least don't keep sabotaging yourself, right?"

"It's not the men. We know that. But until Kelly figures out it's her, she's going to call them losers and keep searching outside herself for the answers."

Claire was shaking her head. "That's why I'm not looking for anyone anymore. If I've got lessons to learn, I'll learn them on my own, thank you very much. Cuts the pain in half, maybe." She looked at Isabel. "Do you think we're ever done with these lessons? Do we ever get to graduate and become enlightened about our path? Do we ever get to relax and enjoy it, Issy?"

Grinning, Isabel said, "I think we're done when we're done. And graduate?" She shrugged her shoulders. "Maybe that's what death is? We graduate, or we have to repeat the grade?"

"Ah geez . . ." Claire stood up. "I was always so good in passing tests, but I have a feeling like maybe I'm not doing so well on this life one."

"Why is that?"

"Because . . ." She looked back at Isabel. "I really give

you credit, Issy. Taking a chance like this. You call me a warrior, but I don't think I have your courage."

"Sure you do, Claire. Bravery isn't being free of fear. You're scared, but you do it anyway. And in my case, look what my reward will be at the end of it. A miracle."

Claire smiled and walked around the bed to her. "Well you and your little miracle get some rest. I brought the soup anyway. Do you want me to get you a bowl?"

Isabel shook her head. "I'm just tired. Thank you so much for running out for me."

"Any time, kiddo." And she bent down and kissed Isabel's forehead. "Call me tomorrow and I'll arrange for one of us to come breakfast, lunch, and dinner until you're back on your feet. Too bad Jen's gone, now that you could really use her."

Isabel shrugged. "She has her own life now."

"Okay, so call me. Now that I know where the extra key is, I'll come barging in here to annoy the hell out of you if you don't pick up the phone."

"I promise. Good night, Claire . . . and thanks again."

"Go back to sleep," she said, leaving the room. Then she yelled out from the stairs, "*And call if you need anything!*"

"*I will,*" Isabel yelled back. "*Thank you!*"

She smiled, thinking about Claire and her no-nonsense attitude. How would Claire have reacted if Joshua had come into her life? She probably would have driven him out with her tongue, which could be just as sharp as a sword when she was riled. Shaking her head, Isabel pushed herself upright and grabbed the bag from the bottom of the bed. She took out the package of super-sized sanitary napkins. Claire wasn't taking any chances, she thought as she slid her legs over the side of the mattress.

Okay, just stand, she told herself. It's going to be all right. She'd fix herself up, put on a comfy nightgown with long sleeves, and sleep until morning. And tomorrow she'd have her reunion. Tonight she needed sleep.

Isabel stood, then smiled as she walked into the bathroom. It was just a bit of spotting, that was all. Nothing to be—

And then she felt it, just like when she was younger and had her period—that unmistakable sensation of something passing out of her body. With her thighs together, she rushed into the bathroom and pulled up her nightgown. Slowly taking away the washcloth, her mouth opened in horror.

More blood. Red, this time. And a clot.

Dizzy with shock, Isabel threw the cloth into the sink, then ripped open the package with shaking hands. She pulled out a napkin and attached it to her panties. Pulling them back up, she held her hand at her crotch. "Don't do this!" she whispered. "Please . . . please . . ."

She couldn't hold back the tears as they streamed down her face. This wasn't happening. It couldn't! *"Claire!"* she yelled, but it came out like a tight squeal. She tried to swallow down the fear that was closing off her throat. *"Claire!"*

Nothing. And then she heard a car engine starting.

"Oh God . . ." She was all alone. Again.

"Help me, Joshua! Please . . . !" she called out in desperation. "I can't do this alone anymore!"

Even in the midst of her terror, she felt the air in the small room charge with electricity, the hair on her arms rise in response.

She closed her eyes and felt his arms wrap around her from behind as he supported her weight.

"It's all right, my love," he whispered into her hair. "Why did you wait so long to call out to me?"

She was sobbing, in fear but also in gratitude. "I . . . I wanted it to be . . . special," she cried, grabbing his hand under her breasts and holding on tightly. "I'm so scared now."

"Don't be frightened, Isabel," he said, reaching down and easily lifting her in his arms. He held her tightly and walked out of the bathroom.

In some far corner of her mind, Isabel registered him

carrying her and was surprised at how effortless he made it seem. "I . . . I'm pregnant," she sobbed into his shoulder.

"I know, my love," he answered, bringing her to the bed.

"And I'm losing the baby, Joshua!"

"Shh, calm down. No, you're not," he said firmly, placing her gently in the center of the mattress.

She curled into a ball of protection, wrapping her arms around her belly as though it might save her baby. "I am!" she sobbed. "I'm an RN. I know what I saw. I know what's happening."

She felt the soft fleecy blanket she had folded on a chair now placed over her body. Joshua climbed in bed behind her and cuddled her up against him.

He placed his hands over hers and said, "And I am connected to the source of all creation, Isabel. You will not lose this baby. . . ."

Within moments her hands became hot, buzzing with an energy that was peaceful and calm. Whatever Joshua was doing, she didn't want it to stop. Her eyelids fluttered open, and she was surrounded in tiny white lights that sparkled in prisms like the colors in a rainbow. Her body became energized, tingling with well-being, and she closed her eyes, trusting Joshua, trusting the lights. . . .

All she could think about was saving their baby.

The next thing she was conscious of was the sound of soft music playing somewhere around her. She stretched her body and reluctantly opened her eyes.

It was morning. The sun was shining.

She was still dressed in the nightgown and kimono, and she blinked her eyelids, wondering if it had all been a dream.

Joshua!

Leaning up on her elbow, she looked around the room for any sign of him. There was none. She touched her belly and then had the overwhelming urge to use the bathroom. Carefully rising, she made her way across the bedroom while paying attention for any signs of trouble coming from her body. Everything felt fine.

She held her breath as she pulled down her underwear and sat on the toilet.

Nothing on the pad.

It had to have been a dream. . . .

And then she remembered hearing music. Someone was downstairs. Of course. It had to be Claire, or one of the Gang making breakfast for her. She must have fallen back asleep after Claire left and . . .

But it had seemed so real. The terror and then Joshua . . . saving her, saving their baby. The lights, the feeling of well-being, that everything was all right and the baby was fine.

She pulled her act together and stood up, letting the night-gown fall back into place. Caressing her belly, she said, "You gave me quite a scare, little one. I even had a nightmare. . . ." And that's when she saw the washcloth she'd thrown into the sink the night before. Fear once more rushed through her body as she saw the dried blood. Picking it up by a clean corner, she threw it in the trash and pulled the thin plastic liner out of the container. Tying a knot in it, she dropped it on the floor as she turned on the cold water.

She scrubbed the sink; then she scrubbed her face, wanting to clear out that horrible memory. Joshua *had* come to her last night. It wasn't a dream. She patted her face dry and looked at her reflection. Maybe it was wishful thinking, but she really did appear younger. Her complexion was nearly glowing with good health!

"I'm radiant . . . ," she murmured in awe, touching her cheek.

"You are beautiful, my love."

She spun around and saw him. Standing in the doorway, dressed in jeans and a blue shirt, holding a tray in front of him with a bowl of cereal, fruit, and a mug of something hot. "You're here!" she breathed, filled with a surge of love.

Grinning, he nodded to the bedroom. "Come and get back in bed. You should eat something."

He turned around, and she hurried up to him and wrapped her arms around his waist. With her head on his back, she said, "I thought it was a dream, but you're here! You really are back!"

"Yes, Isabel," he said, unable to move forward. "I really am back. Now you get back into bed."

She kissed between his shoulder blades and nearly danced around him to hop back into bed. "I missed you so much. I kept wondering why you didn't return with Manny, and I thought it must have been because I was so disagreeable when I sent you away. But you do forgive me, don't you?" she asked in a beseeching voice as she scrambled under the comforter and watched for his reaction. "I'm not really like that."

He was still smiling as he placed the tray on the comforter and handed her the bowl of cereal. "There is nothing to forgive," he answered, sitting down on the side of the bed. "Now eat . . . for both of you."

Isabel picked up the spoon and dug into the cereal, willing to do whatever it took to make him happy. He was here with her, and she had no intention of fighting or arguing ever again. It took her some time to finish half of the cereal, and then she put it aside, really wanting to talk.

"Our baby is going to all right now?" Isabel asked, nodding her head as if that would make him answer in the positive.

"Our baby is growing, Isabel," he said, handing her the bowl of fruit, "and that means you have to supply her with the energy she needs."

"*She?*"

He nodded, and his smile increased. "Yes, last night as I held you I made contact with her. We are blessed, you and I, to have created the space for another beautiful soul."

"A girl . . . ," Isabel breathed in awe. She was filled with happiness and thought she felt a flutter in her belly. It was too soon, wasn't it? "Joshua. I'm so glad you're pleased. I thought you might think I was trying to bind you to me or . . . or something," she finished lamely.

He stroked the hair back from her eyes. "Isabel, I was bound to you the first time we achieved unity together. You are a part of me, as I now am a part of you. We are family. We always were, but now it is tangible, more real for you."

She reached up and held his hand. "Manny said that too. About family. I didn't understand exactly what he meant. He said you would explain it."

He cupped her face with his hand and looked tenderly into her eyes. "It is true human beings are unique, but you are all connected to one another, to all of creation, in all dimensions and in all universes."

"So you and I . . . we're like cousins?" Isabel asked.

"Distant cousins, if you will, separated by fear."

"Our fear?"

He nodded, taking his hand away. "You so fear the unknown, but more important, you fear one another. Your science has finally shown through DNA that all of you, every single one of you, has at least one ancestor that originated in sub-Saharan Africa and migrated north, east, or west. Every human alive on this planet right now is part of the same tribe, the same family. All your fights, your wars, are in actuality family problems. It will take some time before humans accept this science, for they have spent over forty thousand years in separation, allowing the ego reign. Yet if you knew everyone you met was connected to you, no matter how angry you were with your sister . . . would you kill her and leave her children motherless? Would you allow your nieces and nephews to die of starvation or disease?"

Chewing an apple slice, Isabel shook her head. "So we're a great big six-billion-member dysfunctional family," she muttered.

"And until you can make peace within yourself, you can't

make peace in your family, or be reunited with your distant family. It can only begin with each individual healing the past, living in the present, and creating a better future."

Isabel stopped eating. "That's what you and Daniel and Manny are doing?"

Joshua looked surprised. "You know about Daniel?"

"I figured that one out," she said with a grin. "So that's what you guys are doing?"

Nodding, he said, "It is happening all over this planet. In all countries. This next generation, of which our daughter will be a part, is going to support that healing. She will be born with the knowledge of oneness, and never forget it. We won't allow her to forget it. She and thousands of others will help humanity remember. Think of that word, Isabel. *Remember.* 'Put back together again.' It is time for the human family to come back together again, to heal past differences and create a better future. The survival of your species depends on it."

Isabel cradled her belly with her hand. "That's such a big task," she whispered. "I was hoping our baby would have a carefree life, a gentle life. Saving the world is beyond anyone's ability, especially a little girl's."

Joshua's smile increased. "The world doesn't need saving. Humanity does, from itself. All that is being asked is she live her life, carefree and gentle. Being herself, she will affect others. There are beings today, Isabel, already on this planet, who enter a person's life and because their energy vibrates higher than eight point two hertz in this third dimension, they speed up the energy of those around them. Fears and traumas come up to the surface much more quickly. Healing begins."

"Like you?"

He shook his head. "No. Like Jennifer. She was born with great gifts, but shut them off when her mother left her. It was time for her to heal, so Emmanuel manifested in her reality.

What was never originally planned was the effect you women were going to have on us. It seems impossible to resist you."

Isabel grinned. "You fell in love."

"We already loved you."

"But now you're *in* love with us?" she asked hopefully.

"Now we seem unable to resist being drawn into your presence. The way humans achieve unity . . ." He paused, closing his eyes as though remembering.

Isabel giggled. "We may not be as evolved, Joshua, but we've got something pretty great going on, huh?"

Opening his eyes, he looked at her with an intense desire. "Pretty great indeed, Isabel."

Knowing she wasn't about to risk sex, even with Joshua, she cleared her throat. "Okay, back to Jen. Manny came into her life to help her remember her gifts?"

"Yes. But it wasn't enough. We needed a human to help, someone she could trust. That was you."

Isabel felt a tightening of her muscles. "Wait a minute . . . so you came into my life because of Jen, not me?"

"I have been in your life, Isabel, since you were a child, remember? When the call went out for assistance with Jen, I knew you would be perfect. A quick scan of those Marcia could trust produced you. It's all very complicated to explain, but it comes back to that big six-billion-member family. Drop your prejudices for a moment and you will see how perfectly the universe provides. All of you are interconnected. Find the appropriate pathway and the connection is made. You were the pathway."

"I was . . . *used*?" Isabel demanded, feeling a little sick to her stomach. "For Jen?"

"It was time for you to heal your own past, Isabel. That is why I manifested in your reality using this body suit."

"But all this . . . was for *Jen*!?" Oh, she was going to throw up the cereal, and she didn't care if she did it right on him!

"Isabel, your aura has changed. Why are you upset again?"

Breathing deeply, inhaling through her nose and exhaling through her mouth, Isabel managed to say, "I thought you came for me!"

"I did. I told you I have been with you since you were a very young child."

"But . . . you just said Jen was the important one. I was a side job, or someone instrumental in helping Jen."

"You were. But she was also instrumental in helping you. She taught you about faith. It is about connectedness; can't you see that? When one is uplifted, all have the opportunity. Because of your gifts, you were able to assist Jennifer in regaining hers. But first you had to believe her. What better way than to have your own childhood imaginary friend manifest in your reality? Anyone else hearing her story would have doubted her, but you left the door open because of what you, yourself, had just experienced."

"So . . . you made love to me . . . because of Jen?"

His jaw dropped with the very human expression of confusion. "Why would I have done that?"

"So I could relate to Jen!"

A smile started to replace his confusion. "I will say this gently, Isabel. My intention upon meeting you was not to engage you sexually. However," he quickly added, before she could make a protest, "you became irresistible to me. Unity, physical unity with you, is exquisitely beautiful."

She stared into his dark eyes as he placed his hand on her belly.

"And in that exquisite beauty we created this new being. Please drop your doubts and calm down for our daughter's sake, if not your own."

She felt his energy infuse her, and she saw a great love radiating back at her through his eyes. "Maybe it's the hormones," she whispered, tears coming into her eyes. "I don't want to argue with you again."

His expression became even more gentle. "Don't ever doubt that I love you, Isabel. I am here because of you, and I will remain because of you."

"Then you're staying?"

"As long as I can. But you can call out to me at any time and I will be with you, just not always physically."

"Cristine said Daniel can stay up to eight hours now."

"He's been here longer than I." He tilted his head. "You spoke to Cristine . . . about us?"

"I had to, Joshua. I thought I had been abandoned. Try and put yourself in my place. Pregnant, at my age, and alone . . . It was too much to handle myself. I needed someone."

He nodded. "You could have called out to me, but I'm glad you have Cristine. She will help you understand better, having gone through carrying a special child."

"Special . . . I remember you saying that none of us are special, or we all are."

"Which do you think it is?"

"We all are?" she asked in a hushed voice.

"Every single one of you is uniquely you, rare. Do you want to know who you are?"

She nodded.

"Since the beginning of time there has never been another person like you. Nobody has your exact smile, your eyes, your nose, your hair, your voice. No one else has your handwriting or sees things just as you do. In all of creation, there is no one who laughs like you or cries like you, and what made you laugh or cry will never provoke identical laughter and tears from anybody else, ever.

"You are the only one since the beginning of time who has your set of abilities. There will always be someone who is, perhaps, as good or better, but no one in the universe can reach your combination of talents, ideas, abilities, and feelings. Like a room full of musical instruments, some may excel alone, but none can match the symphony when all are played together in harmony."

"That's beautiful, Joshua. I wish people could hear that."

"Tell them, Isabel. Tell them they're special, and they were created for a special purpose that's theirs alone. Out of all the billions of applicants, only one is qualified, only one has the right combination it will take to fulfill that unique purpose. Remind them of what they knew as infants new to this dimension. Help them remember their brilliance and put it all back together."

"How?" she asked, feeling overwhelmed.

"Just by being yourself, telling your story to those who ask. All you have to do, Isabel, is *be* you. That's good enough."

"My story?" She laughed. "No one will believe me if I tell them about you."

He grinned. "No, they probably won't. But you have a wealth of experience to relate, and perhaps you will begin to see things in a more expansive way now."

"About the human family," she murmured.

"About the universal family, of which you are a part. What happens here affects not just this universe, but all of creation. We are all interconnected and—"

"Isabel!"

She stared at Joshua in surprise. "Claire!"

"Breakfast from Cote'," Tina's voice called out from the stairs.

Isabel grabbed Joshua's hand. "Stay. Please. You're going to have to meet them sometime."

He smiled into her eyes and turned to the doorway.

The two women stopped as one, grinding to a halt, staring into the bedroom.

Isabel sat up straighter. "Come in, come in, but you're too late with breakfast. Joshua brought it up earlier."

Claire nudged Tina, bringing her back to life, and Tina slowly walked into the room followed by Claire.

"So this is the famous Joshua?" Claire said, coming around Tina and holding out her hand formally.

Joshua smiled and took her hand. "It is a great pleasure to meet you. You must be Claire."

Claire stared up at him, her eyes wide, her lower lip dropping about a half inch. She didn't remove her hand and looked like she was falling into a trance.

Isabel cleared her throat. "And this is Tina."

Tina came forward, now shouldering Claire out of the way. "You have a great singing voice," she murmured, almost preening as she presented her hand.

"Thank you, Tina," he answered, closing his other hand on top of hers. "It is an honor to meet you."

Tina blinked, closed her mouth, and then looked at Isabel. "Is he for real?"

Isabel laughed. "He's for real."

Claire put the large white bag from Cote' on the bottom of the bed. "So you're back, Joshua? For how long?"

"Claire!" Isabel reprimanded.

"Well, we *all* want to know," she retorted.

Joshua smiled. "It's all right, Isabel. Claire is concerned for you, as any good friend would be." He turned to Claire. "I know how precious Isabel is, and I intend to honor her as long as she welcomes me in her life."

"Which is forever," Isabel added, holding out her hand for Joshua. He sat down again on the bed. "So now that you ladies have met him, can we postpone the inquisition until later?" She wrinkled her nose, embarrassed. "You're kinda interrupting our reunion."

"Oh!" Tina, quicker to catch on, pulled Claire's jacket sleeve. "Got it. We're outta here. Glad you're better, Issy. You *are* feeling better, right?"

"Oh yes. Much better. Why don't—" She was interrupted by the ringing of the telephone. "Excuse me." Impatient to get rid of her friends, Isabel grabbed the phone receiver. "Hello?"

"May I please speak with Isabel Calloway?"

Not recognizing the voice, Isabel said, "Speaking."

"Oh, good. I'm Mary Ellen Fenerty, Linda Wilson's sister-in-law and talent coordinator for A.M. *Philly.* You helped my nephew Terry? I believe Linda called you and told you I'd be contacting you."

Closing her eyes briefly, Isabel exhaled. "Yes. Hello. I'm afraid I told Linda this wouldn't be a good time. I . . . I'm very busy at the moment," she added, looking at the three people who were staring at her.

"I'm sorry. When would be a good time?"

"I'm not sure," Isabel answered, not willing to lie in front of witnesses, especially one who would know she was lying immediately. "Perhaps in a month or so."

"Okay, there's no rush. I just feel it's important to get an alternative to medication out there for the thousands of parents and kids who are suffering. I saw what you did with Terry, and quite frankly, it's miraculous. He's thriving."

"I'm very happy for him," she said evasively.

"And I'm very excited by the results. I've already talked to the show's host, and he's willing to give you an entire segment. We could demonstrate your technique or have Terry and Donna talk about their experience, or anyone else you might want to use."

She looked at the audience in her bedroom and lowered her voice. "I'm just not that comfortable asking someone who's come to me in confidentiality to appear on television."

She heard Tina whisper in an excited voice, "Ohh, *television!*"

"I understand, Isabel. May I call you Isabel?"

"Certainly."

"How about I give you more time to think it over and get back to you next month?"

Anxious to get off the phone, Isabel smiled. "Thank you, Mary Ellen. That would be fine."

"But please, really think about it, Isabel. You could help so many, just by telling your story."

A rush of electricity passed through her when the woman repeated almost the same words Joshua had spoken only minutes before. Still, she could also picture Marcia freezing in place like a terrified deer in the headlights, so she said, "I will think about it."

"Okay, thanks for listening."

"You're welcome. Good-bye."

She hung up the phone as Tina said, "Television! What was *that* about?"

Isabel straightened out the bed linens, biding for time, but she knew with Joshua sitting right next to her, she couldn't lie. "One of my client's aunts is the talent coordinator for A.M. *Philly*, and she wants to do a show on alternative methods for treating children with learning disabilities."

"Why didn't you tell her yes?" Claire demanded, sitting on the bottom of the bed. "You would be great, Issy."

"May I remind you what a disaster that conference turned out to be? I like my quiet life, especially now . . . being pregnant."

Claire lifted one eyebrow in question. "Ah, I'd say that conference turned out to be anything but a disaster, my dear. Look who's sitting next to you."

She touched Joshua's hand. "Okay, I agree about meeting Joshua, but my seminar was torture, and that was in front of only fifty people. Television would be thousands."

"Hundreds of thousands," Tina said. "All the more you could help."

"I can't think about it now, all right? Too much has happened, and I just want to rest up and regain my strength."

"But you did say you would think about it," Joshua said.

"What? You're on their side? You were there at the seminar. You saw me freeze. I can't bear the thought of doing it on TV. I'll write a book, anything so I don't have to get up in front of people again."

"But we'll be there," Claire said. "The Gang will be your audience. Just talk to us. You trust us, right?"

"Can we discuss this another time?" Isabel asked. "It's a reunion, remember?"

Tina hit Claire's shoulder. "C'mon. She doesn't have to make up her mind today. We've got time to wear her down."

Shaking her head, Isabel said, "You're not going to wear me down. I have other priorities now."

Claire stood up and grabbed the white paper bag off the bed. "Fine. But we're taking our goodies from Cote' with us. Merry Christmas Eve, by the way."

Isabel's mouth dropped. "It's Christmas Eve?" she asked in shock.

"It is," Claire said. "And here we came over to sing carols."

"We did not!" Tina said with a laugh, pulling on her friend's arm. "She's just saying that to make you feel bad for kicking us out."

"Sing us a song, Claire," Isabel asked. "Please."

Claire sobered quickly. "I was kidding, and you know it. I'm not the singer," she answered. "You've got one sitting next to you. But tomorrow, if Isabel is feeling better, you can both come to Cristine's. She called this morning and invited everyone for a big party at her place. She knows it's last minute, but she says we're her family, and she wants family around for the baby's first Christmas. Even Paula and her tribe are going to come after they open their presents. She told me to ask you, if you're up to it."

"Maybe. That sounds like fun." She turned to Joshua. "Would you like to go?"

"I would very much like to meet the rest of your friends."

"Then I'll tell Cristine to expect you both."

Joshua rose and walked over to Tina and Claire. "Thank you for coming for Isabel this morning. I know how much you both love her, and I want you to know I do too. She is more than precious to me, and I promise I will do everything in my power to make sure she remains well."

Claire sucked in her cheeks while Tina nearly swooned.

"So . . . I take it you're sticking around?"

"Claire!" Isabel warned.

"It's fine, Isabel," Joshua said, then smiled again at Claire. "You may rest easy on that matter. Isabel and I are a family now. As I hope you are, both of you, and all of the Yellow Brick Road Gang."

"Wait till you meet the rest," Tina said with a chuckle. "You may want to rescind that invitation. We can be a bawdy bunch of broads."

"Oh God . . . ," Isabel muttered, shaking her head with embarrassment. "Will you two just go!?" She waved them out, would have pushed them out if she could. "Let him make up his own mind tomorrow!"

As Joshua grinned and turned back to Isabel, Claire and Tina stood in the doorway, like giggly teenagers. Tina was patting her heart, and Claire had both thumbs up in approval.

"I love you guys," Isabel called out with a laugh. "Now, *please*, go away!"

She heard them laughing as they hurried down the stairs, and she looked at Joshua.

"Alone at last," she breathed, holding out her arms.

He removed the tray and placed it on the floor. Isabel made room for him, and he came into bed with her. Holding her in his arms, he seemed to inhale the scent of her.

"I have missed you," he whispered.

Raising her head from his chest, she looked into his beautiful and exotic eyes. "You have no idea how much I've missed *you*." She swallowed deeply. "I didn't know this was going to happen to me again . . . to fall in love so deeply and completely . . . not twice in a lifetime."

"Aren't you blessed, then?" he whispered back, right before his mouth came down on hers. He kissed her gently, almost reverently, and then the kiss deepened into an intense desire. He moaned and then suddenly ended the kiss, letting his head fall back onto the pillow.

Isabel gasped at the abrupt loss of intimacy. Breathing heavily, feeling the desire still snaking through her body, she murmured, "We have to practice self-control . . . at least until the baby is firmly in place. I'm sorry. I just don't want to take any chances."

"I know. You are still frightened for the baby's safety."

"I am. I can't help it. To have been told I can never have children and then . . . this miracle happens. I just don't want to do anything to jeopardize it. You understand, don't you?"

He leaned forward and kissed her nose. "Of course, Isabel. But our daughter is safe now. I don't want you worrying."

She touched his cheek and ran her finger over his lips. "I can't help but worry. Maybe it's a mother thing, being overly protective. I just want her to come into this world peacefully, calmly, with love all around her."

"Have you thought of a name?"

She shook her head. "No, not yet. Have you?"

"You would want me to name her?"

"Well, I would want you to contribute in naming her. We would both agree to a name."

He looked up to the ceiling. "What about Hope? I do so like what it means."

She grinned. "Doesn't it mean . . . hope?"

"It means 'to trust in the future.' "

"Trust in the future . . . ," Isabel said, thinking about it as she rested her chin on his chest. "I guess that's what we're doing all the time, isn't it? And she is our future."

"Not just ours, my love. You will have to share our daughter with the world."

"I don't want to think that far ahead. Hope." She repeated the name. "I like it."

"You do?" he asked with a wider grin.

"I believe you've just named our daughter, Joshua."

His chest seemed to expand, and Isabel laughed at the very human male display of pride.

"You're very pleased with yourself," she said with a laugh.

He wrapped his arms tighter around her and grinned. "That is a great honor, to name a child. Is it not?"

"Oh, a very great honor, Joshua." She tried to keep her laughter under control.

"Why do you think of it as amusing?"

"I'm teasing you, because you're showing a very human male reaction."

"I am?"

She nodded. "Perhaps you aren't as evolved as you think," she said, leaning forward and staring at his mouth as she ran her fingertip over his bottom lip.

"Isabel . . . ?"

"Hmm?

"You know, my love, we have never achieved unity my way."

"Your way?"

He nodded. "Very safe for the baby."

"What happens?"

"Why don't I show you?" he asked, pulling her up and beginning to kiss her again.

"Wait!" She pulled back. "What are you going to do?"

He paused, staring at her eyes, her mouth, and back at her eyes, and then quicker than she could have believed possible he turned her over onto her back and said, "This!"

In one moment he was kissing her and . . . in the next she was enveloped in the most beautiful whirlwind of color and light. Every pore on her body seemed to open to it, allowing the most exquisite pleasure to race through her until she became dizzy with the sheer joy of it.

"Oh God," she called out, feeling herself transported out of her room, out of her life, into nothingness and everything at the same time.

"Exactly," came the answer from somewhere in side of her. *Yes. Exactly.*

Epilogue

Four months later

Isabel watched the television crew prepare for returning from the commercial. She could barely see Cristine, Claire, Tina, Kelly, and Paula through the three cameras that held position in front of the small stage. Joshua was standing in clear view, and he held his thumb up with encouragement. She smiled weakly, wishing he was rubbing her lower back. Just her luck that today she'd awakened with an odd pulling sensation. It had to be the weight. Almost forty pounds. She was like a beached whale, barely fitting into the uncomfortable chair. The first part seemed to have gone well, she thought, resisting the urge to spread her legs because her upper thighs felt like they were going numb from the round mass resting on top of them

"Welcome back," John Lawson said into the camera. "If you're just joining us, we're speaking to Dr. Isabel Calloway, a clinical hypnotherapist who works with learning-disabled children. In our first segment we spoke with Linda Wilson and her son Terry, and they told us how Terry, with help from our guest, went from not being able to read on his grade level to excelling." He turned back to Isabel. "Okay, so you were saying that students like Terry *are* learning, they just have trouble sometimes retrieving the information?"

Isabel nodded at her host, a young handsome man with a shock of black hair and intense eyes. She was glad Terry and Linda were now off the stage, for she felt awkward speaking of the child in front of him. "Yes, John. When children are labeled so young, they begin to believe those in authority over them and forget how brilliant they are. A part of them shuts down or is blocked, but we can form new ways around the blocks or teach in a way that clears the blocks and doesn't create more of them. Labeling a child is a very serious step. Perhaps we might weigh very carefully the benefit of the label and its ability to command additional assistance against the negative self-image that develops in the process."

"But some of these kids are lost," John replied. "You have to admit that."

Isabel smiled, surprisingly comfortable in front of a camera that was two feet from her face. She knew the Gang was sitting in the darkness supporting her and could feel Joshua's presence. "To be lost, John, means that at one time we weren't in that state. We were fine, when we knew we were brilliant."

Her host laughed. "Well, I don't know that I have ever considered myself brilliant."

"Why not?"

He seemed startled. "I don't know. I was an average student, I suppose."

"During your first year of life you were absolutely brilliant. Think of all you learned. From being barely able to lift your head at birth you learned to manipulate your body and direct that vast machinery of muscles, nerves, bones, and consciousness. Of course you are brilliant. You learned most of your language during that first year. By your first birthday you understood most of what was being said to you, and you could make some of your own needs understood. You were born brilliant, and that same brilliance is still you, still within the adult you. It has been active all these years, absorbing information and storing it. It was only when someone labeled you as less than brilliant that you believed differently and forgot all your successes. All human beings don't learn at the same rate, or in the same way."

John laughed self-consciously. "Well, I know who to call if I ever feel depressed. You do have a very calming and supportive way about you."

She grinned back at him. "Just remember yourself, before anyone put any labels on you."

"You have a thing about labels, don't you?"

She blushed. "I guess I do. Instinctively, she put her hand on her huge belly. Trying to ignore the feeling like her lower back was being pulled out from the weight of it, Isabel asked, "Have you ever misspelled a word?"

He nodded. "Of course."

"Have you ever been embarrassed at forgetting the name of a friend? Do you remember directions exactly the way they were given? When someone is talking to you, are you always listening completely, or sometimes are you planning your next statement for when it's your turn to be heard? Have you ever made a mistake in balancing your checkbook? Does the *ummm* sound occasionally steal into your speech patterns?"

"Yes, to all of those questions," John answered, smiling into the camera. "And I don't think I'm alone."

"You aren't. But do you consider yourself learning disabled?"

"No."

"You might want to reconsider your status, according to the Education of All Handicapped Children Act. It states a learning disability means a disorder in one or more of the basic psychological processes involved in understanding or in using language, spoken or written, which may manifest itself in the imperfect ability to listen, think, speak, read, write, spell, or do mathematical calculations. Now I'd just like to know who the perfect prototype is and who decides where to place a label on a child who is judged as not perfect. The rate of children being labeled learning disabled is alarming in this country. I, personally, don't think medication is the best or only route to take."

"But you have to admit some children are born handicapped. No one likes to use the word *imperfect,* but . . ." He left his sentence hanging.

Isabel inhaled, wishing she had picked a day for this televised interview when she didn't have a backache. She'd gone along with the makeover, had even allowed the Gang to pick out her outfit, but she was becoming more and more uncomfortable sitting in the chair. Glancing at Joshua, looking so handsome and proud not ten feet away, she decided she would still give it her best shot. Smiling, she turned her attention back to her host.

"You know, John, that reminds me of something that happened to me years so. Do you mind if I tell you a little story? I'll try to keep it as brief as possible."

John sat back and smiled. "Go ahead. I find you fascinating, as I'm sure our viewers do."

Isabel blushed again, picturing the Gang giggling behind the cameras and cables that separated them and congratulating themselves for months of pestering her to do this interview. The story, she reminded herself.

Tell them your story. . . .

"Years ago my first husband and I were visiting Africa and traveling from Victoria Falls in Zimbabwe to a town in Botswana. It was a rough trip, and when we arrived at this small town I was looking forward to a nice rest before dinner. We checked into the only hotel, a bungalow of major proportions compared to the mud huts that stretched endlessly in all directions from the center of town. This place had a thatched roof and a wraparound porch that served as the dining hall for the guests. It definitely was not a Hilton, or even a Motel Six, but it was Africa, and that's what we had come to discover.

"So as my husband reached for our bags and I had visions of cool shower, this young man shoots out from the shadows and picks up our luggage. He was small in stature, less than five and a half feet. His back had a twist to the left that brought the right shoulder up around his ear level. His face followed the line of his shoulders, his eyes near his left shoulder, his chin almost on his right shoulder. He blinked spasmodically in time with his facial grimaces. His speech was thick and very difficult to understand, but it was abundant and accompanied by a beautiful sincere smile."

She grinned at her host. "Now you and I, John, would immediately label him as disabled, handicapped. We might even use the word *imperfect*."

John nodded, involved in the story.

"He introduced himself as Lombongo and held out his hand for our room key. He opened the door with a flair and ushered us inside, hurrying to pull up the shades. Then he perched on the most comfortable chair and settled in for a visit. I wanted a shower and a nap, but I didn't want to appear rude and ask him to leave. My husband looked at me and shrugged, and we both tried to listen closely to his speech and to repeat any phrases that we could capture and use to communicate with him. This seemed to thrill Lombongo each time we understood him, and gradually his speech improved. An hour passed and I looked meaningfully at my watch a few times, but our visitor was oblivious to the hint. Then we heard the dinner bell ring, and I gave up all hope of anything except food. The three of us walked out of the room to the dining porch, and when the staff saw Lombongo they fussed over him, wondering where he had been, telling him they had prepared his favorite dishes, saying they had waited so they could all eat together. Obviously this man was well cared for, and his needs were provided by the hotel staff. He giggled at all the fuss, thanked us for the visit, and shrugged in helplessness. What could he do but honor their invitation?"

"So who was he?" John asked.

"We asked that during dinner. One of the guests was in the Peace Corps and knew of Lombongo. She told us that in our world he would be pitied for his disability. In Botswana, in that small town, he was regarded as a very special human being—closer to God, if you will. They say that creation is an ongoing event, and the Creator never tires of creating new beings and environments for them to function in. He, or She," Isabel added with a grin, "is always looking to improve the creation. Most of us are alike, created from the same mold in different combinations, but sometimes the Creator makes one special, hand thrown if you will, not of the same mold. This special being is God's experiment. God will observe his life, and if something is better than in the current mold it will be incorporated into the next. These beings are very important to God, so he always has his eyes on them. The people of that town know that God watches Lombongo, and so they reason if they want God's grace it can be best had by honoring his creation, his hand-thrown work of art."

"So you were fortunate to have had a visit from him?" John asked. "I can see where you're going with this. Here, Lombongo would be labeled in a negative way, maybe even pitied. But in another part of the world he is a gift to be shared?"

Isabel nodded. "Labels again. We think we are so advanced, and perhaps those people in Botswana are simple folks, but to me it made sense how they measured status. In their part of the world wealth is not displayed ostentatiously with big houses or fancy clothes or expensive cars. They say that if their house were bigger and more luxurious than their neighbor's, their neighbor would not feel as good around them. They would live farther away from the other village

houses and the center of the community. They might be left
out of activities, and it might make their neighbor envious,
and that might then cause problems. Yet status is very important to them. A good marriage that produces happy children brings status. Caring for aged parents and sharing good
fortune with your neighbors brings status. But the highest
status is given to those who host God's special creations.
The dwelling chosen to shelter someone like Lombongo for
a night is recognized to have sheltered God. Does status get
any higher than that?"

John was smiling. "That's a fascinating story. Another
way to look at our differences. I'm sure there are parents listening whose hearts swelled as they heard your story."

"But what if we could learn from our friends across the
world, that our works of art are as priceless as theirs and had
their own brilliance to be shared? If we could just listen and
acknowledge . . ." Her words trailed off, and Isabel tightened
in disbelief.

From her seat came a rush of water, staining the dark rug
beneath her feet and spreading toward John.

"Oh my God! Her water broke!" It was clearly Claire's
panicked voice carrying to the stage.

It all happened so quickly. John jumped up from his chair,
as though the spreading stain were the avian flu. "Live television, folks," he muttered, making sure his shoes were not
damaged. "Maybe this would be a good time to go to a commercial?"

"Maybe this would be a good time to get her to a hospital!" Claire declared, pushing past the cameras and reaching
the stage just as Joshua wrapped his arm around Isabel's
shoulders.

"I am *so sorry,*" Isabel murmured, feeling like she was
about to cry. "Your rug and—"

"Who *cares* about the rug?" Tina demanded, joining Claire
with the others right behind her. "Let's get her out of here."

"Get that microphone off her," Cristine yelled.

"Can you walk?" Joshua asked.

"I don't know. I think so," she muttered, biting her bottom lip as Cristine pulled the wire from her body. "My new outfit," she whined, pushing up on the arms of the chair and standing. More water trickled down her legs. "This could not be more embarrassing," she gasped, tentatively taking a step. The entire male crew was staring at her like she was a sideshow freak. "I'm just going to have a baby," she said, breathing heavily. "Hope is coming," she added, smiling weakly up at Joshua.

John pressed his hand to his earpiece. "No, *help* is coming. My producer called the EMTs. An ambulance should be here soon."

Kelly turned to John. "Hope is the name of her baby."

John looked embarrassed. "Oh. Sorry. But there is an ambulance coming. Oh shit . . . we're coming back from commercial." He grabbed Kelly's hand and pulled her to the side, away from the gaggle of women surrounding Isabel. "Just follow my lead," he said to Kelly, who looked horrified when she realized what he meant.

"Welcome back to live television. If you were with us a few minutes ago, you were witness to our guest, the very fascinating and very pregnant Isabel Calloway's water breaking. We're waiting for an ambulance to assist her, and we'll follow her progress because my producers say our phone lines are jammed with callers. Right now I have with me a good friend of Isabel's. And you are?" John took his mic from his jacket lapel and held it before Kelly's mouth.

Kelly looked down to it and then back up at John. "Kelly. Kelly Young."

"Is the baby coming early?"

Kelly pleadingly looked back to her friends as though they could save her. "I guess. . . ."

Isabel shook her head. "Poor Kelly."

"Poor Kelly?" Paula demanded, wringing her hands. "And we don't even have our red high heels on for this birth!"

Claire grabbed Paula's arm. "Knock it off. The heels are just tradition."

"But traditions are important. And they bring good luck and—"

"You want to go back to Haverton and get them for all of us?"

Paula shook her head. "But we did it for me and for Cristine. . . ."

"I'll be fine," Isabel said, clutching Joshua's waist as he held her close to him. "The most important thing is that you're all here with me."

"Where *is* that ambulance?" Tina asked a woman who was rushing to the stage.

"On the way," she answered, handing Isabel a big towel. "What can we do? Would you rather sit down to wait?"

Isabel smiled feebly at Mary Ellen Fenerty, the woman who had called and asked her to appear on the show. "I'm so sorry, Mary Ellen. I've ruined everything."

"Are you kidding?" the woman asked with a big grin. "The phones are off the hook on this one. From what I gather half of them want to ask you questions and the other half want us to follow you to the hospital."

"That's out of the question," Joshua said.

"I want my privacy," Isabel said to Mary Ellen's waved hand.

"I know, I know, but maybe you'll allow us to do a follow-up? You know, happy mother holding her precious little bundle? That kind of thing?"

"Give her a chance to have the precious little bundle, will you?" Claire asked, looking over the woman's shoulder to the studio door. "They're here!"

"And we're out!" an overhead voice boomed.

The energy in the room seemed to dissipate slightly, and all attention was turned to Isabel as the emergency medical team wheeled a stretcher in her direction. They stopped beyond the thick cables that snaked the flooring.

"Can you walk to them?" Joshua asked.

"I think so," she murmured, taking a step. Just as she was about to take another, a sharp pain gathered in her lower back and slowly wrapped around her belly. She gasped and held herself.

"Contractions," Cristine stated. "They're starting!"

Joshua didn't seem to need any more permission. He reached down and gently brought Isabel into his arms. Carefully, he started to walk over the tangled threads of cable.

"How can he see over Isabel?" Claire demanded, watching in awe as Joshua seemed to sense each time he had to lift his feet in order to avoid a cable.

"How can he carry her like she weighs nothing?" Paula asked.

"Let's get our purses and follow them!" Tina declared.

They scrambled back to the row of folding chairs the crew had set up for them and began picking up their belongings. "Kelly!" Claire yelled. "Get your purse and let's move it!"

Kelly started to leave John, but he reached out and took her wrist.

"I'll see you at the hospital? For the follow-up," he added.

Kelly looked over to her impatient friends and nodded. "I'll be there."

"Good."

She smiled and hurried to gather her things.

"That was chummy," Claire said with a smirk. "We have a baby being born, you know?"

"Will you two knock it off?" Tina demanded. "Why is it in chaos we completely lose it like this?"

"I haven't lost anything," Claire said.

"Well, we're about to lose Isabel," Cristine yelled, pointing to the gurney being wheeled out of the studio. "And we don't even know what hospital they're taking her to!"

Five normally intelligent and graceful women suddenly became the Keystone Cops and bumped into one another picking up purses, jackets, and stumbling over cables. The first to emerge with all her things and upright, Cristine yelled to the others, "Hurry, or we'll lose them!" And then she took off out of the studio to follow the EMTs.

"Wait!"

"Don't leave without us!"

"I have to be there! I'm the godmother!"

"Who made you godmother?"

People came out of their offices to watch the women running and yelling down the hallway that led outside.

"Isabel said I was godmother."

"We're *all* godmothers!"

"Yeah, like in Sleeping Beauty. Bippity bobbity boo!"

"They were fairies!"

"They were godmothers!"

"I don't care if they were genies, we're gonna lose them!

"You guys have your fairy tales mixed up."

Claire glared at the young kid holding open the outside door for them. "I'm telling you, they were godmothers!"

"Whatever, lady."

Cristine ran up to the ambulance as Isabel was slid inside. She clutched Joshua's arm. "We have to go with her."

"Just the father," the EMT said. "There's no room for all of you. Meet us at U of P hospital. Emergency entrance."

The rest of the group caught up, wheezing from the sprint out of the building.

"He says we can't go."

Claire shouldered her way to the front. "I beg your pardon? We're her family. We have to be there."

"No way," the man answered.

"Please?" Isabel asked. "I'd feel so much better if they were with me."

Joshua asked the man, "Could they possibly go with her?"

He started to shake his head, and Joshua placed his hand on the man's shoulder. "It would mean so much to my wife."

The man blinked a few times and then inhaled, as if coming up for air. "It'll be tight."

"We don't care about tight."

"The closer the better."

"We showered this morning, right, girls?"

"Right."

"One of you will have to sit up front with the driver."

"Kelly will do it," Claire said, shoving Kelly toward the front.

"Why me?" Kelly demanded, looking insulted.

"Because you're always wanting to meet new men, that's why. Here's your chance."

Joshua climbed in, helping Cristine, Paula, and Tina followed by Claire.

"This is highly irregular," the EMT stated, closing the doors behind him as Kelly got into the passenger seat of the ambulance.

"And *illegal*," the driver yelled out from the cab. "Hello there," he added with a sexy grin as Kelly shut her door and turned around to the back.

Ignoring the man's overture, she said, "I'm not going to forget this, Claire."

"Yes, you will."

"Can we please go now?" Isabel asked, clutching Joshua's arm after the EMT slid past the women to sit at her head. "I don't want to have my baby here."

"Hit it, Joe," the man said, and with lights flashing and sirens blaring the ambulance took off out of the parking lot.

"This is kinda exciting," Tina said, holding onto Claire as they turned a corner.

Grinning like a fool, Claire nodded. "We did it again, you know?"

"What?" Paula asked in a loud voice, bracing herself against Cristine as the siren seemed to absorb all conversation.

"Made fools of ourselves," Claire yelled back, shaking her head. "Did you see those people coming out of their offices?"

"That's because you kept insisting you were the god-mother. You know we all are, so stop trying to bully your way to the top of the list."

Ignoring her wonderful and wacky friends, Isabel pulled on Joshua's hand. He bent over her face to listen to her words.

"I love you."

He squeezed her hand. "And I love you, Isabel."

"She's going to be okay, right? You promised."

"She's going to be better than all right. Just like you. She going to be brilliant, very special, a gift to the world." He kissed Isabel's fingertips. "Trust the future."

And two hours later Hope was born.

Acknowledgments

PATRICIA ANN TROWBRIDGE, DCH, RN—FOR BETTER or worse, after fifteen years of friendship, I think you are my mentor. I know you roared with laughter when I said I was basing Isabel on you, not your life, and I hope you weren't disappointed by my portrayal of a woman of intelligence, integrity, and a sense of humor with which to laugh at herself. Thank you for permission to use so many of your words in this book, especially the story of Lombongo. For the interested reader, Patricia has written a nonfiction book, *Breaking the Memory Barrier.*

Victoria O'Day—for your continued assistance in the mundane part of writing. Thank you for the help with galleys, research, and checking everything twice.

Richard Curtis, my agent—for understanding sometimes life gets in the way.

Anna Genoese, my editor—for your *patience*! I thank and acknowledge everyone at Tor who has contributed to the success of this trilogy. Now to Claire's story!

And though the author is unknown, a deep acknowledgment for the writing of "I'm Special." May we all remember.